BRIGHTFIRE

a story of Sutton Hoo

P.M.SABIN MOORE

authorHOUSE®

AuthorHouse™ UK Ltd.
500 Avebury Boulevard
Central Milton Keynes, MK9 2BE
www.authorhouse.co.uk
Phone: 08001974150

First published by AuthorHouse   8/23/2010

ISBN: 978-1-4520-5609-8 (sc)

Front cover photograph: Gary E.Sanford (with permission)
detail of sword: statue of Byrhtnoth,Eorl of Essex, Maldon,
created by John Doubleday.
Back cover: photograph of 'Storm Frost' cover:Richard E. Moore

This book is printed on acid-free paper.

This book is for Bud

and for all those

who work or have worked

in so many different ways as

National Trust Staff, Guides and Volunteers

at Sutton Hoo

for he and they know what dedication means

ACKNOWLEDGEMENTS

My warmest thanks to:
Christopher Moore, my husband, for frequently saving the computer from destruction.
Anne Hartnett, who lent me her quiet house as a bolt-hole to write in.
Robert Anderson, for enthusiastic support and for proof-reading!
Gary Sanford for invaluable help with presentation and the front cover photograph.
Paul Mortimer (King Raedwald), Ormsgard re-enactor, for much enlightenment.
Brian Ansell, stonemason, for demonstrating his consummate skill.
Andrea Eichhorn, for constant support and helpful advice.
Dr. Sam Newton, historian, of Wuffing Education for answering so many questions.
Stephen Pollington, author and lecturer, for sharing his knowledge.
Neil & Gro Barrie, of Aalesund for giving time to help and a beautiful space to work in.
Rev. M. Hatchett, Rector, St. Andrew's Church, Melton, for generous support

Any howlers are mine alone.

Thanks are also due to Penguin Books Ltd for kind permission to quote (on page 116) some of the words of Pope Boniface in his letter to King Edwin:

AUTHOR'S NOTE

What we do know of this period (608 – 630 AD) comes largely from Bede's "Ecclesiastical History of the English People", but he does not tell us some things: for example, the name of Raedwald's queen, or how Raedwald died.

Bede is, naturally, biased in favour of those who uphold Christianity. He regards Raedwald as an apostate, but nowhere does he accuse Raedwald of attacking or killing Christians, as he does Aethelfrith of Northumbria. Furthermore, he was writing a hundred years after these events, and much of his information has to come from hearsay.

I have tried to remain true to what seems reliable fact, including what we know of the lifestyles, customs and practices of the people of this period, based on archaeological evidence, folklore, herb lore, poetry, sagas, illuminations etc. (See Background Reading at end.)

I have taken a liberty over the practice of using the Anno Domini system, making it earlier so that readers may realize what is the period being covered here.

As is evident in my list of characters, some of them are historical figures, and a few of their actions are known. The archaeologists at Sutton Hoo found no rings on the sword of the king, and we do not know for sure what such hilt rings meant: I have offered my own twist on this practice.

For the rest, I am free to write fiction.

P.M.S.M.

BRIGHTFIRE

In this sequel to **"Storm Frost"**, Niartha remains a key character and so does her son, Ricberht, now a goldsmith: though the tale of **"Brightfire"** can stand alone.

The story is set between 608 – 630 AD, when Christianity is struggling to take hold on the eastern side of Britain.

"Brightfire" covers important events during and after the reign of King Raedwald of Sutton Hoo and is set mainly in and around his homestead nearby, with some scenes set in Northumbria and elsewhere.

Eorpwald, Raedwald's son, is hostile to Christians, jealous of other successful young men, including Ricberht, and is a cruel bully in spite of his father's efforts to master him during his lifetime. When Raedwald dies, no-one can control Eorpwald. Even his own people, the Wuffings, are in danger.

We see fighting and feasting, rescue and rape, cruelty and kindness, laughter and tears, in a story which rises to a strong climax.

LIST OF CHARACTERS

(In bold = historical figure)

IN EAST ANGLIA

IN NORTHUMBRIA

THE WOMEN AT RAEDWALDSHAM
Raedwald's queen
Niartha: Ricberht's mother, a healer
Gilda: Niartha's servant
Idunna: Beorn's wife
Ulla: Randulf's wife
Maura: rescued by Ricberht
Guthrun: Aelfric's daughter
Fritha: Maura's 1st child
Morwyn: Maura's 2nd child
Gurth: Raedwald's cousin
THE MEN AT RAEDWALDSHAM
Ricberht: trainee goldsmith
Diuma: his master
**Raedwald: King of the Wuffings
later High King (Bretwalda)**
Garmund, High Priest of Woden
Raegenhere: eldest son of Raedwald

Eorpwald: 2nd son of Raedwald
Sigeberht: 3rd son of Raedwald
Onna (Ánna):
Aelfric: Hall Steward
Arnulf: blacksmith to the King
Randulf, his brother, King's sword maker

AT YEFRIN
Aethelfrith: warlike king
Aethelberga: Edwin's wife
Ecgric: Hall Steward
Grimwald: King's Smith

AT RIVER COCKET
Prince Eni : brother of Raedwald
(called Wulf) now dead

Bertha: matriarch
Eadwacer: Niartha's betrayer
Wilhelm: headman of village
Lukas Lukasson: shipmaster, trader

IN KENT
**Aethelbert: King and
High King
(Bretwalda)
Eadbald; his son and heir
one of Raedwald's nephews**

FROM ROME
**Paulinus: Christian
missionary**

Borgil: King's shield maker

Beorn: Arnulf's son

Bedwyn:

Plegmund:

Boniface: Pope following Gregory.

Felix: a monk

village elder

Eorpwald's crony

PLACE NAMES
Raedwaldsham = Rendlesham

AT WEDRESFELD

Aescgar; elderly king

Ulric: invasive neighbouring king

Yefrin = Ad Gefrin = Yeavering

Eofric = Eorfric = York

Northumbria = Bernicia + Deira

(Humber to Berwick on Tweed)

R. Cocket = R. Coquet (no 'q' in Anglo-Saxon)

NIARTHA

People often ask me if I am lonely living here under the great oak tree, but I just smile and say no. Very few people know the story of my life before I came here seven years ago, and those who do have the sense to say nothing to me. They are probably afraid to bring back old griefs, to stir up old troubles.

For thirteen years I lived safely in the tiny northern fishing village where Raedwald's cousin Gurth had become headman, and where my son Ricberht grew up – unaware of the treacherous man who had been his father; unaware of my hunt for my beloved: Wulf, whose real name was Prince Eni. Great-hearted and forgiving, Raedwald had ensured my safety, and then he fulfilled his promise to me to give Ricberht an honourable living. So now we have lived in the kingdom of the Wuffings for two years.

I worry that old Diuma, the jewel-smith will not let my son work soon to show his potential. When he talks of his jewellery, Ricberht's face lights up. He has learnt so much in two years and he has ideas for new designs. Too often he complains that he is kept making preparations, tidying the smithy, working the bellows. I warn him against impatience, but if he gets bored he may never be a craftsman like Diuma.

Nothing I can do now will help the old man's eyes, and soon he will need Ricberht's fingers. It must be hard to let go, to lie idle, like a rusting sword, unburnished, losing its fire. But soon he must let Ricberht begin to prove himself. My son has talent, I think, and also now the physical strength. I have watched him listening intently when in the hall the *scop* sings of strange creatures. I know he has also learnt the signs of some runes – Garmund does not share the knowledge willingly, but he has helped Ricberht to understand the meaning that lies behind the world we see. Sometimes I have wondered if he might wish to become a priest, but he laughs at the idea. He says he does not need to meddle with the gods, he is happy to make this world more beautiful.

1

Ricberht was anxious for me, I know, when my uncle Edgar died a year ago, but sees that I am busy and contented. Diuma needs him more than I do, and relies on him more than he is willing to admit.

Some day soon the time will come. I wonder if Raedwald will let my son come to live with me here in Edgar's small but pleasant house.

1

Old Diuma raised his head, as he heard the quick footfall and rustle of clothing which announced the arrival of his assistant. He tugged his woollen cap more firmly on his sparse grey hairs and turned his head at Ricberht's greeting.

"Why are you late?" he asked rather gruffly.

"Am I late? The sun has barely risen. Here, I've brought you your breakfast." Ricberht put a flat, wooden board into the old man's hand and, fishing out of his bag a knob of bread and a chunk of goat's cheese, he laid them on the platter. "There's some beer when you're ready."

Diuma grunted and then coughed, clutching at his food to stop it spilling.

"Are you warm enough, my master?" the youth enquired anxiously. "Would you like a fur wrap?"

"I shall be well enough. The sun will soon do its work."

"I wish you would come into the hall at night. It is warm there."

" I keep telling you! It is warm here, too. I have only to step over to the kiln. The smithy does well enough. Besides, I have to watch over the tools."

Ricberht said, "I could do that, if you'd let me." He was thinking that the old man's cloudy eyes could not see much, especially in the dark. Nor was his hearing too good.

The old man licked his fingers noisily and held out his hand for the horn beaker. He patted his beard where some beer had spilt and gave the beaker back to Ricberht.

"Time to work now, boy," he said.

Only two years ago Diuma would have been the one to haul a sack of charcoal, to hew the logs for the fire and to pump the small bellows at the kiln until his muscles screamed. As time passed he allowed the boy to take a turn - ostensibly because this was necessary for his training, but actually because he needed to rest more often, though he would not admit it.

The wooden hut behind them was not a blacksmith's large forge; that would have worked iron for weapons, armour, cooking pots and horse-shoes. Diuma's smithy was the jeweller's workshop, set beyond the black forge, even further from the houses, off the trackway that led away from Raedwaldsham towards the great oak forest. This protected from fire the settlement and, not least, the royal hall of the Wuffings, the ruling family, and home to the powerful king, Raedwald.

It also preserved the privacy of the goldsmith, and, wittingly or not, enhanced the sense of the arcane... smiths of all kinds were held in awe, sometimes even in fear of their being in league with supernatural powers. Who else could create objects from lumps of ore, chunks of metal, or even of pieces of gold? In times past, gold had been offered to the gods. Iron was strong and gave protection: the strength of gold lay in its emblematic power. Magic was dangerous.

On shelves were strewn blowpipes, used to build heat in the small kilns (Diuma had two), during smelting. There were many small crucibles of clay to melt gold or silver, and moulds of clay or antler to shape the melt. There were the plates for making wires of different thickness and the tool for making beads from wire The precious tools for beating even thin sheets of precious metal, for stamping impressions, punching tiny filigree holes, for engraving or incising – all these were kept high on a dark shelf to the rear, together with a honing-stone for keeping blades sharp. Dumped in the darkest corner under a pile of stinking skins, filthy sacks and rubbish, Diuma hid a store of small silver ingots and blanks of thin gold, together with remnants of jewels and glass, in a cloth, then wrapped in leather on a bed of birch-bark. Ricberht was flushed with pride, honoured to be shown this secret hoard only a few months after he joined Diuma to be trained.

A jeweller needed many of the same skills as the blacksmith. He had to know the signs that his metals were at the point of melting in the heat of the kiln. He had to draw off the liquid melt as it oozed down its channel into a shallow pan to cool. He had to beat, roll, stamp or smooth it to the requisite thickness or shape to create any of the pieces forming in his mind.

Ricberht had been quick to learn, and at the same time was careful, practising the assessment of the heat of the kiln and the differences in gold, silver or even bronze or tin when they could trade for these. Like all smiths his fingers suffered burns and cuts and his tunic was pitted with spark-burns, but he shrugged off the pain and showed such persistence that the old man relented and gave praise where it was due.

Now, coming to a decision, Diuma lifted himself off the stool with the aid of a bramble-stick as thickly gnarled as his wrist.

"Come, boy," he said and began to limp towards the village centre, coughing as he went.

"Where are we going?"

"We are going to get the pieces we need."

"What – for the new shield? For the king's shield? That means we get to ask – get to see…"

"Yes, boy. Be quiet now, and see how this is done. Another time I might send you on your own."

Ricberht fell quiet, his eyes shining and his lips tight in a smile of silent excitement. At the hall the door-thane met them and greeted Diuma, who asked to speak to the king's steward.

" I have the lime-wood board for the shield from Randulf, and the alder for backing some of the shapes. Now I can begin to make the jewels while the grips and rim are being prepared. I come to ask for the treasury to be opened."

The door-thane bowed and ushered them to a bench inside the door. He hastened off into the interior. They waited in silence.

To Ricberht's amazement the steward himself came and beckoned them to follow him through various areas of the hall into the king's smaller room at the end. Here the queen sat on a carved stool. She rose as they bent their heads, and spoke their names. For some reason, Ricberht always felt uneasy in her presence. She knew who he was, of course, and he had attended feasts, though sitting at the far end of the youths' table far from the high seat. He knew she disliked his mother, for some reason, but he had never had to speak to her directly, himself.

Now she crossed to a great, oaken chest, ornately carved, in a corner of the room, and raised a bronze key from one of the chains on the belt at her waist. She bent to open the heavy, tubular padlock, and lifted the hasp it held, before raising the heavy lid, carved with writhing dragons, gilded and with eyes of inset garnet. Inside the chest were smaller boxes and bags knotted at their necks.

"What do you need, Diuma?" she enquired.

"Gold, my queen, for a great bird and a dragon, more for the plates, rim-clasps, the boss itself, and garnets and blue glass. Randulf and I will work closely together."

" And when will this be ready?"

"About a month, lady."

"As long as that? And with two of you working?"

Ricberht twitched and reddened. He was longing to be allowed to work on this piece. He was also sure that his sight was keener and his hand steadier than Diuma's, but would never say so.

"The king needs this soon, Diuma. Raedwald has called a moot in three weeks' time. The new shield will look splendid hanging over the throne-stool at the feast."

Diuma merely bowed. The two men took from the queen bags of various sizes and she fed into them rough red stones, one broken blue glass jar, one small, misshapen goblet, some odd pieces of gold and several gold ingots.

"If you need more, come to me again. Remember to return any pieces you do not use. Make the spare gold into ingots as usual. You may go now." The queen swung back to relock the chest, not heeding as the two turned away, to be escorted back through the hall.

Diuma trusted Ricberht to make up the fire in a kiln. He showed him some figures carved in wood, as an example of the sort of shapes he wished to make, and pulled a bag from a cord round his neck, hidden in his tunic. Here he kept a few, flat slices of gold, again with designs scratched on them. Naturally, he did *not* give back all the gold left from his work, why would he? He had to show his apprentice what was in his mind. Ricberht raised his eyebrows but nodded in understanding. There was obviously more than one hoard!

The old man led the youth to the stools placed near the kiln, so they could tend the fire for several hours before smelting could begin. He took up a sharp twig and leant forward, scratching in the flattened soil at his feet. Soon two dragons writhed, head to tail on the ground.

"You try now," said Diuma and scuffed the soil to obliterate the image. Ricberht took the twig and produced a rather uneven version. Frustrated, as this was not the first time he had practised, he swept the dust with his foot and began to try again. "It's the heads. Make them larger. Make the eye dangerous – no, the nose of the beast longer. Yes. Now the bodies must be stronger. Thicker here, then narrow. Yes, good." He took from his bag one small tongue of gold and showed it to Ricberht. "Fetch a board and my bag of carving tools from the shelf."

To his delight, the old man handed him the gold and a slender, sharp-ended iron tool.

"Now mark this piece, just as you did the earth. No! Don't copy that." A grubby shoe made the dragons vanish. "Take your time. Be careful. Use your eyes and feel the creatures move."

Ricberht had watched over the years and had even been allowed to scratch designs on thin iron sheets and once on a silver dish to give to his mother. But this was the most important thing he was to do: work for the king's own shield. He raised his hand and turned the tip of the tool toward the gold.

Just as he did so, Diuma gave a cry, startling Ricberht so that he dropped everything and leapt to catch the old man as he toppled from his stool. He lay, propped against the wall of the little smithy, one hand gripping his left arm, with his face in a rictus of agony, gasping for breath. His lips turned blue in an ashen face. Then his head dropped forward and his weight slipped to the earth. He uttered a harsh sound and was still.

Ricberht called his name many times and tried to pull him into a sitting position, but to no avail. He felt sure Diuma was dead.

He scrambled to his feet, ready to run, instinctively, to one who could help him, but luckily had the wit first to grab the bags with the king's treasure. He raced toward the oak-wood. In the heart of it lived his mother, Niartha, wise-woman and healer. She would know what best to do.

2

So distraught was Ricberht that, leaving Niartha to watch over his master's body, he rushed into the hall just as the king and his thanes were about to leave for a day's hunting. The news caused natural distress, as the old goldsmith had been much respected. They had seen men carry items of bronze, iron or wood to place them in his hands. Sometimes it took many days, but these would reappear, transformed into something rich and rare.

The king commanded a warrior's funeral for Diuma and a feast. The queen enquired of the shaking Ricberht what had happened to the gold, glass and garnets she had taken from the treasure chest. Mutely, the boy proffered the sacks, but Raedwald held out his hand to stop her.

"What of the shield?" he demanded. "Has the work started yet?"

"The kiln is lit, lord," began Ricberht and his eyes widened in shock as he realised the fire needed tending. "We had begun to make the design..." He faltered and stopped. There was silence.

"Well, boy," said the king, fixing him with a steady, blue-eyed gaze from under strong brows, "can you do the work? Diuma always said you were quick to learn – how much have you learnt?"

The queen made a small sound and moved as if to speak, but again Raedwald hushed her. Ricberht took a deep breath and, straightening up, looked steadily back at the king.

"Yes, lord. I can do it. But..." he stopped again.

"Go on."

"My pieces are not the same as Diuma's. I see things in a different way. I..." As if sensing that he was talking too much, he paused again.

"How different?"

"I want dragons, eagles and boars to be so beautiful that their magic touches you. But it must not. Magic is dangerous. I shall put a border round each body so that we may be protected."

Several people shuffled nervously and looked askance, fingers went to amulets – what was this boy likely to do?

"Do not let the priests hear you talk like that," suggested Raedwald mildly. "At least not the ones who worship Christ. They think magic is evil, not just dangerous."

"Such nonsense!" snapped the queen. "A thing as strong as a shield needs strong magic. If this boy can find it, then let him bring it to his work."

So Ricberht began working for the king. It was necessary to reassure the other craftsmen with whom he would have to collaborate: the shield-maker, swordsmith, armourer, leather-worker, whose crafts were to be embellished with jewels and gold. They would need some convincing.

For the moment, he and Niartha had to deal with the funeral for Diuma, being the closest to a family that the old man had. As he paused outside what was now his workshop, he saw Niartha at the doorway.

"I will help," she said. She had laid out the old man, put a clean tunic and leggings on him and wrapped him in his blue cloak. "The grave-diggers are already at work. They tell me the king has commanded an honourable funeral. You must speak in Diuma's memory."

"What of the priests?" Ricberht demurred.

""What of them? Diuma was no Christian. Surely they may attend, but they will have nothing to say. Garmund will do the rites."

Niartha was not altogether right. Paulinus, the Christian priest, had plenty to say. Diuma's was, surprisingly, the first significant death to happen since Raedwald had been summoned by the High King to be baptised in Kent and had brought the Christians and their new religion to Raedwaldsham, six years previously. On the site of Woden's shrine on the hillside half a mile from the hall, Raedwald had built a fine wooden church, perhaps not quite as large as his hall, with an altar to Christ, next to Woden's. The church was dedicated in due course to Saint Gregory, the recent Pope, responsible for the Christian mission to the east of Britain. This Gregory had advised his missionaries to avoid confrontation with hostile pagans; he had been sure that exposure to this new, gentler religion would be sufficiently persuasive, though baptised kings could enforce change, if necessary.

Raedwald was a baptised king, but everyone knew that his

wife and many elders of the people were antagonistic. Raedwald cleverly took the path of least resistance, and turned a deaf ear to the pleadings of both sets of priests. In the last six years only a few slaves, one or two old women and some children had died here, to be buried as usual in the cemetery field outside the palisade.

Now, it seemed, conflict was inevitable. Paulinus demanded a Christian burial for the king's goldsmith, but the elders, the queen and Ricberht declared that Diuma preferred the ancient rituals. Furthermore, Raedwald had entrusted important ceremonies to Garmund, the old high priest, all his life.

There came a day of wrangling. Diuma had never been baptised, so special pleading for his soul would be needed if he were to receive Christian burial. Traditionally, he would be taken to the grave-site of the warriors, up on the hoo, on the way to the royal mounds. There he would be buried with some of his choice possessions, ready to meet Woden with honour.

"Let the gods fight it out between themselves," said many. But feelings ran high – not least in the family of the king.

PAULINUS

O God let me turn the heart and mind of this stubborn king!

Let thy mercies come also unto me, O Lord, even thy salvation, according to thy word. So shall I have wherewith to answer him that reproacheth me: for I trust in thy word.

And take not the word of truth utterly out of my mouth; for I have hoped in thy judgements. So shall I keep thy law continually for ever and ever. And I will walk at liberty: for I seek thy precepts.

I will speak of thy testimonies also before kings, and will not be ashamed.

And I will delight myself in thy commandments, which I have loved.

My hands also will I lift up unto thy commandments, which I have loved: and I will meditate in thy statutes.

Remember the word unto thy servant, upon which thou hast caused me to hope. This is my comfort in my affliction: for thy word hath quickened me. The proud have had me greatly in derision: yet have I not declined from thy law.

I remembered thy judgements of old, O Lord; and have comforted myself.

Horror hath taken hold upon me because of the wicked that forsake thy law.

Thy statutes have been my songs in the house of my pilgrimage. I have remembered thy name, O Lord, in the night, and have kept thy law.

They draw nigh that follow after mischief: they are far from thy law.

Let thy hand help me; for I have chosen thy precepts
Amen

3

In his short but heartfelt speech at the graveside, Ricberht expressed his admiration for his beloved master. Standing by the deep grave he drew the listeners' attention to some of Diuma's skilful work: on one man's sword-hilt, another's neck-collar, a gilded brooch on a woman's dress, a beautiful chain worn by the queen herself.

"All I can hope to do," said the young man, "is to make jewelled pieces as fine as I can to honour his memory. He had agreed to allow my designs to go forward for our next work – the king's shield – and I am ready to begin. I pray to whichever god..." (here he faltered, noticing the frowning gaze of both priests) "whichever god will give me the craft in this making."

Now, of course, he would have both breathing down his neck, urging him to employ their symbols.

"I shall work in secret," he boldly announced, "until the work is done. Only the king will approve it." Ricberht glanced at Raedwald, who stood impassively at the foot of the grave, and received a cool gaze and a slight nod in acquiescence. Beside her son, Niartha visibly relaxed. She had obviously thought he had gone too far.

"Naturally," the young smith assured the company, "I shall depend on the knowledge and advice of those whose crafts need jewels for their final embellishment." Here a few heads nodded. "But I have to say that I have some new ideas." This time a few eyebrows were raised.

Then Ricberht fished in the bag hanging from his belt and drew out some small, thin sheets of gold. Those closest to him could see marks scored on these.

"Go to your gods, old friend," said the new smith. He gently tossed these onto the simple fir-wood coffin, then unhooked a slender iron tool from his belt and dropped that on top of the gold. "Use these to please the spirits that you meet, my master, I..." but here his voice failed him. He brushed a sleeve across his eyes and stepped back. Niartha placed a hand on his arm.

Raedwald nodded to Garmund. The priest of Woden, bony skull covered with a wolf-head, blind in one eye, like his god, began a series of incantations and placed on the grave some pieces of bark inscribed with runes.

At this, Paulinus turned sharply away and retreated, accompanied by his usual pair of clerks. Raedwald began to turn away, but the queen clutched his elbow, whispered fiercely in his ear, and stood her ground. Raedwald stayed.

Then came the feasting. The people gathered in the hall in response to the call of the steward's horn. Outside the autumnal darkness thickened to a velvet blackness; a chill wind blew from the river and rain threatened. Inside the hall a long hearth blazed, over which hung cauldrons of broth and stew, while girls carried in platters of meat, fish and fruit. The king and queen fed from silver dishes. The king's sword, Beorhtfyr, lay along the table before him: the only weapon in the hall. It shone, bejewelled. On the walls, lit by torchlight, hung the shields of the warriors, many glinting with gold emblems, crafted by Diuma's hands. Soon, thought Ricberht, his work would gleam among them. He hoped Diuma would be proud of him. Brooches and pins twinkled from gowns and cloaks. Niartha noticed how many people fingered these, perhaps conscious of the old man whose life was being celebrated.

The trouble began after most of the dishes were cleared, and the mead, ale and beer, so swiftly guzzled, were starting to take effect.

The custom was for the priest to pray the gods to receive the spirit of the dead man, so that he might use his skills in their honour. Then the new smith would be presented to the people, and the gods invoked to grant the craftsman strength, creative imagination and protection from the dangers of his work. A deep cut, burn or scratch could kill a man in days, if it turned bad, and dust or fumes associated with firing a fusion of gold and mercury, or some other metal, could leave a man coughing or heaving for breath for years. Diuma was fortunate to have lived so long and died so easily.

Raedwald presented Ricberht with an engraving tool, crafted for him by Randulf, the swordsmith. As the young man knelt to receive it and the king stepped back, both Garmund and Paulinus moved, simultaneously, arms outstretched towards Ricberht. They glared at each other, and the youth flinched and sat back, looking from one angry man to the other.

Paulinus turned to the king. "Enough, lord," he said. "The old

13

man was buried in the old ways. Let this boy receive the blessing of the One True God." As Raedwald made to reply, Garmund interjected angrily. "Lord king, as all here know, if we do not observe the old rites, then our lives are endangered. Without the old gods we cannot grow our food, without their favour our hunting will fail, our people will..."

"Once again, king," interrupted Paulinus, "this man misleads you – all of you." He gestured toward the assembled people. "God loves you. He cares when one sparrow falls, much more when one man dies. If Diuma had been Christian, his soul would now be in heaven, where there is no more age, no more pain..."

"Save it for your day in the church!" shouted Garmund. "Is it not enough to have to listen to you there? Lord king, let me give this young man the sign of the *fylfot*. Thus he will be..."

"Condemned to burn in hell forever," cried Paulinus. "If I am allowed to bless this young man's work, I know the saving of his soul will follow."

There was silence as the murmuring crowd stilled, waiting for the king to decide. Ricberht had risen quietly and looked toward his mother, who lifted a finger as a signal to wait.

This kind of argument had gone on for years, though perhaps not quite so openly, publicly, as this. Most of the folk felt that the queen and the elders were right. It had been a shock when Raedwald came back from his visit to the High King, bringing this Christian stuff with him. And he did not, for once, seem so sure of himself. The funny business of the church with two altars was unsettling. And in spite of Garmund's thundering, Paulinus's influence was subtle and persistent. Not everyone was set dead against him. He was allowed to preach on the sun's day and quite a few went to listen.

Over time, this quiet, strangely-robed figure had begun to celebrate festivals which more or less coincided with those of the old religion, so that it was hard to tell which god was being honoured at harvest, or Yuletide. Sometimes the old festivals prevailed: midsummer rituals were held in the face of all Paulinus's objections. He absented himself from what he saw as licentious, immoral behaviour.

Confrontations were more obvious at ceremonies to name babies, celebrations of hand-fast or wedlock, but this at the funeral was proving fiercer than usual.

In the silence of the hall, Raedwald lifted the ivory wand,

inherited from his forebears, passed down from Wuffa himself, ringed with a band of gold bearing the imprint of a wolf. It signified that his word was law, not to be gainsaid.

NIARTHA

In an instant my mind flashes back, not to the last time Garmund had tried to outface Paulinus, but to a small hall in the tiny village in Bernicia, the land far north of the Humber River, where Raedwald had meted justice on the man who had killed my lover, the man who had fathered my child, the man who had betrayed me.

Although my father, the king at Wedresfeld, had given me in marriage to Raedwald, it was his brother, Eni, whom I loved for his sensitivity, his courage and his passion. Once our love was betrayed, Raedwald left me. Outcast by my own people I sought my lover, my Wulf. I travelled far to the north, but was found by Eadwacer, my betrayer. He took advantage of the pitiful state I was in, and got me with child. When he found us again in the village of the fisher-folk, he lied and killed; he stole my baby, but was caught by Raedwald and given justice. He stood before Raedwald as we do now, and just so did the king hold this slender ivory staff, full of the power of his kindred, of his kingship.

Eadwacer's death he brought upon himself.

Thanks to Raedwald's judgement, I was left safe to rear my son until we were brought here, to Raedwaldsham, where Ricberht could be given honourable work, as the king promised.

Now my son stands ready to prove himself, and yet he is not free. They wrangle for his spirit, these two priests, but who knows what path his soul is treading? If only they would let him alone!

I wonder if Raedwald realises how the folk are divided in this matter.

4

Raedwald stood up. Garmund was on his right, red-faced, priest's staff in one hand and a small bowl full of the burnt ash of a yew-tree in the other. On the king's left stood Paulinus, apparently calm as he gazed at the assembled people, but his face was set and his fingers white, where he clenched the pendant at his breast. It was silver, inlaid with deep red jewels, indicating the figure of Christ crucified.

Raedwald made his pronouncement. "Let us settle these arguments once and for all. I declare that any man who has chosen to be baptised shall, if he has not transgressed the laws of that church, be given Christian burial at the church."

He raised the ivory wand and held it outstretched, upright before him, a sign that a Wuffing lord had spoken.

A low muttering was making itself heard as the king finished speaking. Suddenly someone left the table of the youths and approached the trio of men at the high seat, just as Garmund opened his mouth to speak

"Father," said the boy, clearly, "Lord king, will it be unlawful then to observe the old customs of our people?" There were some growls and calls of support from all round the hall. It was not clear what the king intended. Even the women were speaking out. This was Eorpwald, the king's second son, daring to make what seemed to be a challenge. Because of the fuss he had made about being the king's son, he was given a place on the youths' bench, even though his voice had not yet broken.

"Silence, boy," commanded the king, but the queen touched his arm and murmured something in his ear.

"Our customs are good and honourable," she said aloud.

Paulinus broke in. "And some, lady are unworthy and barbaric." For a few minutes there was hubbub until the king signalled the hall steward to thump with his staff on the wooden platform on which Raedwald stood. The king's eldest son, Raegenhere, was pulling his brother's arm, but Eorpwald was shouting, "I demand the right to choose!"

"Be quiet!" thundered Raedwald. "You are a child! You have no right to speak in this assembly!" People fell quiet – but they, too, were not sure if they had the right to choose between these gods.

"And what of this young man?" demanded Garmund, gesturing toward Ricberht, standing silently before him. "Will the lord of the Wuffings rely on the strength of the puny Christ to protect him? Everyone knows that magical powers are woven into a smith's works. He uses the fire of dragons, the swiftness of eagles, the might of the great boar – he needs the symbols of the gods to shield him in his craft."

Raedwald put up his hand to stop Paulinus replying. Then he beckoned Ricberht forward, to stand beside him on the platform, facing the company, king's hand on his shoulder.

"The king's jewel-smith is a special case," he affirmed. "He will receive the protection of our gods – our old ones," he interjected in response to Paulinus's gesture of objection. "Garmund! Prepare to make the *fylfot* and we shall go to the shrine to make the sacrifices as usual." He raised the ivory wand and held it outstretched, upright before him, a sign that a Wuffing lord had spoken.

Anxious to absent himself from a pagan ritual, Paulinus and his two clerks left the hall. A few people followed him, Raedwald observed, those who were committed Christians

"Let us drink to the health of the new smith," the queen suggested. Amid the hurly burly of filling the drinking horns, beakers and cups, Eorpwald turned his back and left the hall. Raegenhere sighed. His brother was so headstrong! Then the prince was among the first to raise his beaker, and soon the place filled with shouts of good cheer, stamping of feet and clapping of hands.

At the king's signal, an informal procession wound from the hall to the church. It was a handsome building, roofs crowned with thatch, and gables and eaves ornamented with a rare mixture of old and new symbols. Dragonheads protruded from the timbers, and one end bore a cross, the other a rooster. Inside, serpents writhed up polished pillars of wood. At the end of the dark, wooden building, lit only by candles on one of the altars, was a crucifix and Paulinus's copy of the book he carried wherever he went. To the Wuffing people that book was at least as mysterious and incomprehensible as any of Garmund's runes or the craftsmen's emblems.

Garmund stalked up the centre of the church and stood at

Woden's altar decked with birch twigs and sprigs of yew. He turned to face those entering the church.

Paulinus came from where he had waited at Christ's altar and came down the church to the door. Here the trail of people halted. Raedwald, Raegenhere and the queen stood beside the three low steps leading to the door of the church, and Ricberht and Niartha paused below Paulinus. The monk signalled to his crucifer, and followed the cross down the steps, sweeping past the king and firmly closing his holy book in silent protest. Most, but not all the folk followed Raedwald into the church.

From a small door Garmund's servants dragged in a wild boar, struggling against the ropes that bound it. They heaved it onto Woden's altar, yew and birch scattering to the floor, while Randulf, the swordsmith, whetted the sacrificial knife. He proffered this to the king, who with one clean thrust slit the throat of the shrieking beast. Suddenly all was silent. Garmund caught the blood in a wide bowl, carvings bloodstained from previous use. When the flow stopped and the boar lay still, the wolf-headed priest made a sign, and the creature was lifted away. Its flesh would, on this occasion be divided between the king, the priest and the new goldsmith.

As Ricberht knelt before him, Garmund marked his forehead with the sign of the *fylfot* and spoke the runes of power. He invoked the mysteries of Woden, Frey and Yng to make the smith skilful and productive and to keep him safe. As he spoke the words of the charms, people listened in awe, accepting in awe, though without much understanding, the quality of his words.

In starlight and torchlight they returned to their homes. Ricberht went with Niartha to her place near the great oak. His new life would begin tomorrow.

EORPWALD

What Ricberht did not reckon with was Eorpwald's growing jealousy. As a child he had always been quarrelsome, overeager to copy what the older boys were doing. Ricberht was about two years older than Raegenhere and over three years older than Eorpwald.

When Niartha brought her son from the north, Ricberht had surprised the other boys by his skill with sword and spear and his physical strength. Raegenhere, the elder, the atheling, never minded being bested in the training bouts in which all the boys participated: he rubbed his bruises ruefully and quickly improved his technique. Eorpwald hated being beaten at anything, grew sullen and fractious. Now Eorpwald's resentment grew stronger after the king silenced him so abruptly in the open hall – and then so markedly honoured Ricberht.

Ricberht's new position as the king's goldsmith brought automatic assumption of manhood, without the rites of initiation. At fifteen and a half years, Ricberht had reached this goal, and it made Eoprwald fume to think of the years of waiting that he faced.

He took his frustration out on the younger boys, so he was soon feared as a bully. If any of the older youths rebuked him it made matters worse. Eorpwald would find ways of getting his victims into trouble, setting them up and quite prepared to tell lies.

Some day, he was sure, he would find a way to get at Ricbehrt. He found it hard to curb his impatience.

5

Raedwald rewarded his new goldsmith for his work on the shield in a way that startled the elders and fuelled Eorpwald's envy: the king gave him a horse. True, it was not young, but nor was it a carthorse. 'Steady and well-travelled' were Raedwald's words. Ricberht was grateful. Now he could dwell with Niartha, rather than dossing down in the hall, and it would take only a few minutes to reach his smithy.

His smithy! Ricberht's stomach still quivered at the thought. The first thing he had done was to fix a stout door with a bar, latch and key, to safeguard the place in a way Diuma had resisted. True, he had spent many hours day and night, working on the shield. For twenty days he had smelted gold, pouring the melt into moulds he had fashioned from antler or clay. He had beaten thin plates, made wires, twisted them, fused them to the shapes he had designed. He worked from dawn until his eyes blurred in the light of his lanthorn, and his fingers could bear no more pain. Often he stayed by the kilns to watch for the melt, falling into troubled slumber on a bed of bracken.

Each morning he was roused by Brand. Brand had been body-slave to Niartha's Uncle Edgar, and, though Niartha had freed him when Edgar died, he had stayed on to look after her and the dwelling she had made comfortable for the old man. Realising how much help Ricberht would need if he were to finish his task for the king in time for the moot, Niartha sent Brand.

At first the man was afraid, even though he had known the lad for two years. To help a goldsmith was a scary business, and not just because of fire and molten metal. But Ricberht was mild-mannered, not unkind, and seemed normal enough, even if a bit too preoccupied at times to notice missed meals or the yawns of his sweat-streaked helper.

So Brand helped to watch the kilns, kept the tools clean and sharp, fetched the charcoal, fed titbits into Ricberht's mouth when the lad was too busy to stop the work process. They kept pails of cold water to hand, sometimes to use to quench metal, or to shrink it to the lovely stones, so carefully cut, and thus inserted into the work. Often the cold water soothed burns or Ricberht plunged his head to wake himself up.

Borgil, the shield-maker, Arnulf, the blacksmith, and his brother Randulf, the swordsmith came often to check their pieces or simply to watch the young jeweller at work. They may have had doubts, but Diuma had spoken well of the boy. They sat on the crude bench by the door, occasionally peering more closely, but too tactful, or even too impressed to interrupt.

For this Ricberht was grateful. They all knew the importance of this work. Adorning the king's shield was as much a rite of passage as his first battle was to a young warrior. Staggered at the beauty and the symbolic power of the pieces, Arnulf willingly offered to help with fixing them to the leather, stained red with oak-bark, which covered the great board. All three were involved in matching the leather rim and the gilded clasps around it. What was more stupendous? Ricberht's embellishment of Arnulf's great central boss? Or his own figures of the eagle and dragon and the intricate patterns of the strap-work?

All three stared at the finished shield in silence. Randulf squeezed the young man's shoulder, smiling.

"Please," he begged them, "say nothing of this until the king has seen it." He winced at the strong grip of the swordsmith.

They nodded in understanding. The king's eyes should be the first to give approval to such an object. The brothers proclaimed their satisfaction when Ricberht was given his horse. They recognised the skills of the new smith. He deserved it, they said. Eorpwald seethed.

NIARTHA

Time passes. Ricberht has been the king's goldsmith for five years now. In the spring after Diuma died, Raedwald sent my son to the great courts across the eastern sea, so that he could see the work of master craftsmen in the lands from which the Wuffings' forebears had come. For two whole years he watched and learned so that on his return he could make beading from wire, melt glass inlay to form a hard surface, and could mount lovely stones in gold, so that they were held in place to form whatever shape he chose.

Yes, for those two years I was lonely enough. I had only Gilda, my house-girl and Brand, who came to dig over the plot of ground I kept for my herbs. It was easier to uproot them from the woods, hedgerows and fields and plant them near my lodging. I could cut them for use, dry them and hang them for use out of season. As usual, I made salves and powders for poultices and tisanes, and when in need, the people came to me for help.

In Ricberht's absence, I went to the hall only when called to a full feast. The wives of the thanes were civil but cool. They took notice of the queen's manner towards me. If we met face to face, I bent my head and knee as was due and correct. She usually made a slight inclination of her head in response, but never gave me my name.

As for Raedwald: for weeks I might not even catch a glimpse of him; then he would ride by the oak to go hunting, and cast a hasty glance at me as I stood in the doorway. If this happened, he was likely to pause, hours later, send his troop onward to the village, and come to me. He did it openly enough. I wondered if the queen knew. There was not a lot to know! We sipped wine from little burr-wood cups and nibbled my oatcakes. He asked if I had news of Ricberht or even brought me word, come from a trader, that he had been seen somewhere. He did not take me to bed. He was king. I was his – what? A kind of vassal, though I had never had to swear allegiance to him. He could have taken me as a bed-mate (he had had plenty of those) but then he never did. He seemed to want to know that I was content.

When Ricberht came home, he asked permission to replace the great eagle-mount on the king's shield, and intersperse some of the rim-clasps with dragon-heads to show what he had learned. From his fingers, creatures of power take life, and lend their forces to the objects they adorn.

Ricberht's workmanship is so fine that the king has rewarded him with a large piece of rock crystal. I know that Prince Eni, (Wulf, my lover) gave this to Raedwald, his brother, after a journey to far mountains. Not only is the crystal beautiful, but when you peer through it, you see things enlarged. This is a kingly gift and useful, indeed, to a jewel-smith.

I know from Brand how it rankles with Eorpwald that my son is endowed with skill, by the gods. Eorpwald is furious at the gift of the crystal. He resents such a rarity being given, as he puts it, "to a mere workman," and has openly vowed in the hall that one day he will have it back.

Ricberht says Eorpwald is a stupid bully and that he can take care of himself. It is true that he grew in height and muscle while he was away, and is now a man, full-grown, and still gaining power. Yet I begin to fear Eorpwald's angry jealousy might harm my son.

PAULINUS

Far to the north of this land, a most violent king is slaughtering hundreds of monks: how can God permit this?!

O God, the heathen are come into thine inheritance; thy holy temple have they defiled; they have laid Jerusalem on heaps.

The dead bodies of thy servants have they given to be meat unto the fowls of the heaven, the flesh of thy saints unto the body of the earth.

We have become a reproach to our neighbours, a scorn and derision to them that are round about us.

How long, O Lord? Wilt thou be angry for ever? Shall thy jealousy burn like fire?

Pour out thy wrath upon the heathen that have not known thee, and upon the kingdoms that have not called upon thy name.

Help us, O God of our salvation, for the glory of thy name.

Amen

6

About eight weeks into the year which Paulinus called Anno Domini 615, the High King, Aethelbert of Kent, died. His son was said to lack wisdom and ignored the strength of the Christian churchmen to whom his father had entrusted much governance. At the grand gathering to honour Aethelbert, after his Christian burial, the Kings' Moot elected Raedwald as Bretwalda, Lord of Wide Realms, High King.

This was not altogether to the liking of the Christians; certainly Raedwald had merely paid lip-service to their god, but he held powerful sway by domination, alliance, inter-marriage and military power over most of the south and east. He returned from Kent to Rendilsham, now officially renamed Raedwaldsham, and in the month of Eostre he held a great feast to mark his new status.

Kings brought rare gifts, which would have been fit for some Roman emperor of ages past. Among these was a lovely hanging-bowl made of bronze, ornamented with gold and garnet plaques, and holding in the centre a small, jewelled, swivelling fish. There was also an antique silver dish from Byzantium, its base impressed with the head of a Roman emperor. Some gave fine textiles, woven with costly thread and bright colours.

From his jeweller's workshop, Raedwald commissioned a pair of jewelled shoulder-clasps, and a lid for a kid-leather purse to hang from his belt. Once again, Ricberht worked night and day. This time he had Arnulf's son, Beorn, to help him, as well as the faithful Brand. This freed him from the time-consuming tasks of the fire, and left him to deal with design and crafting.

The clasps of gold he made, each in two matching halves, which hinged on a gold pin through their centres. At each end of the pins he put an animal head, a bit like a wolf, Ricberht thought. Staples would hold the back of the clasps to a leather garment. The inner areas of the clasps held a complicated pattern of garnets and millefiore glass encased in a network of strengthened gold. Beyond a border of double-twisting dragons, he built the curving backs of two boars, garnets and glass marking their spines, jaws and tusks, and pierced gold at their feet. Each element of each half-clasp was bordered by gold, to preserve the inherent powers of each symbol.

Luckily for Ricberht, he had already made (for whatever purpose seemed appropriate) several plaques: two of a man between two protective wolves, and two of a predatory, hook-beaked bird with another in its talons. He had taken the ideas from jewels he had seen on his travels. He found in Diuma's secret store four circular pieces with blue glass centres, surrounded by gold and garnets. There was also an incomplete plaque of four intertwined creatures, needing garnets to be fitted. He made two more patterned pieces, drawing intricate, symmetrical designs and using Beorn's nimble fingers to cut the glass and stones to fit.

Now he took the precious sheet of ivory he had traded on his travels, and which Borgil cut into a sizeable, curving shape, comfortable to wear below the belt, even when riding. With infinite care, Ricberht attached each piece, within his usual boundary of gold and garnet. Wolf and eagle, they could do no harm. Nor could they receive it. The magic was preserved.

At his original coronation, Raedwald had been given his great, gold buckle. Now, with the helm of Wuffa on the table beside his throne-stool, Ricberht's shield glowing on the wall behind, shoulder-clasps, buckle, purse-lid and bejewelled sword-belt the panoply of a High King was almost complete. Raedwald held his ivory wand and across his knees he laid Beorhtfyr, hilt and scabbard refulgent.

Each king came to him, bent the knee and laid head and hand to touch the sword in allegiance. Though each one came splendidly dressed to honour him, none was more resplendent than their High King. No-one could guess how strongly his leadership would be put to the test.

EORPWALD

As his seventeenth birthday approached, and two years on from attaining manhood, the king's second son found even more cause for resentment.

For some weeks, months even, the Wuffings had given shelter to a man called Edwin. He had come to seek Raedwald's help in reclaiming his kingdom. All his life, and he was thirty now, he had been moved hither and yon, from Wales to Eire and latterly from Mercia, fearing for his life. Now he felt sure that, with the aid of the powerful king of the Eastern Angles, he could raise an army great enough to tackle his enemy.

The enemy was Aethelfrith, King of Northumbria – the mighty double kingdom of Deira and Bernicia – all the land between the Humber River and the Tweed. He was feared far beyond his realm, having raided and slaughtered to the western coast, into Wales and up into the northwest.

Only Lindsey lay between Raedwald's lands and Aethelfrith's. Surely, said Edwin, the people there would prefer to live under Raedwald's rule, and would join with them? Raedwald privately sent messengers to sound them out. He sent Edwin to the burgh over the River Alde from Icanhoo, to wait for his answer.

Aethelfrith must have had spies, even in the land of the Wuffings. Hearing that Edwin was under Raedwald's protection, he despatched three separate messengers to Raedwald, bearing gifts of gold – victor's gains, no doubt, taken from the battlefields and monasteries he had despoiled. The last message threatened war, if Raedwald did not give up Edwin to certain death.

Why did Edwin not flee again? Perhaps he had nowhere to go. He told a trusted companion, whom Raedwald had sent with him to the burgh, that he would rather die at the noble hand of Raedwald, than be subjected to the ignominious death likely to be dealt by Aethelfrith. In the end, he may have trusted no-one.

The young men in Raedwald's hall were wild with excitement.

It seemed that, one way or another, they would soon see battle. Even if Raedwald gave up his guest to Aethelfrith, surely there was no longer room for two such powerful men on the eastern seaboard.

What all but the elders either forgot, or did not know, was that Raedwald had actually met Aethelfrith twenty years before, coming in peace and leaving hostages as a sign of good faith, when he dealt with the problem of Wulf, Niartha and Eadwacer. His own cousin, Gurth, exiled from East Anglia, along with Wulf, dwelt in Bernicia, living as headman in the tiny village Niartha still remembered as home. Gurth had even, at Raedwald's suggestion, sworn allegiance to Aethelfrith and had fought for him twice, though he was more use to him as a warden, watching one of the vulnerable eastern approaches to the kingdom. Neither king, Aethelfrith or Raedwald, had, so far, sought to challenge the other's strength.

Raedwald might well be tempted to take Aethelfrith's gold, but he had fed and sheltered Edwin, and the laws of hospitality were deep-rooted in centuries of tradition, and so he was reminded. The queen said, "Friendship and honour are worth more than gold."

So Raedwald called in fighters from all parts of his wide realms, and Edwin summoned assistance from the Mercians (to whom he was allied by marriage).

You do not cross over heath, through forest, marsh or fen easily or willingly – there are too many dangerous paths, dangerous beasts, dangerous men, dangerous spirits. You take ship on the waters you know how to handle, especially when you need a speedy journey. So they sailed their keels up the coast to the River Witham, all the way to Lindum.

But Eorpwald was not with them. Raedwald had left him at home. The king took his eldest son, Raegenhere, and his twin nephews (sons of his dead brother). He left the eldest nephew, Onna, to guard the Deben, the Alde and the Ore, with Eorpwald's help and under the guidance of the old king of the Helmings and Raedwald's own queen. Raedwald also took Ricberht along with the other smiths. They would be needed, he said.

To be told you are lacking in experience, and then not to be given the chance to gain it is, to say the least, frustrating. Eorpwald was incandescent with rage.

Naturally, he took it out on an easy victim. The queen's third child was a thin, sickly boy called Sigeberht, now aged seven. Raedwald allowed Paulinus and his clerks to teach the boy his letters and, although the queen did not like it, Sigeberht was soon reading the holy book of the Christians. The child soon became the butt of Eorpwald's spiteful scorn. When Paulinus went to the Alde and then north with Edwin, Sigeberht looked for sanctuary elsewhere. Niartha found him in the forest, bruised, cut and sobbing, and took him to her house to salve his wounds and comfort him. After that Sigeberht came often, when his lessons were over, eager to escape his brother.

THE BATTLE OF THE RIVER IDLE

Raedwald and Edwin made swift passage to Lindsey, where their army immediately grew in number. One over-night camp on the hillsides beyond the town allowed the men from the Wash, even some from Mercia, and many from the wolds and plains around Lindum to join them.

Next day, they followed the Witham for several miles, until it became unnavigable even to the smallest boats. Then, with slaves and the horses, they hauled the boats, using treetrunk rollers, for about two miles, to the great Trent River. Raedwald sent single spies west and north to seek news of Aethelfrith. He knew already that his enemy had left the north-west (where he had been fighting) and that he was heading east. He also knew that most of Aethelfrith's forces had yet to join their king from his northern strongholds. Could Raedwald cut him off before they came?

They waited overnight at a strong burgh about twelve miles from Lindum. As the moon began to sink, news came in. They had found the enemy. Under four miles away, the Trent was joined by the River Idle. Not far from the confluence there had once stood a Roman fort, now long disused. Aethelfrith had camped there, on the eastern bank, waiting for his army to reach full strength. He had sent outriders in hope of meeting the auxiliaries, and to discover Raedwald's army, but his scouts had been dealt with easily enough by Raedwald's men, before they could report to Aethelfrith.

Just before dawn, Raedwald and Edwin moved silently, leaving their boats at the Trent, with Paulinus and a small band of men to guard them. There was no need to mark out a traditional battle-field with willow-sticks. Only two sides were exposed. The river made one boundary, the wall of the fort another. A small force could easily watch for men trying to escape over the ruins. On the last two sides, Raedwald and Edwin formed their shield-walls. Light grew.

A horn sounded a sudden alarm. Aethelfrith flung his men

31

into action. They grabbed swords, spears, knives, shields, helms. Raedwald held his ground and waited. It would not be honourable to attack defenceless men. Some of the Northumbrians even gobbled bread and sloshed down beakers of ale, as they tried to make some sort of formation. A few leapt to horse, but most animals were still tethered inside the walls of the fort.

Aethelfrith rode forward, halting a few yards from Raedwald's shields. It was easy to recognise the High King Raedwald on his horse, with Beorhtfyr, his sword, at his belt, ready for use. He wore chainmail, and held the royal shield before him, though this would very shortly be exchanged for a less ornamental one. His menacing helmet had long brought fear to many hearts. Beside him a thane held the battle-standard, barbed with bulls' horns. The Northumbrian king did not quail.

"We meet again," he called. "Eh? Raedwald? Have you come to bring me what I asked for?"

Edwin's heart may well have lurched. Was he to be betrayed at the last minute? But Raedwald kept silent. Behind the mask of his helmet he may have smiled, but who could tell?

"I have come," finally he pronounced clearly, "to give you what you deserve. This is war."

"Be careful, pretty king! My main army is not far off!"

"Not far off is too far off!" came the response. "Make ready!" Shouts echoed along the angled shield-wall. Ash-spears formed a hedge behind the shields. Thanes on horseback now moved forward, restlessly, ready to press in when required.

Aethelfrith turned his horse and crossed the square of open ground to meet his men. Comparatively few they may be, but they were experienced, hardy and bold.

There was a moment's stillness before the calling of horns was outdone by the yells, then screams of men. Spears whistled through the air. Shield-boards thundered and cracked under the blows of hard axes. Knives slashed, swords clashed. Horses trumpeted, hooves flying, teeth bared, swerving between the blades.

Foot by muddy foot the Northumbrians were pressed. Forced against the wall to their rear, they were cut down as they tried to climb, or get past the corner of the old fort. Later, men would say the river ran red with blood. This was true. Aethelfrith's men fought bravely, so that the battle lasted for hours. Many injured Northumbrians leapt into the stream and bled to death or drowned. Those few who tried to flee, or who made no effort to fight, were cut down without mercy, so that, beheaded, they could not hope to reach the Hall of Heroes, Valhalla. Their bodies were tossed later to the flood.

At the end of five hours the fighting stopped: there was no-one left to fight.

PAULINUS

God has given us the victory. Now Edwin will be mine – a gift to God.

Praise ye the Lord. Praise God in his sanctuary: praise him in the firmament of his power.

Praise him for his mighty acts: praise him according to his excellent greatness.

Praise him with the sound of the trumpet: praise him with the psaltery and harp.

Praise him with the timbrel and the dance: praise him with stringed instruments and organs.

Praise him upon the loud cymbals: praise him upon the high-sounding cymbals.

Let everything that hath breath praise the Lord. Praise ye the Lord.

Amen

7

The night before the battle, Ricberht and the other smiths had, on Raedwald's orders, moved past the far wall of the fort and put up their bivouacs at first light. At the sound of the first horn, they lit fires, ready for work, when need there was. Arnulf and his boy and some servants stayed to nurse these furnaces. They would call for help if threatened.

Randulf, with Ricberht and a group of bowmen, clambered over the ruins of the fort and up onto the wall overlooking the battle. From here it was easy to pick off those who attempted to escape among the stones. What sort of men were these Romans, Ricberht had time to wonder, who used the strength of the earth to make towers and to employ them in the destruction of honest folk? It was, for sure, an unnatural act. Then he realised that he was using this same high wall to his advantage. That day, he must have killed half a dozen men.

The killing was not what shocked him. All men could wield a spear or knife, and as a growing child he had been taught by Gurth to use a sword, and was trained with Raedwald's sons before Diuma died. The bloodlust fired his veins as the noise of the fight grew louder and he slid down to where Aethelfrith's men had been forced to leave their horses tied. He loosened one and, using a protruding stone as a mount, he swung onto the horse, bridled but not saddled. He did not have time to push forward into the mass of men before he became aware of Raegenhere, shield up, sword high, about to bring his blade crashing down onto the head of a grizzled warrior.

Time froze, and in one second, Ricberht's spear took the force of the prince's blow, splintering, bending but also trapping the blade of the sword in its length. He knew who Raegenhere was trying to kill. It was Gurth. He yelled at them both: "No! No!" He tried desparately to free the blade, to ride between them, but the horse would not respond. Gurth's own sword flashed up and took Raegenhere through the chest from one armpit to the other. His body slid down to the hilt of the sword, and Gurth, almost tenderly, took his weight as he fell to the ground. In another second he had retrieved his weapon and was sweeping round towards Ricberht.

"No! No! Gurth! It's me! I'm Ricberht! Stop!" He managed at the last instant to dodge the blade and drop from the horse to stand before the slayer.

The hubbub seemed to fade. Beside them was the din of massacre, but they stood, facing each other in stunned silence. Tears ran down Ricberht's filthy face. His sword hung from his hand. Gurth appeared to wake from some nightmarish state. His grimace faded as he gazed at the youth. Then he took a lurching step forward and clasped him to his great chest. They clung together in a moment of strange peace.

"Come with me," urged Ricberht. "We can talk over here." He nodded toward the wall. Gurth took a deep breath, hefted his great sword and made to follow.

Then, in a moment which Ricberht would for ever after recall with horror, a figure on horseback swung past, took in the black and yellow colours knotted to Gurth's leather helm, saw the lifted sword and, with a loud yell and a swift manoeuvre, used his horse's flank to nudge the warrior off-balance, swinging a strong blade to split Gurth's helm asunder so that the brains spilled on the bloody ground and spattered the wall beside him. The rider leapt his mount over the corpse of Raegenhere and disappeared into the battle-throng.

The rider was Raedwald.

Later, Ricberht found it was hard to say which was the worst moment of that day. Telling the High King that his beloved eldest son was dead by Gurth's hand. Telling Raedwald that he had killed his own cousin, Gurth. Clearing the battle-ground of corpses only happened after the smiths had removed from the enemy all objects of value or use, and that was foul work. The property of their own men was kept, bagged up, to be returned to their kindred.

Next day, they raised a huge pyre, to send the honourable dead in glory to Asgard, to join Woden with the respect they deserved, friend and foe alike. These dead heroes included Aethelfrith, found among the heaps of slain. A pity – he would have brought useful ransom. But it solved the problem of the kingdom of Northumbria.

Raedwald put Edwin on the throne of Northumbria, and he would surely become a great ally, a just and powerful king. With his alliances and dominion in the east and south-east, Raedwald had

36

now brought the possibility of peace to the eastern seaboard. This was, indeed, a mighty High King.

But he had lost his likely heir – for, surely, no-one would have raised a voice against that fine young atheling. Amid the victory celebrations, Raedwald mourned. And so did Ricberht. They both mourned the same two men.

NIARTHA

We heard about the victory, of course, weeks before the *Sea Witch* returned with Raedwald to the Deben. They had sailed from Trent to Humber, then up the tricky coast to one of Aethelfrith's strongholds at Dunstanburgh on a cliff above the shore. From there Raedwald and his force took Edwin to Yefrin – the great royal hall of his people in a wide valley in the high hills. He proclaimed the new king at the greatest Kings' Moot anyone could remember. Representatives from Mercia joined the tributary kings of Northumbria and of East Anglia. There were a few "minor skirmishes", we heard, but Aethelfrith had been so generally feared that the people accepted the change. The new king seemed brave enough, wise enough and had the strongest of allies. They longed for peace.

Three weeks later, after the throning, where apparently Paulinus had plenty to say, Raedwald left them to it. He returned to the village at the mouth of the Cocket river to bring them news and see them settled - but it was not for another week that I knew what the news was.

They came to me together, Ricberht and Raedwald, leaving the thanes to sit under the trees, while I set mead before them both. Ricberht pulled me gently to sit beside him and took my hand. He looked at me, then turned his head away.

"What is it? What is the matter? Are you hurt – ill?"

"No, no, Niartha," Raedwald spoke, and leaned across. "But our news is ill indeed."

So they told me, simply enough, and with few details, that Gurth was in the great battle; that he had killed Raegenhere – that lovely boy! – and that - here Raedwald broke off, turned away, head in his hands, so that Ricberht had to find the words to say that Gurth was dead.

"Did Raegenhere kill him?" No, of course not, he had killed the prince. "So, who?" Ricberht opened his mouth, then shut it. He broke down, choking back sobs, so that I pulled him to me, cradling his head, patting his hair in a way I had not done since he was a child.

Raedwald stood up. "It was I." He stopped. "I did not know who it was, Niartha. I saw someone lift a sword against Ricberht and I just..." He lifted his hand in a helpless gesture. Then he stood silent, head bent.

"Not Gurth, no, not Gurth. You are wrong! I know you are wrong!" I moved free from Ricberht and flung myself on Raedwald, beating him with my fists. My head-cloth slipped so that my hair fell free like a veil as I wept in grief and fury.

Ricberht clasped me tightly, dragging me away from the king. "I am sorry, my lord. Forgive her – she is distraught. Please..." He obviously feared reprisal. No-one touched the king, except for the queen and his body-slave. Only the swordsmith was permitted to measure his hand for the grip of his hilt.

Raedwald opened his arms and took us both firmly into his embrace, so that for a few moments we all shared our grief.

"Oh, Raedwald," I found my voice. "I am sorry. I know you would never have done – you did not know, did you? You did not know he had killed Raegenhere."

"I did not know then that the boy was dead," said Raedwald. "Ricberht came to me after the battle. He watched over both of them."

I could only hold my son and kiss him gently. I could not imagine the horrors he must have seen and I could see in his face that he would never tell me.

"Do the people at the Cocket know? Does Bertha know?"

"Yes, Niartha. I went to see them. Erik has been acting as headman while Gurth was away. I think that, in the end, it will be young Wilhelm who becomes headman. Gurth and Bertha between them have made him into a fine young man. They will do well now that Edwin is king – all they want is peace."

Peace. We all need that. I did mean to talk to Raedwald about young Sigeberht, but this is not the moment. Right now, I have to give the king time to recover himself and return to his hall. Most of all, I need now to help my son to recover from wounds you cannot see.

BEORHTFYR

Even sheathed, the king's sword is well-named. Brightfire, indeed. Light glows from it. The scabbard is the combined work of master-craftsmen. It is made of wood, beautifully carved then impressed with gold so that it becomes a flaming yellow. It is ornamented from hilt to tip with writhing dragons. The rim is bordered by the curving backs of wild boars. Dragons show fierce power. Boars show strong protection. These are qualities not just of a good sword but of a good king: one who protects his people.

The king's hand grasps the hilt, concealing its intricate brightness, but at his wrist the jewelled pommel gleams, golden and glowing with garnets. As he shifts the blade, small chains dangle from the crosspiece of the hilt. Each one marks a battle won. Beorhtfyr bears seven, four on one side of the hilt, three on the other. Each victory means an enemy killed, a people subdued, new land acquired – a strengthening of the king's position, a broadening of his sway.

The hiss of steel, a flash of fire: the blade lights the sky. To make a sword for a king is every smith's dream. Smiths have even made swords for the gods.

EORPWALD

Repairing the king's sword brought Ricberht into close contact with the other craftsmen. Working alongside them he was drawn into their company, accepted by them, part of their tight-knit group. He sat with them in the hall, learned the board-games, drank the ale, Before, he had always felt awkward. He was no man's son that they knew of. He had been given privileges that their own boys did not share. He seemed to have an easy manner with the king, because of the strange friendship Raedwald had with Niartha. She was rather strange, herself, they felt, though the women liked her. All except the queen.

After the loss of Raegenhere, perhaps because she had not been able even to bury the ashes of her eldest child, she had become even more remote than usual. She performed her function as queen perfectly well, opening the granary for feasting, unlocking the treasure chest at Raedwald's command, greeting guests in the time-honoured fashion, seeing to it that the people celebrated Midsummer, Harvest and the annual slaughter of beasts to provide the winter's meats. Here she was, queen to the great High King, but she seemed preoccupied, distant and unaware of the needs of her other sons.

True, Eorpwald was fully involved in maintaining the skills of a warrior, and had even been sent by Raedwald on a couple of visits to Kent and to Essex. He was not a successful ambassador, as the older thanes reported, rather shamefacedly to the king on their return. Eadbald now ruled in Kent, and had none of the noble qualities of his parents. He rejected the teachings of the Christian church, scandalising his folk by marrying his stepmother (this marriage was the reason for Eorpwald's 'official' visit) and generally preferring a wild life, to which Eorpwald took readily enough.

On his way back to Suffolk, Eorpwald encountered the sons of the late king of Essex. He had been met by messages from Raedwald sending him to attend the funeral of this King Saebert. At a place called Prittlewell, he feasted at their royal hall. Much drink was, of course, consumed. As a result Eorpwald got embroiled in an unseemly confrontation between the three Essex princes and the holy Bishop Mellitus. They were demanding why they were not fed white bread of the kind partaken by their late father, with others in the church. The bishop explained that they would have to be baptised first, in holy water. Amid howls of laughter, the young roisterers refused to have anything to do with *water!* What they wanted was this magic, strong, white bread! That - or nothing... So they threw out the Bishop and his priests– literally shoving him out of the door - and cast his followers into exile.

Next morning, thoroughly hung-over, Eorpwald sailed from the tiny port at the south end of the river Thames and spent a miserable day on board a tossing ship. But, on the whole, he felt, things had gone pretty well. It was left to Raedwald to disabuse him, if he wished.

The next evening, drinking alone in the hall, after a dressing-down by his father, Eorpwald heard laughter from what was becoming known as Smiths' Corner. He lurched over to their benches, caught Ricberht by the shoulder, swinging him round to meet a fist in the mouth. Ricberht slid backwards helplessly, toppling to the floor, and Eorpwald leapt on him. Before he could do more damage, Arnulf seized him in his great paw and, aided by his brother, dragged the two apart.

The hall steward had summoned Raedwald immediately, and he arrived to see Ricberht sitting on the floor, nursing a split lip, and Eorpwald struggling in the arms of Randulf and Arnulf. Order was restored, and the group stood below the king's seat. Eorpwald told how they were mocking him. Ricberht looked startled, and shrugged in denial. The smiths refuted any such thing. They had been talking about Beorn, Arnulf's son, who was apparently absent tonight because – well, because he'd found a woman. Or she had found him. They could not help smirking even before the king.

"Go home, now," Raedwald ordered the smiths. "Get that cut seen to." He made a gesture of dismissal

When the hall was empty, he stared at Eorpwald in silence for a moment.

"Is it not enough that you behave dishonourably when I send you abroad? You know how any guest should behave. You were there to represent me! There is no difference – no! By Thunor! Hear me speak! It is no different here. Brawling in my hall brings no honour to you or to me. If you wish one day to be chosen as my heir, you will have to prove yourself worthy. Who will follow a drunken, quarrelsome oaf?"

He stepped down from the low platform, pushed past Eorpwald and vanished into the darkness of the door at the far end of the hall.

Eorpwald left the hall, staggering into the blackness of the night. A few houses were lit by torches or dim candles, but as the cold hit him, he stumbled to a tree outside the palisade and was violently sick, as much with fury as with drink. He reeled further up the slope, away from the hall and began to move faster. He could hardly see, as the moon was misted and few stars were visible, but he veered from one tree to another, past Arnulf's forge, eventually coming to a halt at the barred door of Ricberht's smithy. He beat at it, growling and sobbing in rage, then suddenly stopped, felt in his scrip for something, and drew out his firestone. He ended up on his knees, hopelessly scrabbling for something dry to ignite, and that was how Beorn (swaggering home toward the village) found him.

"Is all well, lord?" asked Beorn. "Have you lost something? Let me..." he bent down to help. Eorpwald gripped him by the neck of his tunic.

"What is it with you people? Why can't you leave me alone?" He scrambled to his feet, pulling on Beorn's cloak as he did so. Then he seemed to realise who Beorn was – it was not difficult. He had the same sturdy build and crinkly red hair as his father and uncle, showing even in faint moonlight. "Let me go, Beorn, curse you."

"This is no place for a fire, lord. Let me help you home." He caught the king's son as he began to slide back down, and picked up, too, the firestone and Eorpwald's scrip. Then he heaved Eorpwald across his shoulder and marched back to the village. After leaving his burden with the watchful door steward, Beorn took himself home. His father, Arnulf, was eager enough to tell him about the unprovoked attack, and began to ask for details about his evening, when Beorn pulled out Eorpwald's leather bag and the firestone. His face hushed them, and he described what happened.

"We must tell Ricberht," said Arnulf. They nodded. This was no joking matter. It seemed that Eorpwald had turned nastier than they could have foreseen.

NIARTHA

I could see how shaken Ricberht was. I bathed his cut lip in comfrey water, and gave him a hot posset to steady him, while he told me what had happened in the hall. We were just going to our beds, when Arnulf thumped at our door and called our names.

Ricberht let him in while I hastily wrapped myself in a long cloak and offered him something to drink. He shook his head and indicated Beorn, standing beside him.

"The lad has something to tell you," he said, and they squatted down on stools, while I stirred up the fading fire. The story was soon told. It seems that I was right to fear Eorpwald. Yes, he always was a jealous bully, but this is something more. This is dangerous and wicked.

Under High King Aethelbert, folk were subject to a code of laws, with strict punishments for those who broke them. Raedwald had pretty well maintained this code. I did not know what all these penalties were, but felt sure that firing of a man's house could cost a hundred shillings. What about the workplace of the High King's jewel-smith? If it was counted as the king's property, then the penalty might well be loss of a limb, or even death.

"Will Raedwald believe us?" I asked.

"I have the proof," answered Beorn.

"But you know Eorpwald," said Ricberht. "He will say you stole it. Was anyone with you when you came across him? What about Idunna? Had she – had you left her?"

Beorn's face fell. "No, I was alone," he said.

"What should we do, Niartha?" Arnulf asked. "This could cause big trouble – and I don't mean for Eorpwald." We all sat, staring at the embers, thinking of the possible consequences of taking this to Raedwald.

"Leave the things with us, " I said. "Ricberht will pretend that he found them at his workshop door in the morning. He can take them into the hall and leave them with the hall steward. He can ask whom they belong to. If Eorpwald confesses, then it is up to Raedwald what happens to him." They all snort with derision. We all know that is unlikely to happen.

We have forgotten how crafty and unscrupulous Eorpwald can be.

8

Ricberht's tale was believed, naturally. One of the house-carls recognised the scrip as Eorpwald's and it was returned to him in all innocence, when he slouched into the hall late next morning. Beorn and Arnulf kept busy at the forge, and Ricberht stayed at his smithy, tidying the place up and turning a few pieces of gold and silver into little ingots, lined up in their moulds like piglets at a sow's teats. These he would return to the treasury.

Randulf sat in a corner of the hall, beaker to his lips and peered over the edge as Eorpwald received the scrip. He turned it over a few times, gazing at it as if not sure it was his. He accepted the fact that it had been found, seemingly not too tense about hearing the exact whereabouts, and fastened it to his belt. As he turned his head to look around, Randulf dropped his knife and ducked down to retrieve it, avoiding Eorpwald's eyes. Left alone, Eorpwald opened the bag and pulled out the flint, fingering it abstractedly. He appeared to be deep in thought. How much could he remember of last night, wondered Randulf. When Eorpwald suddenly turned to look straight at him, then left the hall abruptly, the swordsmith felt sure Eorpwald knew what he had so nearly managed to do the night before.

Eorpwald could remember being at the door of the workshop, but he recalled nothing of the encounter with Beorn, or being helped back to the hall. If he had just dropped his bag, then no-one could prove what he was trying to do there: touching the firestone had reminded him. He was certainly going to say nothing, and hoped Ricberht was stupid enough to make no more of it.

He sent for his horse-carls, collected his hunting spears, bow and arrows and went out hunting. He felt like killing something after the last few days.

From inside the door of his smithy, Ricberht watched him go. With the aid of his friends, he would keep an eye on the king's son. He sighed. Suddenly he felt trapped. If only the king had work for him – special work, not just pins and brooches, however fancy.

Or if only Raedwald would send him travelling again. Sometimes he even wished that he and Niartha could go back to their home in the north again, though not forever; but with Gurth not there, it would not be the same. He wanted to be free of all this – this what? It was a kind of insecurity, a feeling that he was in Eorpwald's power.

Then he straightened up, pulling himself together. He was the king's jeweller. He would find out from Garmund about protective runes and find a way to bind fast the hands of his enemy. He had the craft. He began by making a plain-looking disc brooch, engraved with just a few circles on the gold-plated front. Below the pin on the reverse side, he etched the sign of the *fylfot*. He wore this perpetually, as protection, hidden inside his cloak.

EORPWALD

It was unfortunate for Sigeberht that, on his way back from a visit to Niartha that afternoon, munching on a crisp apple, he did not hear the horses' hooves until they rounded a bend in the forest track and came upon him. Eorpwald let out a bray of laughter, and gave the sign to encircle him. As if he were a trapped boar, they lowered the points of their spears and hedged him in, yelling as they surrounded him. The child was terrified. He began to cry, then screamed as Eorpwald made as if to pierce him with the spear-point. It was an angon, a throwing spear, with a barbed blade, cruel and sharp.

"Squeak, piggy, squeak!" jeered Eorpwald. Some of the men drew back so that the circle widened. This was no longer funny. Sigeberht was distraught, running helplessly, blinded by tears, round and round, until he found a gap and fled through it, back, as chance would have it, towards Niartha's cottage. So far unaware of the child's love for Niartha, and even forgetting how nearby she lived, Eorpwald let him go and galloped off to his supper.

It was growing toward dusk by the time the little boy was missed, and servants were only just beginning to look for him, when Ricberht and Niartha carried him home to the hall. Exhausted by fright and weeping, the child had fallen asleep in Niartha's lap after she had persuaded him to tell her what had happened. Here was something Niartha *could* deal with.

As Ricberht laid the child on a bench covered with wolf-skin, she told the hall steward that she must speak with the king.

"*Must*, lady?"

"Yes, indeed. You can see that all is not well with the child. I need to tell his father what has happened."

When Raedwald came, the queen was with him. She sat by her youngest child, held his hand but did not wake him. Neither of them spoke while Niartha told Sigeberht's tale.

" He was afraid to come home," she said quietly. "It is not

the first time his brother has frightened him. I wondered..." she stopped and looked steadfastly at Raedwald. He could see she was both determined and afraid to speak.

"Say it." The king spoke calmly.

"I wondered if you had thought that maybe he needs a gentler place. He loved the Christian priests, and he misses their lessons. We all know there are houses for schooling the young, in this island or across the Frankish sea. Might he not be..." again she hesitated, then said the word. "Might he not be safer there, in such a place? Other kings send their sons to courts abroad, and now even to monasteries." She fell silent, and stood, head bowed. The queen remained motionless. It was impossible to tell what she was thinking.

Raedwald put his hand on Niartha's shoulder. "I understand what you are saying. Perhaps all that has happened since I became Bretwalda has been too much for him. I had forgotten about the monks. I wonder if, perhaps, we might think for the time being of sending him to Helmingham. If he seems happier away from here, we could think about what to do best for him." He took the queen's arm and they moved quietly away, though she was gesturing, with passion.

Ricberht beckoned a house-carl to lift the sleeping child and take him to his bed. Then he went to one of the tables, poured two goblets of wine, and drew Niartha to a seat by the hearth. "You need to recover from that," he told her. "It would be good to know the little one is safe.

NIARTHA

I wish I could keep us all safe. Ricberht told me last night how uneasy he feels about Eorpwald.

I had just cleared away the crumbs from the breakfast table, and was throwing out the water from the bowl I used to clean the pots and beakers, onto my plot of herbs, when I heard voices and the neigh of a horse. To my astonishment I saw it was the queen, accompanied by one of the thane's wives and a couple of horse-carls.

"Lady!" I exclaimed. "What a surprise! What brings you here, and so early?" The queen had never come before. If medicines were needed, she sent a servant for them. She had never sought my company. "Will you come inside? I can offer you a drink..."

The queen had been helped to dismount, and stood, looking round, and then at the open door I was indicating. She took one step forward and then hesitated. I saw her eyes flicker, as she noticed the symbols scratched on the lintel and doorposts. In a flash, I understood. She was afraid that if she came inside, I would cast some sort of spell on her. No Christian, she, but one who knew of the practices of old lore.

"It is a pleasant morning," I said. "Would you like to sit outside?" I indicated the rough bench against the wall, reached inside the door for the woollen rug I kept at hand for the purpose, and, as she and her woman sat down, I fetched a stool and joined them, bringing some elderflower wine. We drank. I waited. What was it she wanted?

"Are you alone?" she asked.

"Yes, my son is at work, and my girl is at the river, washing bedding before the winter comes. Do you need something?"

"I have come to tell you that you have no right to meddle with what goes on in our family. Coming along and telling the king what he should do with his own son! How dare you?"

"Lady, please, the child was frightened!"

"He had no need. His brother was merely playing with him!"

"Playing? I have seen too often the results of Eorpwald's playing. Sigeberht has come to me before, hurt and..."

"He will not come again." She rose. " I will not have you enticing him to this place. I forbid you to interfere again! Whatever Eorpwald does, it is nothing to do with you."

"Only when he threatens my son!" I could have bitten my tongue out, but it was too late. The words were said.

"Ah, yes, your fine son. So skilled, so favoured by everyone, but still only a craftsman, after all. Why should my son bother to threaten him? And with what did he threaten him?"

"With fire, queen. He was going to burn the workshop." Something snapped inside me. "The workshop of the king's jeweller. It belongs to the king – to Raedwald."

Perhaps it was because I used Raedwald's name like that. She glared at me with such menace that I moved back. She stepped up close, using her height to stare down into my eyes, and hissed so that I felt her moist breath.

"And you can leave him alone, too...he is not your husband now!" Ah, so she *did* know my story! "I think you will find that his visits here will cease. We do not need your advice. If Raedwald decides to send Sigeberht away to be educated, that is his own decision – do you understand?"

What could I do? I bowed my head and moved toward my door. I wondered if she would call me back; she had not given me leave to go. Then she turned abruptly, her full cloak swirling, and was helped to her horse. Shutting my door, I could hear the angry hoofbeats as she retreated.

I can settle to nothing today. It seems that I have made matters worse for us all.

9

That night, the queen was taken ill. She was feverish, vomiting and with griping pains. Her women tried the usual remedies – making her swallow a cool drink made from the leaves of mint and marjoram, and using the boiled leaves with some wormwood to bind round her stomach, like a sort of poultice, to try to relieve the hardness of her belly. Nothing seemed to work.

Only when the king returned that evening from Helmingham, where he had taken Sigeberht, and suggested that they call for Niartha, did the queen's woman mention their morning visit. The queen refused to allow Niartha near her and became so distressed that Raedwald summoned Garmund instead. Perhaps the aged priest's runes and prayers might work.

It was Eorpwald who asked what the queen had eaten or drunk that day. There was nothing unusual – nothing, except, said the woman, the wine Niartha had given her. Elderflower, she had said. From his questioning, the king learned of the queen's encounter with Niartha.

"Well, there you have it," said Eorpwald. "The woman has poisoned my mother."

"Nonsense!" snapped Raedwald. "Niartha would never do anything of the sort."

"Ask her, lord," urged Eorpwald. "Let her place be searched. She may have some of her concoction left. I will fetch her, here and now." Before the startled king could speak, his son had gone.

Garmund arrived, leaning on his staff more now for support than to create an impression.

He placed strips of birch-bark, marked with runic signs, on the queen's coverlet, burnt some fragrant stems in his small, bronze bowl, and muttered charms.

"This may need a sacrificial offering, lord king," he said. "If I were you, I would send for Niartha."

"She is coming." The king did not say under what circumstances.

In the great hall, people were coming together. Word spread fast that the queen was ill; that Niartha had been summoned; that there was talk of poisoning. Many had also heard some version of the queen's extraordinary visit that morning. They came with offerings of blankets, broth, advice, and above all curiosity. The noise in the hall was beginning to cause disturbance in the queen's quarters, when there fell a hush.

Eorpwald rode up, together with Ricberht, Niartha clinging to his back on the stout old horse the king had given him years before. A half-circle of men drew up behind them, and stayed at the hall-door, as the others passed through. Niartha was clutching a soft, rush basket. There was a rustle of whispers and a shuffle as the people parted to let them through.

"I have brought her, father," cried Eorpwald, dragging Niartha into the room. At the sight of her, the queen moaned piteously and began to wave her arm and twist on the bed. Garmund stepped forward.

"This is not good, king," he said firmly. "Take these people out of here. If Niartha can be of help, send her in. But make haste," his voice dropped low. "I do not think the queen can survive this for long."

The group reassembled in the second chamber, shut away from the throng of people in the main area of the hall. Raedwald took Niartha from Eorpwald's grip and seated her on a carved stool, while he placed himself on another before her. Ricberht came to stand behind her, a hand on her shoulder, Eorpwald to one side, together with the woman who had witnessed that morning's visit.

"Tell me," said Raedwald gently. "Just say what happened."

"We know what happened!" shouted Eorpwald. "She gave my mother poison!"

Raedwald stood and faced his son. "By Thunor!" he said quietly, but with a voice of steel, "If you cannot be silent, then leave!" He sat again, took one of Niartha's hands and rubbed it softly.

"I heard you quarrelled. Is that true?"

"Raedwald, you know that, all these years, I have never quarrelled with the queen. She was angry because I had advised you to shield Sigeberht from his brother's bullying." Niartha outfaced Eorpwald, who was held silent by the king's raised hand. "She did not wish to enter my house, so I brought a drink outside for us all to share." She raised the rush basket and lifted from it a pottery bottle, with a stopper of wood.

"Is this the drink?" asked Raedwald. The waiting-woman nodded.

"It looks the same, lord."

"It is the same," said Niartha. "It was the end of last year's making. The rest is new, from this last spring. This is all that is left."

"Did you all drink from it?" The woman nodded.

"Father, this woman's house is full of jars of ointments, powders, liquids – she could have put anything into a cup of wine."

"But I did not. Why should I? Until we had started to drink, I had no idea the queen had come to tell me of her anger. I was surprised to see her, but had no idea she felt so – so hostile to me. I still do not understand," Niartha said to the king. "Why would she not wish to protect the child? Where is he now?" she asked, aware that Sigeberht would be even more upset now, with all that was going on.

"Helmingham," said Raedwald rather grimly. "For the time being." Eorpwald scowled.

"There is one way to prove that this is a lie," said Ricberht suddenly. He took the bottle from his mother, pulled out the stopper and drank. There was a stunned silence, then Niartha retrieved the wine and did the same. With a small, mocking smile, she offered it to Eorpwald. "*Waes hael*, prince."

To everyone's surprise, the waiting-woman intercepted the bottle. "It is true, king," she said. "It happened exactly as Niartha says." She, too, drank. "She makes a fine wine." Niartha smiled at her, warmly, and squeezed her arm in gratitude.

Raedwald roused himself. "I know that any ill-effects could well take time to show, but I am satisfied. We can forget any ridiculous ideas about poisoning. Niartha, come with me. You too. The rest, wait in the hall." He, Niartha and the woman returned to the queen's room.

A few minutes later, Garmund hobbled out, and a large group followed him to the church. A sacrifice had to be made, sufficient to placate the gods. Several slaves went with them. One of them would not return.

Once the queen lapsed into semi-consciousness, Niartha was able to touch her, feeling the heat and tumescence in her lower belly. She gave her a draught to stop the nausea, and cause sleep, but knew there was nothing that could save her patient. She made it clear to Raedwald and the women exactly what she was doing, what was the nature of the medicine, to allay any lingering suspicion. She warned them quietly that there was no hope of recovery.

The queen died inside twenty-four hours. She was buried below a mound, necklaces of beads, chateleine belt, ivory comb and her favourite gaming-pieces beside her. She was clothed in splendid garments, adorned with golden brooches and jewelled pins. Ricberht had made several of the jewels. He was not, on the whole, sorry that he would not look on them again.

NIARTHA

After the queen's death, Eorpwald was kept busy, and often absent. When it was evident that Sigeberht was still longing for the books and gentle conversation of the Christian priests, Raedwald sent him into Gaul, to a monastery, where, he thought, the boy would either thrive, and make a life for himself, or would grow sick of the peace and quiet, and come home, ready to be trained as a warrior. We have no news. I hope the child has found happiness. He will be well-grown by now – he must be fifteen. He has not returned to pursue the rites of manhood. Perhaps he will become a monk. Raedwald does not mention him.

Sometimes he sends with Eorpwald the fine young man, Onna, who is one of the sons of my long-dead love, Wulf. How proud he would have been of him, I thought. Unaware of my history, Onna has always treated me with respect, and is well able to handle his twin brothers (who came back from the battle at the Idle much too big for their boots) and even to control his cousin Eorpwald, being both more able with a sword, and less hot-tempered than any of them. Together, or variously, they are despatched to Raedwald's territories, over-seeing their management, settling disputes, or bringing to Raedwald matters of serious import.

Ricberht used to watch their comings and goings, and I think he sometimes feels restless, but Raedwald has the judgement to see that the king's goldsmith and his son are kept apart. I feel relieved.

There have been, from time to time, minor clashes with kingdoms on our borders, sometimes involving the East Saxons, or those who confront the Mercians. Several times, Raedwald has gone, taking Ricberht and the other smiths with him; or he sends forces to the aid of Edwin in his campaigns in the north. He tells me there is much to do to bring peace across the huge kingdom carved out by Aethelfrith. It will take many years, says Raedwald, but he approves of Edwin. He handles his people well. Just as you do, I think to myself.

Apparently, the Christian priest, Paulinus, still visits Yefrin, and has much influence over Edwin's queen, Aethelberga. He has also tried his best to get Raedwald, as High King, to relinquish the worship of our old gods, but Raedwald persists in letting folk have freedom to choose. He allows a monk to preach when one comes on his travels, but does not wish to impose such a change upon the people. There are a few who worship Christ, but we are getting used to their ways, and they are peaceable enough. The lesser kings follow Raedwald's example, and, by and large, we have little trouble now.

In fact, we have a strange situation here at Raedwaldsham. Last year, written down by the Christians as the year DCXXI, apparently, Garmund died. No-one could tell his age, but he was as gnarled as the staff he bore – or rather that bore him. He could hardly crawl from bed to table. I know, for it was I who nursed him. I brought him to my house, fed him nourishing titbits and tried to ease the pains of his poor old joints. We even had him carried on a litter to the church so that he could preside at his altar, but in the end he was stricken and lost his speech and his strength. He would lie there, gazing at me as I moved around, and I tried to do what he wanted. When Raedwald came, he would cling to his hand and fall asleep. When he died, Raedwald wept in a way I had never seen before.

Raedwald had Garmund's ashes placed in a great, bronze bowl, and buried below the altar to Woden in the place he loved. He brought priests from nearby settlements, and on the night of full moon, they performed a sacrificial ceremony. Only the king and these priests were present, apart from one slave. He was never seen again.

Now we have no High Priest of Woden. Yet we still go to the altar, and one of us lays the oak, birch or yew. Often it is Ricberht or I who will bring the runic charms to offer in prayers. I make mine, stitches on cloth, which can be burnt in Garmund's old bowl. Ricberht will make small rings or pendants, and these can be re-smelted in the fire of the kiln. Occasionally the king will, himself, perform the sacrifice of some beast, to ensure victory in a battle. Sometimes he uses a priest of Woden, from nearby Helmingham.

Yes, Raedwald does come to me. I know his queen would hate it, but I am glad. We have always – well, nearly always – been honest with each other. I go to the hall when he asks for me, but the times he comes here are what I treasure. Now he comes alone, no troop following, no-one waiting to question him on his return. At first I felt uneasy, and I think he did, too. But one evening, as he left, he bent his head and kissed me, quite naturally, and I knew he could sense my joy.

He was away for several weeks after that, so I was not sure if that kiss was meant as a possibly final farewell. I was not left in doubt for long. On his return, I waited. He came just after noon, alone. He took my hand and kissed the palm. I was startled. No-one had done this since Wulf. I gasped.

"Do you mind this, Niartha?" He asked quietly. I shook my head, and somehow we found ourselves beside my bed. He began to loosen my clothing, slowly at first and then we tore at each other. I felt his beard at my neck, my breast, my legs, and then I was lost as he came into me, again and again, till we both lay gasping, clinging to each other. He just turned on his side and gazed at me. I smiled.

"You have improved with age," I said. Then we both roared with laughter.

"Let's do it again," he suggested. So we did. Many times over the last few months. I have been anxious lest I might conceive, but I believe my time has passed, rather early as it does for some women. And I know what to do to prevent a pregnancy.

So where is Ricberht in all this? He has found himself a woman, too.

PAULINUS

We battle still against savage, lawless men: even under King Edwin's shield, I am afraid.

Deliver me from mine enemies, O my God: defend me from them that rise up against me. Deliver me from the workers of iniquity, and save me from bloody men.

For, lo, they lie in wait for my soul; the mighty are gathered against me; not for my transgression, nor for my sin, O Lord.

Thou therefore, O Lord God of hosts, the God of Israel, awake to visit all the heathen: be not merciful to any wicked transgressors. They return at evening: they make a noise like a dog, and go round about the city. Behold, they belch out with their mouth: swords are in their lips: for, they say, 'who shall hear?'

But thou, O Lord shall laugh at them: thou shalt have all the heathen in derision.

Because of thy strength will I wait upon thee: for God is my defence.

Amen

10

As it happened, Ricberht was quite aware of his mother's new relationship with the king, and he was almost entirely happy with it. He had, all his life, seen how Raedwald had cared for Niartha, whatever the mysterious rift between them in the past. But what worried him was what would happen if – or probably when - Eorpwald found out.

Ricberht knew because Maura told him. He had rescued her, a slender, dark-haired girl, from a battlefield up in the area of great lakes. It was on one of Edwin's campaigns, the previous year, where Raedwald had allied himself against the Pictish enemies of Northumbria, daring enough to raid deep into Edwin's kingdom. Years before, Maura had been taken as a child, for a slave, on one of Aethelfrith's raids, and was now in terror of both sides of this particular battle, Picts or Angles.

Ricberht was working at the kilns that night. It had been raining, and he was anxious that the fires were kept hot. They had been busy since dusk, repairing sword-tangs, forging spearheads and fixing pieces of harness. With no time, or need, for fine jewel-craft, he lent a hand wherever it was needed. At first he did not notice the shrieks, against the din of the forge. No wonder they were kept out of the main encampment! No-one could sleep here, with the hammers ringing.

In a sudden lull, he heard her and stepped to the door of the barn the smiths had taken for their workplace. Some ruffians were pushing something around, as if in a ball-game. When the shapeless object dropped to the ground, they fell on it, as it screamed. With a roar to alert Randulf and the others, Ricberht leapt into the affray, wielding his hammer. The smiths made short work of the mob of drunken men, who fled with cut lips and wrenched arms. What Ricberht found was a girl, clad in the remnants of rags, her skin filthy and her hair matted. She tried to scramble away, but Arnulf held her. She took one look at him and fainted.

When they had finished laughing, Arnulf carried her inside and laid her on a pile of sacks beside Ricberht's anvil.

"Here," the big man said. "I'm busy. You deal with this."

Ricberht fetched water and began to bathe the girl's face, streaked with mud, blood and tears. As she roused, he put the bowl to her lips, and she gulped at it thirstily, staring at him with terrified eyes. She was trembling violently, with both cold and fear, so he lifted the woollen blanket Niartha had woven for his bed and wrapped it over and around her.

She snuggled into its softness, so that her limbs seemed less tense, but still said nothing, watching him warily.

"What is your name?" he asked gently. At the sound of his voice she shook, then sat quiet.

He asked again. "Your name?" Perhaps she did not understand him. He touched his own chest. "I am Ricberht. You?" He put out his hand towards her, and she shrank away. "I will not hurt you!" He smiled at her and waited.

Quietly she said her name: "I am Maura." She spoke his tongue, with a sweet lilt to it.

It took nearly a whole hour, but at length Ricberht heard some of her story. She was obviously exhausted, so he led her to the pallet he had made at the back of the barn, passed her one of his tunics, and left her to sleep.

Next day, after she had bathed in the nearby stream, he brought her to the king, who allowed her to find shelter with his servants, some of whom had brought their wives, of course. But it was to Ricberht and his friends she came, as often as she could. It took several days of gentle handling before she completely trusted him and his companions.

By this time, Ricberht had become entranced by her. She could remember little of her life before being captured, but had been held, far from home, in the hall of a strong, fierce man, as she put it. She worked in the cookhouse, and in the fields, served in the hall, trying to keep out of the way of the men. She had been able to hide under a hedge when this battle started. When night fell, she was afraid in the darkness and, seeing a light in a barn, she was crossing the field to reach it when the soldiers found her. They were very drunk and would not listen to her when she pleaded with them.

Ricberht saw to it that she was fed and adequately clothed. He asked the king's permission to bring her home with them. Raedwald considered the dark-haired girl with a kind enough gaze.

Perhaps he was wondering what Niartha would make of her. Trust Ricberht to do something like this. It was not the first time a man had found himself a woman on the road, or after battle, and at least she seemed compliant and free from constraints of ownership or of marriage. She was also, now, good to look at. Ricberht could have found worse. Raedwald declared her a free woman and gave his approval.

On their arrival back at Raedwaldsham, Ricberht begged Beorn's wife, Idunna, to take Maura in, while he set about building himself a house beside his smithy. He did not fancy sharing his life with her under his mother's roof, however loving was Niartha's care.

Maura was nervous with Niartha, for no good reason, other than being in awe of her as a wise-woman. It was from women's gossip in the bakehouse that now, after she and Ricberht were tied handfast, she told him what was being said about Niartha and the king. In a few weeks their tiny house would be finished, and the king had said they could marry then. In the absence of a father, there was no bride-price to pay. It could be said that Maura was now a free woman, so Ricberht was not dishonoured in the wedding.

Dishonour! He felt that he had won a rare gift. One night they lay on a wolf-skin rug on the floor of their unfinished house, gazing up through the open roof-space to watch the stars. When she turned towards him in wonder, he could not help himself. He lifted off her overmantle, undid the ties of her dress, and she slid out of her skirts. He was gentle with her, as she seemed so frail, but she responded with such uninhibited abandon, that he was soon lost in her warm centre. Nothing had prepared him for the blended feelings of tenderness and power, or for the release that came so strongly that they both cried out aloud. It changed him.

Niartha was glad her son had apparently made an easy transition to full manhood, and Maura seemed practical, neat and willing. Niartha risked a lot in the asking, but knew enough to find out that the girl had been left clean and free of disease after her slavery. Now she and Ricberht could be allowed to get on with their life together.

11

There was something else that Ricberht had brought back from the north. Among the trophies from a battle against some northern tribe, Arnulf had found a huge whetstone, as long as a man's forearm, carved with four heads squarely below the round knobs at each end. Someone had broken away fittings from the knobs at the ends, but there were a couple of curved tangs of bronze. He showed it to Ricberht. Surely something could be done with this?

Ricberht had measured the piece with cord, admiring the precision of its dimensions and the symmetry of its gentle curves. Arnulf had decided it was actually a stone for honing, putting the final sharpness on a sword or knife. The stone was so strong that no blade marked it. When wiped, it kept no trace of greasy fingers. But this was so long! How could you use it? Lying on his pallet one night, after working late on his house, Ricberht suddenly saw what he could do.

Next day, he drew an image for Arnulf, of a mighty object, fit for a king's fist, fit to hold on his knee as he sat, throned.

"As soon as I have finished my house," he declared, "and I have made my morning-gift for Maura, we shall be wed. Then I will make this. I shall need you and Beorn to help me. I only wonder who cut this stone. I have never seen anything like it. Say nothing of this to anyone, not even Beorn yet."

"No," grinned Arnulf. "That Idunna can get anything out of him. And if she does, it'll be all round the village. We know what women are like!"

Ricberht smiled, but in truth he did not know much about women in general. His mother could be trusted with anything, and he believed that Maura's faith in him would lead her to keep silence if he asked her. Nevertheless, he knew about village gossip, and would give her no chance to join the chatter. Meanwhile there was a house to finish.

His friends helped, of course. Each evening they brought their tools and their strength, so that ash staves formed the walls, with beams of split oak, and a roof of reed thatch rose over the clay-lined hearth. They made a bed-space, with much ribaldry, in a cosy corner to the rear, and built shelves.

" However shall we fill all those?" asked Ricberht, but everyone smiled or laughed outright.

Niartha provided many of the essentials, and took Maura on a day's outing to the market. They borrowed Arnulf's cart, loaded with baskets of eggs, goat's cheeses, and sacks of down from the fowls as well as a few chickens to sell alive or dead. They came back with baskets and panniers full of cloth, pots and pans. Maura had really enjoyed the experience, was excited and happy. Best of all, thought Ricberht, she was relaxed with Niartha in a way she had not been before.

"Your mother is going to show me how to make salves for the burns and cuts you keep getting!" she reported to her betrothed.

"As long as it's you that rubs them in," he grinned. "Then I'll be a happy man!"

Niartha had seen to it that Maura was beautifully dressed for her wedding. She wore a dress and kirtle of fine cloth, colourfully dyed and embroidered, and a headdress edged with gold thread, which Niartha had made, herself. Ricberht thought his bride was fit for a prince.

Raedwald performed the function of a priest at the wedding. He pronounced the prayers to the gods to bless the marriage with fruitfulness and prosperity. He draped the ribbon over their wrists, and gave each of them a gold finger-ring, which, naturally, Ricberht had made. There was dancing on the grass of early summer, feasting and drinking, and people brought gifts – mead, wine, dishes, cups, knives and spoons. Arnulf had made a fine new anvil, Randulf a shining curved knife, a splendid *seax*, not for battle, but a useful size for butchery and carving. It would be the last blade he forged. Beorn brought four horn beakers set in graven leather, which he had gilded from secreted scraps of gold when Ricberht was not looking. Idunna gave Maura a woven bedspread.

To honour each giver, Ricberht had made a tray full of pretty trinkets, wrist-clasps, pendants, rings and brooches, and let folk take their pick. None of these was gold, but each was decorated in some way with engraving, spiralling wire, pierced fretwork, or bits of amber from the beaches a few miles away.

The noise grew and the drink passed. As the moon rose between the trees, Niartha began to clear trestles, and to take some of the goods and gifts into the house. She did not wish to be part of any bedding 'ceremony', and she saw the king bid the couple farewell and move away toward the village. She and Brand came to bid them goodnight, and were walking away, when they heard a blare of laughter.

"Time to stoke the fire, smith! Time to put the blowpipe in the kiln! Pity it isn't a big one like Arnulf's! Ricberht's only got a little one!" It was Eorpwald and some of his cronies. Maura had been playing with one of the children, and was just lifting her back to her mother's arms. "You'll have one of your own in nine months!" yelled Eorpwald. "Unless he's already done the business! Eh, lads? Let's see what he can do!" They tumbled off the bench and tried to catch hold of Ricberht.

Quick as a flash he grabbed Maura's hand and swung her towards their door, blocking the path of the drunkards She screamed in fright, and Ricberht's mind flashed to the night he had rescued her.

"Beorn!" He shouted. "To me!" The smiths took in at a glance what was the problem, and strode up to the door. Some of the men went on laughing, thinking this was still part of the fun, but the laughter died on their lips when Eorpwald drew his knife from his belt.

" Let me pass, curse you!" he snarled at Beorn. "We want to see that all is done properly," he jeered towards the couple.

"Let them be, atheling," said Randulf quietly. "We want no trouble here. Let's go and have another drink." He put his hand on Eorpwald's arm. All went still.

Steel flashed in the moonlight and Eorpwald sliced at Randulf, slashing him across his upper arm, so that he fell, bleeding. There was hubbub. Beorn forced Ricberht inside and closed the door, standing outside to guard it. Arnulf gripped Eorpwald tightly from behind, in a great bear-hug, and threw him to the ground, twisting the blade from his fist. Brand and Niartha, rushing back to the scene, knelt beside Randulf. She whipped off her head-dress, using it to bind his wounded arm.

Quickly, Aelfric, the hall steward took command. He put Eorpwald in the charge of several thanes, all armed with knives, and Arnulf still standing over him. The king's son seemed to be in a state of shock, stunned into sudden sobriety. The steward sent boys running to the hall to inform Raedwald. He sent other men to fetch a hurdle to carry Randulf to Niartha's cottage.

The women stopped screaming and gradually things were brought under control. Raedwald ordered Eorpwald to be put in the lock-up until morning, and he was led away, protesting loudly, that he had been provoked, attacked even. Arnulf accompanied his brother, gripping tightly the bandaged arm as Niartha asked. He would stay at Niartha's place that night, he told his wife.

Dismayed, the folk left the little green outside the smithy, and it was left to Beorn and Idunna to quieten the sobbing bride and her furious groom. It must have been almost dawn before they slept.

Only in the morning, well after sunrise, did Ricberht wake to see Maura's sweet face, black hair spread on the pillow they both lay on, and see in her smiling blue eyes how much happiness they still shared, in spite of the way last night had ended. He took her in his arms and began to kiss her in the ways she liked. When they finally arose, he gave her the morning-gift he had made. It was a delicate, gold chain, interspersed with beads of blue glass, rock crystal and amber, a lovely piece, fit for a king's daughter, she said. She wore it constantly, hidden beneath her dress, except at a feast, when she showed it off proudly. To Ricberht, now every morning was a gift.

12

Raedwald kept Eorpwald locked up most of the next day, while he learned what had happened. He rode to Niartha's house to find Randulf, Ulla, his wife, and Arnulf there, and all in considerable distress. Niartha had tried to staunch the flow of blood so that she could attempt to stitch together the severed muscles and sinews of the arm. Then she had bathed the deep wound with water from boiled groundsel, before actually sewing the cut together. She used her smallest horn needle and the thinnest thread of wool. It was a fearful business, by the light of torches and candles, with Arnulf holding his brother until he fainted from the pain. Then she had smeared the wound with a paste of yarrow mixed with animal fat, and bound it with freshly-washed linen.

She and Ulla, Randulf's wife, had stayed by the sick man's side all night, feeding him sips of cordial and bathing his face with cool water, in an attempt to stop fever. Niartha was exhausted, distressed at the violent end to the wedding feast, worried about her son and his wife and, she told Raedwald, quietly, apart from the rest, not at all sure that Randulf would be able to use his arm again, even if he lived. She was only too aware that this man was the swordsmith to the High King. She would do her very best for him, but… here words failed her, and she wept. Now that Randulf was sleeping, Brand led Niartha away, so that she too could rest. Arnulf made Ulla take some rest while he stayed, nodding, beside his brother, and Raedwald promised to return.

Back at the hall, he sent riders to fetch Onna from the Blythburgh. One of the twin brothers could stay there to deal with the trade and the passage of ships between there and the coast. He needed his nephew, and waited for the few hours it would take for him to sail down to the Deben. From the jetty below the raven's wood, he could ride swiftly to Raedwaldsham.

After they had eaten, late that afternoon, Eorpwald was brought to the hall. He was in a foul temper, having been given only cheese, ryebread and water, and his angry yells were ignored. First he saw the elders of the thanes assembled at the benches. When he saw Onna, on a carved stool next to Raedwald's throne, he realised he was in serious trouble. He tried to speak, but Raedwald silenced him. Then he saw the ivory wand in Raedwald's grip, and saw he was to face justice.

Coolly enough, Raedwald said he had had enough of Eorpwald's irresponsible, drunken behaviour. As a potential leader of his people, he should know when to share their fun and where to draw a line. Now he had behaved outrageously as a guest at a wedding feast, and, even worse, he had caused a serious, possibly deadly injury to one of the king's men. And this man was the swordsmith, who had made Beorhtfyr, no less.

Now Eorpwald saw the great sword on the king's knees, and he knew he stood in danger of his life.

"I have taken counsel," said Raedwald, "and you should know what are the penalties for these offences against law and good conduct. If Randulf dies, you will pay the *wergild,* which I set at a hundred shillings, twenty at the open grave, the rest within forty days. I shall also fine you for the loss of my swordsmith, by death or by injury, at the same rate. You will pay twenty shillings to Ricberht to compensate him for your dishonouring of his feast."

"Lord! Father!" cried Eorpwald, "I do not have such money! I beg you..."

" You will have," said the king. "Hear me speak. You are to leave these shores. The king of the island of Odense in Denmark has need of fighters. He is raising an army to sail east, to settle a boundary dispute, which has gone on far too long. He will pay for services rendered. When he has finished with you, you may send a messenger and I will let you know if you may return, and how much you will need to pay in recompense."

It was useless to plead. Onna was to see him safely across the sea to Odense, and leave him in the care of the king of that place. Faced with the implacable faces around him, Eorpwald held his peace. He stalked from the hall, saw to the packing of his goods, chose the permitted two horse-carls to accompany him (but no thanes) and rode to the coast, refusing to speak to his cousin for the entire journey. Onna was unperturbed.

Raedwald watched, that night, as Niartha performed the ritual of the Nine Herbs Charm. She had done it only a few times before, and was chary of letting people find out, in view of Christian attitudes towards the practice of magic. But there was skill in this, she knew. She begged Ulla, Arnulf, Brand and Raedwald to say nothing. Just as she had done so many years before, up in the village of the fisherfolk, she collected the seven herbs, taking their powders from her jars, and mixing them with the softening ingredients to make a paste. She added the juice of an apple and, lastly, boiled it all up with fennel. At every stage of the selection and processing she sang the charms three times; then she smeared the poultice onto every orifice of Randulf's body, and onto the wound itself, again singing the charm thrice, as she did so.

She tenderly wrapped the hurt man in soft coverings, laid a lambskin over the coverlet, so that the hurt arm was cushioned, and stroked his temple until he slept. This time Raedwald stayed beside him. He said he was not tired, himself, and sent them all away. Next morning, when Ricberht and Maura came from the village to tell her about Eorpwald, Niartha understood why Raedwald could not sleep.

That morning, Randulf was lucid, and she had every hope that he would live. But she would not know for many days whether or not he would have the use of his arm. What sort of a life lay ahead for the man who had forged Raedwald's sword?

BEORHTFYR

It takes not skill alone to make a sword, though the craftsmanship is masterly. Cutting stout sheets of iron into bands, twisting some into ropes, then welding them in intense heat, then repeating the banding again and again, before beating them, pounding with hands blistered, bleeding, sweat hissing on the fiery metal. For hours and days the furnace roars, tools clang and the hammer rings.

Where the craft becomes magic is in the way a man's hand and eye gives life to the emerging blade. This blade will swing, cut and slash without breaking; it will respond first to the grinding whetstone, and again and again, until it takes the final sharpening from the hand-held honing-stone.

Its length heeds the height of the hero: it will fit his fist: its strength must match his might. The sword is beautiful. From the forging, welding, beating and polishing, a pattern blooms, silver-soft to the eye, but cold and hard to the touch. But the king alone may hold it.

The smith has taken ugly rocks and created from them the strength of a living king. Is this not magic? To create at once the power over life and death. Such craft is more than magical. It is godlike.

13

Randulf did live, but his right arm withered, the sinews were powerless and the broad muscles thinned through lack of use. Niartha had continued to come to him each day after he returned home. Ulla, his wife, begged her to visit, even when the wound had healed to a jagged, pink scar. She knew Niartha had tried everything.

"So have I," she told Niartha. "I even let that monk baptise me, and I prayed to the virgin goddess they have, to get Randulf better. It's no good," she wept. "He just sits there and says he's useless. He won't talk to Arnulf, even, nor that boy of yours."

Niartha felt that the man's sadness was doing him more harm than his wound, if that were possible. She went to Ricberht's workshop, a few hundred yards away, and sat watching him at work.

"Would it be possible," she asked suddenly, "for you to do that with your other hand?" Ricberht straightened up from where he was feeding some lengths of silver into the device that produced wire. One hand turned a wheel, while the other did the pushing.

"Why would I?" he asked.

"Try it, please. I want to know." Ricberht obliged, but the piece of metal would not go in straight, and buckled so that it snapped. He cursed softly, but tried again, and this time it worked.

"It might actually be easier with a harder metal," he said, and lifted a sliver of flattened iron. "It depends on how strong the other hand is, he said. My hands are pretty equal, because of all the twisting and bending I do. Arnulf's got strong arms, but his right side is bigger than his left. Now Randulf..." He stopped and looked at his mother. "Ah! That's it... you are wondering if there is any work he could do." Niartha nodded. "Well, I'd say he would not have the power for twisting those lengths for the sword. I'd say those days are over for him. But, yes, clever mother of mine! Yes, I think he might be able to do some things here. Shall you ask him?"

"Not just yet," said Niartha. "I shall have to find a way to strengthen his grip, probably in both hands. Look! Give me your hands. That's right. Now squeeze mine – go on, a bit harder. Ouch! Not quite so hard! Hold it just like that." She was staring hard at Ricberht's powerful upper arms. The muscles were working a bit, but not much, while his bulging forearms relaxed the minute she asked him to let go. "I have to think," she murmured. "What kind of work makes you use those muscles?"

"I use mine all the time. What else does a man do? There's scything, but that needs a full swing. There's ploughing, but that needs strength to guide the blade. Digging – no." He scratched his head.

"I have it!" cried Niartha. "I must go, Ricberht. This needs women's work!" She gathered up her basket, leaving some rolls and a jug of ale, kissed her sweaty son, and left.

Women's work it was, indeed. She walked Ulla to the stream with a basket of washing, and talked earnestly to her for quite a while, cajoling and persuading, until at last Ulla burst out laughing and hugged her. "It'll be worth it!" she chortled. "He'll be mighty grumpy for a while, but then he'll be ready!"

When she got home she made Randulf hold one end of a tunic, then a cloak, then a blanket, screeching at him if he dropped it, so that he clung on tight with both hands while she twisted and pulled the things into shape. When they had finished, he sat down and opened and shut his palms, and rubbed his bad arm.

"You've fairly made me ache," he grumbled. Ulla smiled, and gave him some ale. Next day she had him kneading dough. He tried it first with his right, then with his left.

"Quite right, my man," she approved. "This way and that." Day by day she found things for him to do. "I can't have you sitting there, when there's work to be done!" she scolded, and only chuckled quietly to herself, or to Niartha, when he found the strength to pull a chest away from the wall, so she could sweep. Soon he was doing the sweeping, himself, then feeding the chickens, or lifting baskets for her if they were not too heavy, then going to see to the bees in their wicker hives.

One morning the worm turned. "I've had enough of this!" he cried. "I'm going fishing!" He picked up his rod, creel, little wooden box of hooks, and the line Ulla had plaited him of strands of horsehair, skilfully joined to make a good length and rolled round a sort of bobbin. She watched him from downstream, as he fitted the line, tied

72

the hook and flung mouldy breadcrumbs to the water. As he perched on the bank, he took a small trowel from his creel and began, left-handed, to dig for worms. He brought home two fair-sized trout.

"I might see about how to make one of those basket-traps," he said.

"Good idea," said Ulla. That afternoon she went to see Niartha. Time to get Ricberht involved, they both agreed.

Next day, Ulla broke the pin on her favourite brooch. In distress, she showed it to Randulf.

"It was what you gave me when I had the baby." Here she did not need to fake tears, as the child had died in infancy, and they had no more. "Take it to Ricberht for me," she pleaded. "He'll fix it in a wink." She held her apron to her eyes, and Randulf moved off without a word, clutching the pretty jewel.

"It'll only need a new pin end and a bit of solder," Ricberht told his friend. "Good to see you here. Sit down. Pour us some ale, there's a good fellow. Thanks." He cleared a space at his bench, picked up a blowpipe and asked, "Could you just get the heat up a bit, while I find the metal?" Without giving Randulf a chance to object, he busied himself with preparations for the bit of smelting. Soon Randulf was holding in a wad of cloth the tiny tray used to catch the flow, while Ricberht removed the piece as it cooled, and began to shape it. Once he had fashioned the minute end-piece, he set himself to soldering it to the back of the brooch.

"The pin is broken. It's the wrong length. I'll need a new one. Get that wire-frame, would you? Take two, no, three pieces of the thin – no, next one along. Now, if you put them in that clamp there, you'll be able to twist them together." He said no more, apparently not noticing how it took several attempts for Randulf to hold the clamp, position the wires and do the twisting evenly.

"Now I have to let the solder harden. Can you cut the wire to the right length? Just measure it, don't knock the brooch." He sat and drank his ale while Randulf found the diminutive shears. Then Ricberht took the pin to put it in the small furnace on his bench for a minute or two. He lifted it out with his tongs, laid it on the anvil, which Arnulf had made for him, and struck it fairly gently, turning it round and round as he did so. "Make the point for me, would you?" he asked Randulf. "It's not a blade, mind." He wished he had not said that, but Randulf just took the little piece back to the kiln.

He picked up a jeweller's hammer in his right hand and made an attempt to beat the end of the pin. Then he shifted it to the other hand, pressed his right hand to hold the pin, and tried again. He persisted, pausing to turn the tip around until it was shaped to a point.

"Now flatten the butt end just a tad – perfect. Do you want to fix it? Right. Not too much solder. That's it! Just wipe off the extra. Fine! Let it rest now, to cool. Have a drink, man, you've earned it!"

They sat, companionably, and Ricberht showed Randulf the great honing-stone Arnulf had found. He described his secret plans to make it into something for the king.

"Like a sort of sceptre," suggested Randulf.

"What's that?"

"Something he holds."

"But he already has the ivory stick," said Ricberht. "Do you think he'll want something else?"

"If it's as big and beautiful as you say, by the time you've finished with it, he'll be only too delighted!" exclaimed Randulf. "I wish I could help you with it."

"You can," said his friend. "You've just proved yourself. I'll let you know when we're doing the bronze for it. You can help with any gilding, too. Get along home, now, and tell that wife of yours to be more careful!"

"I wouldn't dare," laughed Randulf. He could not wait to tell Ulla what he had done that morning, but he would not mention the sceptre.

Three days later, Arnulf sent Beorn off to help the Helmingham blacksmith, who had suffered a severe burn. He was allowed to take Idunna with him, as he would be away some time. Arnulf's own wife had died when Beorn was ten years old. Maura was staying with Niartha. She had not been feeling well for several days, and needed the advice of the wise-woman whom she had once feared. Niartha thought she could guess at the trouble, and asked Ricberht to spare his wife for a few days.

Arnulf needed his large furnace for smelting the bronze, so they carried Ricberht's two small ones, his workbench and anvil to the larger forge. Randulf brought tools, clay and antler for making moulds. He was to prove invaluable in fetching things, holding pieces and watching the fires. He even managed to do some twisting and shaping, while the small pieces were malleable.

It was the antler that had given Ricberht his idea. He had never made such a complex piece before, and it took days of trial and error. The knob at the base of the stone was held onto an inverted cup (of exactly the same diameter as the faces carved on the stone) by a cage of tines fitted to a circular collar, so the hard, grey rock was gripped in shining bronze. It seemed simple enough work to fashion the moulds for the cup, tines, bars and collar, but they, like the stone itself, had to be measured precisely, fit perfectly smoothly, and the piece had to balance on its base.

They built a similar, clasping cage for the top, then pinned an upright ring of twisted iron wire to it, using a small pedestal base of bronze to hold it to the cage, but allowing the wire ring to swivel on its pin. On top of the ring was the crowning glory. Crafted together was a splendid stag, hooves held to the ring, fore and rear, neck proudly uplifted, antlers with tines to show his mature strength. His dimensions were perfectly matched to the bronze, which cupped the stone. Arnulf's huge hands held the stone firmly upright, while Ricberht welded each piece. Finally, each cage was clipped to the stone and brought to the fire for the final closing. Randulf did not yet have the strength to hold the stone, but was able to help with the polishing. As the stag took life, glowing with the rich colour of the bronze, Ricberht decided not to gild it. Too easily one could rub off such a finish, and this piece was made to be held. No-one could resist playing with the swivelling ring, so that the stag appeared to turn this way and that, before standing erect. They washed the piece to remove dust and fingermarks, then dried it again and repolished it. The finishing touches were made by Borgil, who painted each of the round knobs with red ochre.

What they all marvelled at, even though they had crafted it, was that, with some care, the whole thing stood up on the bench.

"When shall we show the king?" asked Arnulf.

"It's nearly Midsummer. That's when his birthday is, and all the feasting. Shall we do it then?" suggested Randulf, and they slapped his back in agreement. "Keep it safe until then, mind," they told Ricberht.

With everything put back in Ricberht's smithy, they locked the place securely, as usual, padlock at the hasp over the solid plank across the door.

"Fancy a drink, boys?" asked Arnulf. Randulf said he certainly did, but Ricberht needed to get over to Niartha's place to see how Maura was.

NIARTHA

Like one or two other women I had known, Maura was being sick in the evening, as well as in the morning, and felt nausea at the thought of some foods. So I gave her warm milk and steamed fish with some wheat loaf, or scrambled some eggs. I dosed her with a tisane of dried raspberry leaves – it would not be long before we could pick some berries from the hedges.

She complained that her breasts felt sore, and I persuaded her to let me feel her body. True, the nipple area was a bit swollen, and I could feel in her belly what I knew already.

"Child," I said after straightening her skirt, and helping her to sit up. "You are not ill."

"Then why?"

I just looked at her and smiled into her eyes.

"Am I -?"

"Yes! Oh, Maura, my dear, you are going to have a baby."

She gave a little scream of delight and hugged me to her. "When?"

"Well that depends a bit on when you and Ricberht last... well, when he last came into you."

"Well, I've been here for – how many days? Before that we do it all the time!" She reddened, and put her hands to her cheeks. "Is that wrong?"

"No, of course not. I suppose you did it before the marriage? Most people do, as soon as they are handfast," I said, hurriedly. "It would be unlikely to have an effect so soon after your wedding day. Look, Maura, don't be so worried about my feelings, if that's what the matter is. I am not a Christian to fuss over such things. I am the last person to make that kind of judgement." If only she knew, I thought, but I would not tell her. Ricberht had never troubled me with questions, and the tale could wait until he did. "I am so happy for you. Oh! Ricberht! We – no – *you* must tell him he is to be a father!"

A few hours later, he came, looking so pleased with himself,

76

I wondered if he knew already. But how, if Maura had no inkling? Perhaps it was only that his work had gone well that day. I went to fetch in our dry laundry from the bushes it lay on. They needed time to themselves.

I heard Ricberht's shout. "What?" Then the voices blurred into each other, mingled with laughter. When it seemed quiet, I went inside to see them clasped together, and he was kissing her hair, so dark below his own red-gold thatch. He looked up at me and beamed.

"Well done, son," I said, bent down and kissed them both. "Oh! Ye gods! I shall be a grandmother! I'm not sure I feel ready for that yet!" We all laughed. "Perhaps that's why it takes so long to make a child – to give everyone time to get used to the idea!"

"Thank goodness you're not a cat," grinned Ricberht. "We'd hardly have time to make a cradle or anything!"

"Or clothes," I said. "We've got a lot to do, Maura, in the next seven or eight months."

"You will help me, won't you, Niartha?" she asked.

"Of course I will. It will be entirely my pleasure. Take her home, Ricberht. She's not ill. But go gently with her, if you've brought the horse."

"Poor old fellow! He's too slow to jolt anyone now! I'll take care of her, don't fret." He gave me a squeeze filled with pure joy and they left. I heard him tell her, "I've certainly got something to tell the lads!" Their happiness makes me smile. My own pregnancy had not been a source of joy, though I came to love my son beyond measure.

14

As was usual at Raedwaldsham at Midsummer, there was much to do: guests were bidden to celebrate the king's birthday, and there was so much food to prepare that every pair of hands was kept busy far into the night. The difference this year was that Garmund was no longer there to perform the ritual of the Earth mother. Raedwald discussed this with the elders. There seemed no-one who could take his place. Garmund's only acolyte had returned to the East Saxons, to be with his own folk. Onna's Blythings were pro-Christian, and the old priest of the Helmings had lost his wits.

Who knew what were the rituals? Well, most people could put forward some memories. After all, they had watched him each year. They knew the rules about no weapons being carried; they knew about the gathering of herbs – but which ones? Perhaps, suggested Raedwald, Niartha might know. What about the runes? Would she know those, too? Her son might: he sometimes put them onto an amulet. It was decided that they should be called in the next day, to find out. But then? What about the Goddess, hidden in her shrine, until brought out on her wheeled wagon? And what about… here the questioner's voice trailed off, but suddenly everyone knew what he was thinking. Someone had to make the sacrificial offering at the deep marsh-pool not far from the ford. No-one had ever seen what happened to the two chosen slaves. The king knew, because he had made Garmund tell him, many years ago. The year he had, at sixteen years old, been the chosen man. He wondered, idly, what had happened to the girl.

Called to the council next day, both Niartha and Ricberht were at first puzzled to be asked what they knew, then a bit dismayed at being treated as if they could take responsibility for part of the events. Would the people agree to this, asked Niartha? Would the gods approve? asked Ricberht. The chief elders summoned their wives, at Raedwald's command. After much discussion, it was agreed that they were more likely to offend the gods if they did nothing, than if they made the most of what they had.

So, the day before Midsummer Morning, Ricberht drew from its shelter behind the church the little, brightly-painted wagon and washed it down carefully. The king and two elders carried the Goddess from her cobwebbed shrine (and she needed a good dusting, too), put her onto the wagon on her pedestal, and covered the whole lot until dawn broke. Then, drawn by oxen, she made her way, followed by the people, to the field, selected for the ritual.

Here Niartha waited. She was simply dressed, wearing a head-cloth held by a garland of flowers. She had been up at first light, collecting from the field-hands one of every softwood plant that grew on that field. Beside her stood pitchers with the oil, milk and honey she needed. When the procession arrived, Arnulf cut a square of turf from each corner of the field for her to anoint in the time-honoured fashion. Ricberht laid runes, etched onto thin pieces of metal, in their place, and then the turfs were replaced, on top of the cut plants, each in its correct corner. Niartha chanted the words of the prayer to the Goddess, and the people joined in.

As there was no trouble this year with the crops, these rites were done to honour the Earth Mother, to thank her for sharing her fruitfulness and to pray that they might be spared from damaging storms. The selected pair, a young man and a maiden were brought, willingly enough before her, to be blessed. Raedwald pretended to tie them handfast and they were led off to the mock-marriage bed. Plenty of people chased after them, hooting and calling.

Then Raedwald led the wagon away, down towards the river. He was accompanied by four of the elders and two slaves. They disappeared round a corner of the riverbank and the people went back to the village. The two elders returned in a little less than an hour, but Raedwald did not meet Ricberht at the shrine until a further half-hour had passed. He looked grim, and passed Ricberht his sword to be cleaned.

"I prefer a battle," he growled. "This is cold blood. No wonder Garmund used to get drunk!"

In silence, they put away the Goddess and the wagon. In the distance they could hear sounds of laughter and singing voices.

"The people are happy," said Ricberht."

"Let us hope that the gods are, also," grunted Raedwald.

Ricberht said no more, but smiled inwardly, thinking of the

rare gift he and his fellow smiths had made for the king's birthday. Tonight they would give it to him at the feast. He felt that, at the moment, the gods were certainly smiling on him.

Putting the morning's events behind him, Raedwald rode back to the hall, his spirits lifting as he welcomed guest after guest. One of these was Edwin, come all the way from the north. Somewhat to Raedwald's relief, Edwin was being housed by Onna. Indeed every hall and house for miles in the east was filled with guests for the High King's festivities. Not all had chosen to attend the Midsummer rites, some because they would have had to set out in pitch darkness, some because they were pro-Christian. Raedwald knew that Paulinus had remained behind at Yefrin on this occasion, and was not sorry.

As soon as the cooks reported that all was ready, Aelfric sounded his horn. The guests assembled. There was no queen to offer the cup to the king, so the same steward had asked Niartha to do it, insisting, when she demurred. She offered the glass goblet to Raedwald, and, smiling, she told him that, with all his people, she wished him happiness and long life on his birthday.

The drinking horns were filled, and from then on passed man to man, while the platters of food came, were devoured, and were replaced. Ricberht knew that his dream had come true, as he saw his work displayed, not just on the king's shield on the wall and the jewels he wore from his shoulder to the purse at his belt, but also those shining on the cloaks, tunics and dresses of all around him. As Maura carried in a great silver dish, laden with a goose, lying on a bed of mixed herbs, he saw the necklace he had made, glinting on her breast, and he choked with pride. Her body was just beginning to swell and her sickness had stopped, just as Niartha had predicted. Almost, he longed for the night to draw on, so that he could lie behind her and run his hands over her soft belly...

"Wake up, man!" said Arnulf. "We can't sit around here while you watch that wife of yours! You needn't make it so obvious!" Randulf was joining in the laughter at Ricberht's expense. Then they signalled the hall steward, and got his nod to leave the table. Arnulf snatched one of the great horns as it passed across the end of the board, and took a great swig. "Fill it up again, Borgil," he called. "We'll be back in a minute."

The three smiths made their way to the door at the porch of the hall, to the big wooden spear-rack, where the weapons had been put aside for the day. Behind the hedge of spear-shafts, Ricberht drew out the cloth-wrapped stone, loosened it, to check that it was unharmed, then laid one great flap of cloth over it, ready to present it to the king. He walked behind the two large brothers, back to their corner of the table, so that no-one saw what he carried.

Before the *scop* began his singing, Raedwald stood and held up his hand for quiet. From a great chest beside him, he brought out gifts for all. Kings, like Edwin, received kingly gifts, some of which Ricberht had never thought to see. Bronze bowls, some ornamented with gold and precious stones, armbands of varying widths and craftsmanship, horses were promised, even swords. Each man present was given something – a ring, a pin, a bag of flour, each to his degree. The king spoke to each, then turned to sit down.

"Lord king!" Folk fell silent again, as Ricberht and his companions rose and stood before the high seat. "May we be allowed to give you something to honour your birthday?" Raedwald turned in surprise, and for a moment, they thought he might refuse. He actually glanced at Niartha, as she stood among the elders' wives, and saw that she was as surprised as he.

He sat, just as Ricberht had dreamed he might. On the table before him lay his ivory wand. Beside it stood his helmet, gleaming with tinned bronze, gold and garnets, and his own garments resplendent with embroidered bands, standing out against the glowing shield behind him. Above the shield, Beorhtfyr shone, hilt and scabbard gleaming, tied to each other with bright braid as a sign of peace.

The hall steward hurried up, but Raedwald nodded to Ricberht to approach. The young man knelt on the platform at the king's knee, and offered the stone, revealing it as he raised it to the king's hand.

"It is heavy, lord," he whispered, and the king took it in his strong grip and held it out. There were gasps, and even little cries of amazement.

"I have seen nothing like this," said Raedwald. "What is its use?"

"It is a sceptre, lord king. It is to represent the High King's power. It was a sort of honing stone, but so big! So we thought perhaps you could hold it on your knee for important business, maybe. Like the ivory wand, but sort of—well-larger." Ricberht stopped talking. He had forgotten what company he was in, surrounded by kings and the like. He bent his head and knelt in silence. Below him, Arnulf and Randulf also bent their knees to the ground.

Raedwald hefted the huge stone, stood and held it out proudly, then sat, lent forward to take the ivory wand in his left hand, and stood the sceptre on his right knee. The cup at its base might need a pad of cloth to stop the weight from cutting the cloth of his cloak, but it certainly felt, what were the words? 'powerful' 'large', 'important.'

"You made this?" he asked Ricberht.

"My lord, Arnulf found the stone after one of the battles. We all made more of it. The bronze-work to fit it."

"So you thought of this splendid stag?"

"Yes, king, but Arnulf and Randulf helped me." The king looked in some surprise at Randulf, but held his peace.

"This will be my first important pronouncement, then," he stated. "From now on, this shall be one of my royal emblems. I shall use it as you propose," he told the kneeling smiths, and now they dared to look at him. He liked it! "I thank you," he said. Then he put aside the ivory stick, stood the sceptre on the table, and suddenly realised what an extraordinary object it was that could stand so proud, so well balanced. He then found that the stag in its ring turned at his touch, and again the company cried out in awe, as it faced them. The king laid the piece carefully on the board before him, and clasped the hand, one by one, of each of his smiths. When he took Randulf's proffered left hand, he patted it softly after shaking it in both of his.

"It is good to see you back at work, man," he said softly. Then he called aloud for more drink, and gave each of the three a silver goblet. "I have never had a more princely gift," he stated. The hall resounded to the pounding of fists and boots, as the folk echoed his approval and the feast went on. Ricberht, Arnulf and Randulf were helped to a bed beside the hall's hearth that night, returning to their wives next day with very sore heads, and only half-aware of their triumph.

NIARTHA

The summer days are almost forgotten, harvest has been gathered in, animals brought to the near paddocks and bartons, and the king has held his last moot of the year. It grows dark so early now, one month away from the shortest day, that people are busy making candles, hoarding oil and storing bedding and tedding as the bracken and heather turn colour. Logs begin to climb up under the eaves of houses. The noise of sawing, chopping and splitting resounds far through the almost bare trees. Thatchers are finishing the last repairs to roofs and now it is time to show why this is called Blood Month.

Only one or two bulls and rams, boars and cockerels are needed. Some stallions are kept for warfare. A few male animals are gelded, to be kept on and fattened for food if the harvest has been good enough to feed them through the coming winter, or, in the case of horses, trained to lesser tasks than fighting. Some will have been sold to other people. There is a fairly large market-wick growing up about a dozen miles from here, by the Gipping River. I sometimes wonder if Ricberht will be tempted to take his work there, and build a bigger house, now that they are going to have the baby. (Maura looks as if she will go to term.) But I think he is happy, and Raedwald keeps him busy. Many a king has a gift to be proud of, thanks to Raedwald's bounty and my son's skill.

But I stray from the point. This is the month when we cull the surplus stock. Many male creatures, and several females who are injured or can no longer breed are being slaughtered. Of course we make feasts of it all! The hides go to the fell-monger at the wick, bartered for his rugs, hangings and leather for garments. We strip the flesh for roasting, salting and drying. We hang the wild birds and the venison, or smoke them, ready for Yule, and we lay the bones of our beasts like pallets to make fires. The lovely sweet chestnuts taste best, cooked in the ashes, better than saving them for boiling, as we sometimes have to, if the crops have not done well. It is a poor sort of flour, but better than acorns.

I remember when I was glad enough to get even acorns – but I will not think of that. I have now all that I need, except of course the grandchild who will come next month.

Tonight, it is our turn to make the bonefire, and Maura has helped to make the bread while I have put out the cheeses we made a few weeks ago. I have boiled a great many eggs and made a large crock of butter, churning till my arms and back ached. There are nuts, apples and late pears I kept in the cold store There is mead, wine from the market and milk with honey. I wonder if Raedwald will come.

The broth is bubbling in its cauldron. I think we are ready now.

15

Ricberht had built the fire in the centre of the glade, so as not to scorch any of the trees, especially the mighty oak which gave its name to the place. Nor did they wish to risk being too near to Niartha's house. A couple in the village had lost theirs the previous year, when a sudden gust of wind blew the sparks onto their thatch. Now they had gone to live at the wick, where he found work on a trading ship and she kept a stall to trade whatever he brought home, and whatever she could grow or make.

It took only one spread of kindling below the bones to ignite the fire. The residual fat and gristle soon caught, and the bones held the heat. It rose, layer by layer, up platforms of bone and logs, spitting and crackling, with occasional bursts of noise as something split open. Sparks fizzed up into the sky, as if trying to meet the fires that burn there already. The black clouds parted to let the moonlight wash over the faces of the people below, but still loomed threateningly.

Many came from the village, but Niartha had no anxiety that there was not enough food. They carried baskets and platters, covered with cloth, and revealed thick slices of ham, apples for baking in the hot embers, meatballs ready to sit on iron baking trays, their long shafts sticking out of the fire like spines on a hedgehog, too high for children's hands to reach. Trestles creaked and swayed perilously with the press of folk. Ricberht was kept busy, pouring drink from jugs, flagons and leather bottles.

One man began to play his wooden pipe, and soon there was singing. The *scop* strummed his harp in time, and then plucked the strings to make the tunes for dancing. A great circle formed around the bonefire, and, as they sang, the people moved two steps to the right, then six to the left, taking in new dancers, and gradually moving round, until the leader was back where she started.

This was no formal feast, with each form of music in due order and listened to, on the whole, with some respect. Here men reached out their hands to take the pipe or harp and start the tune of some song, well-known to all, and becoming more and more ribald as the night went on. Tonight was not the time for tales of great heroes and battles long ago. They sang songs of drunken sailors, of silly old men, of raunchy girls, with actions in the dances to match. Soon they were nigh helpless with laughter. Finally, they sat down to drink, beside the mellow blaze, on skins laid down on the damp earth, too tired to dance any more. Someone started telling a new riddle he had heard. Cries of "Easy! Too easy!" led to another and another: "a horse!"- "leather!"-"onion!" Eventually one lad began the one about something sharp and pointed, that soon shudders and dies, but his mother boxed his ears, pulled him to his feet and made her husband stand up and help her get home with her weak and giggling son.

No-one would fancy walking back in the dark alone, so soon the baskets, beakers and horns were reclaimed, thanks were called and Niartha's little family were left to collect the remains of the food to use next day, or chuck bits onto the embers. Soon there was only trampled ground and flattened grass to show for the throng.

"That was good," smiled Maura, helping to bring in a tray of wooden cups, resting it on her large belly.

"Yes, it was. Everyone enjoyed themselves so much!" Ricberht agreed. "It was worth all the hard work!"

Maura cuffed him gently, laughing. "What hard work? Pouring a few drinks?"

"And carrying the trestles!" he objected, smiling. "We'll do the rest tomorrow, when we can get the water to wash stuff! Bedtime, now!" They kissed Niartha and went off to the little room they used when they stayed for the night.

Niartha went outside and spread earth and dead ashes over the remains of the fire, to quench it. The moon was covered, so that the night was black as the pitch they used to seal their buckets and their boats. A vixen barked nearby, and an owl swept soundlessly past on wide wings. She dowsed the two torches burning beside the door, in the hooped bucket kept for the purpose, and closed the door, before going to her bed. She pulled her thickly woven blanket to her ears and lay, smiling at first at the memories of the evening. Then she wondered why Raedwald had not come. After all, they were the bones of his animals they had been burning. She kept no livestock, except for ducks, chickens and one nanny goat, constantly in kid, trading the young ones on, or using them for food and hides.

Raedwald must have had something to attend to, she thought sleepily.

He told her about it next morning, arriving just as she had stowed away the last pots and cups on a shelf, and was making a hot raspberry drink for Maura. She knew this would help in the labour to come, and had sent the girl to rest on the bed for a while, now that the work was done.

"I passed Ricberht on the way," Raedwald told her. "He said you all had a good time last night. It was a big fire, to judge by the ashes!" He leaned on the doorpost looking out. "I'm sorry to have missed it." He stood, twisting between his fingers the horn of wine she had given him.

"Did something stop you, Raedwald?"

"Yes." She waited. "Eorpwald sent me a message. He has landed at the Gipping."

"What?" cried Niartha in some dismay. "I thought you told him to wait until you gave him permission to return!"

"Well it is about seventeen months since he went away, so I suppose I should have expected to hear something. At least he has not come home to Raedwaldsham. I have sent Aelfric to find out details. He may be injured, or not have the rewards, he hoped for. Let us hope he has grown wiser, at any rate. Aelfric is making sure he stays at the wick until I send word."

"Does anyone else know? Ricberht? Randulf?"

"Not yet. I will wait for Aelfric's news. I have told him to come straight here to find me. I do not want gossip to spread. I hope you do not mind?"

"Of course not. In any case you can surely do as you please, lord king," she smiled.

"I know what I would like to do," he grumbled quietly, "But not with the girl here, even if she is asleep."

"Let's go and pick up fir cones in the other wood," suggested Niartha. "You can carry the big basket!" Never let it be said that they stood on ceremony with each other.

They strolled off, side by side. Surely it would take at least three hours before Aelfric came to find the king, and that same king was wearing a thick cloak, soft enough to lie on and full enough to cover them. Niartha carried a smaller basket with nuts, cheese, bread and mead. A pity the late blackberries were not fit to eat. Perhaps some mischievous being, like Loki, had bitten them.

In fact, though they kept each other warm long enough

for Niartha to tell the king how she had just remembered the rude riddle from last night, it was looking quite stormy as they lay, gazing up at the high treetops and noticed the black sky. They gathered enough cones to seem useful, and ran back to the house. Maura greeted them demurely enough, but she was smiling as she bent awkwardly to put a pan on the hearth to heat while she found rashers of bacon and fetched some eggs. As she came back in, she told them someone was riding up the track. She and Niartha made themselves scarce, so that Raedwald could hear what Aelfric had to tell him. The little outbuilding certainly needed tidying after yesterday's upheaval and it would be one less job for Ricberht when he returned from the workshop. Niartha removed the pan from the fire as they retreated. The food would have to wait.

That night, Niartha had to tell Ricberht the news that Eorpwald had sailed home, even this late in the year, unhurt in his exploits, amply rewarded by the Danish king, and would be at his father's hall by midday tomorrow. He had greeted Aelfric civilly, enquired of his father's health, and was keen to come back home. He had rewarded the messengers generously and sent his father a huge bear-skin and a silver ladle-bowl with a lip, for raising and pouring wine or ale from a larger bowl at the feast.

Raedwald permitted Eorpwald's return. What else could he do? By no means would everyone be pleased. What would happen about the debt he undoubtedly owed to Randulf? Ricberht sighed. It always seemed as if joy was inevitably followed by grief of some sort. He would keep out of the way.

EORPWALD

The king's son had, indeed, learned that he was expendable. The battles were hard-fought, and he had to recognize that he had still much to learn. One wound had left his leg scarred, but he was luckily kept alive, and did learn more skills with dagger, *seax* and sword. He also learned when to hold his tongue; there was an old saying about an uncontrolled tongue bringing a bad reward, and his babbling got him into a stupid fight, so that for a month he had been banished from the hall of the Danish king, and was forced to live with the seamen. After that, he tried to hold his peace. His courage was not doubted. He was willing to throw himself into the fray, and did his fair share of killing. He also discovered when it was more politic to bring in a prisoner to be held hostage, so that his people paid a good price to have him returned. So he had proved useful enough.

When there came peace, or at least a prolonged lull in the fighting, he was allowed to travel with the Danish king's sons. This he enjoyed hugely. The riding in vast forests, the sight of terrifying mountains, the feel of frozen snow, or of the hot vineyards to the south: all provided the excitement of the unusual. In addition, there were the pleasures of food and drink, offered in hospitality, not to mention other delights to be tasted, rather less openly. A girl at a forest-edge, behind a barn or even in a midnight bed, all brought the satisfactions he had missed. By moving on he and his fellows avoided the penalties of discovery: no fines could be imposed for making free with another man's slave, his daughter, or (once) his wife. Eorpwald was well out of the way next day.

After a particularly cold, long and dark winter, the call to battle again was quite welcome, and Eorpwald was one of the honoured guests at the celebratory feast many months later, and was given much treasure and a fine new stallion. He begged permission next day to return to his father's home. The Dane was unaware of Raedwald's strictures, and let the young warrior go.

As it was no longer in the sailing season, Eorpwald used a coastal trader to sail from place to place, and had to wait for an unusually unseasonable, southerly breeze, to carry him to the Kentish kingdom. He had thought to stay in Kent, enjoying the company of his old drinking-mate, Eadbald – the one who had married his stepmother. To Eorpwald's surprise, he found that his friend had turned Christian, ashamed of his former ways. He had given up his stepmother-wife, and appalled at the treatment of the bishops in both Kent and Essex, he was making amends by building churches and founding monasteries. Quite a few of his people had moved west, some to the island off the south coast, and some into East Anglia. When he tried the Christ-talk on Eorpwald, that was enough, and they parted politely, but not as the closest of friends.

When he arrived at the Gipping wick, Eorpwald suddenly remembered Raedwald's prohibition, and sent a most carefully worded message to his father, and waited to see what would happen.

After the bonefires, people were too busy smoking the meat, drying it or salting it, to need the bother of another feast. Yuletide was just over a month away, and, of course, the Mothers' Night just before Yule. So, in welcome, Raedwald did not do more than invite the elders, with their wives, to a meal of spitted venison, with mashed swede and shredded parsnips, followed by stewed apples topped with breadcrumbs soaked in honey, and thick cream.

To Eorpwald, after several nights at sea, this was enough. It all smelled just as he remembered. After the meal, the men sat with feet propped along the benches by the hearth and listened to Eorpwald's version of events in Denmark and Sweden. He would save accounts of his sexual prowess for a convivial session with his younger companions, some other night.

Other men came in, to take some fire from the hearth, or to sit drinking in a relatively warm corner, but there were no smiths among them, Raedwald noticed. Later, he would have to raise the matter of Randulf's compensation, but for the time being they would steer clear of any controversy. Eorpwald took himself off, still sober, to his chaste bed in his mother's old house, and fell asleep.

The king took a little longer to find rest.

16

Ricberht, Randulf and Beorn were kept busy for the next six weeks, working into the darkness of the short days, to make the things that the community wanted to give as gifts. Arnulf was equally busy mending broken tools ready for the spring, and trying to find time for forging new ploughshares. He made knives and *seaxes*, too, now that Randulf was crippled, and it was fortunate that no new sword had been needed. Maura was now staying with Niartha, and Ricberht returned there each night, ready for the birth. It must be soon! No-one could be as big as that for much longer! She had little rest with the child moving within her, and Niartha did not allow her to do much work now, except to slice vegetables and fetch the eggs from the hens she liked so much for their funny ways.

Sometimes Niartha would watch her, unobserved, as she stroked her child through the cloth and skin that covered it. She would sing a little song to it, over and over. Niartha remembered how she had felt about her own, unwanted child, and sometimes she felt a clawing regret. Baby Ricberht had become lovable to her, in her strange plight, so that when he was stolen from her, she was frantic with distress. Now she was entirely proud of him, and glad to share her love with Maura, who trusted Ricberht with her life.

She would send her house-girl, Gilda, to tell Ricberht when the pains came, and to bring back Ulla to assist her. Idunna had given birth to her baby at the start of the month before Yule, so was in no state to come and help, being cared for by her own mother, and sisters. She had given birth to a large, healthy boy, but had been badly torn in the delivery, and was tired out with the feeding of the child. Niartha sent bottles of raspberry juice and infusions of milkwort, and a salve for the sore nipples and torn privates, but she had to stay to keep an eye on Maura.

Once or twice she had been on the verge of getting help, when she realized it was a false alarm. The day before the Night of the Mothers, the busiest time and most solemnly kept feast of the year, Maura came indoors and dropped her apron of eggs to the floor, with a sudden cry. She clung to the doorpost, doubled up, and looked up at Niatha, mutely.

Niartha helped her to the bed, and placed a hand on her belly, to wait for the next pain. There was no doubt this time.

"Stay there for the moment," she said, and called the house-girl to finish cleaning up the broken eggs and then go for Ulla's help, as they had planned. "Tell my son there is no need to rush home. This will take some hours," she ordered, knowing he would take no heed. "Tell Ulla I need her as soon as she can get here." Gilda vanished into the misty morning, running as fast as she could.

Niartha returned to Maura. She thought she might find her too frightened for her own good, but Maura was quite calm.

"What must I do?" she asked, though she cried out as the next pain came.

"Let's get you off the bed," said Niartha. "It is best for you to stay upright as long as you can. Try to breathe through each pain. Like this." She blew to show her. "Can you walk awhile?" She took the girl's arm and began to help her walk to and fro, pausing for the agonizing spells as the belly tightened. She had just let her lie down again so that she could see how she was opening, when Ulla arrived. It was hard to tell how much the opening had progressed, but, as they stood Maura up, her waters broke, and she yelled in fright.

"It is all right," soothed Niartha. "I told you that is what happens. Now things could speed up a bit. Here, let us put a clean robe on you." They bathed her hot face and body, and were just getting her to walk again, when Ricberht arrived, followed by Randulf.

"And just what good do the two of you think you'll be?" enquired Ulla tartly. "It is all going the way nature intended. Get out from under our feet now. It will be ages yet."

"I told them that," said Gilda, the house-girl. "But they would come!"

"Get back to your smithy now. This is women's work," Niartha urged her son, though kindly. "I promise we will call you when the time comes." He put his arms round his wife, then jumped backwards as she gave a groan; he looked wildly at the group of women and left, followed by a sheepish Randulf, whose wife was pushing him out of the door.

"Peace, at last," smiled Niartha.

"Is that what you call it?" gasped Maura, and held on to Ulla for support.

The morning passed. While Niartha found linen to tear into strips for wadding, Ulla washed the small shears in hot water and laid old cloths on the bed. In between, they all drank the sweet, warm, raspberry infusion. It could not have been much after noon, when Maura's pains grew noticeably closer together, and stronger, so that she could no longer stay on her feet.

"I think this baby is in a hurry, Ulla. Let's see what's happening." To Niartha's surprise, her exploring fingers could feel the baby pushing its way toward daylight. Yes, she could feel wet hair! Any minute now the channel would be wide enough.

"The child is the right way round," she reported. "But it is coming so fast, I have never seen anything like it. Now, Maura, I want you to lie back down again. Bend up your knees. Now, try to stop pushing. Just let things slow down a bit if you can. Pant now! Stop pushing if you can. Hold onto Ulla instead. Steady! And again! Just pant! That's better. Now let me see. Yes, the head is coming... breathe! Now push!"

With a sound something between a yell and a moan, the girl bore down with all her strength.

"I have it! I have the head. Hold still! Wait – yes, the neck is free. Now one more big push! Keep it going! More!" The girl fell back, exhausted, and Niartha's ready hands took the slippery little body. Quickly she checked the airway, clearing the mouth, and lifted the child to slap it. No need. Its mouth opened in a scream and it drew its first breath. One more searing pain for the afterbirth. They tied the cord close to the baby's stomach, cut it with the shears, and Niartha rested the infant on its mother's breast.

"What is it?" breathed Maura.

"It is a girl." Neither midwife knew if this was good news. They had not thought to ask, so they looked a bit anxiously at the new mother.

Maura cradled her babe and beamed at them. "I am so pleased," she whispered. "She is just what I wished for." Niartha hoped it was Ricberht's wish, too.

Ulla filled a wide bowl with warm water, and now Niartha took the child and washed her gently, checking every bit of her as she did so. All seemed well, so she padded the baby, and wrapped her tightly in a soft cloth, then a woollen shawl. Ulla helped to clean and reclothe Maura, and gently brushed back her hair. They placed pillows behind her so that she could sit up, ready to feed the child, helping to place the baby to the nipple, and encouraging them both with little pats and soft noises.

"Now you may go and fetch Ricberht," Niartha told her girl, and Gilda darted off. "There will be enough time to tidy up and finish the feed, and then you can both rest."

"I do feel a bit shaky," said Maura.

"I'm not surprised, the quickness of that birthing!" said Niartha. She gave her some warm milk and honey, and then, when the baby had fallen asleep and was laid in its wooden rocking cradle (made by Borgil), they all enjoyed a bowl of broth.

To their surprise, not to say anxiety, it was almost two hours before Ricberht appeared, long after the girl had come home, saying that he would be close behind her, after locking the smithy.

Ricberht rushed in, straight to Maura's bed and took her tenderly in his arms. "Is all well?" he asked his mother.

"Yes, indeed. A quick and easy birth, and no damage done. Don't you want to see your baby?" she smiled. He stepped over to look down into the cradle, half-embarrassed, half-eager.

"It looks very pink. What is it?"

"We have the daughter you wanted," beamed Maura. "Go on! Pick her up! She's yours!"

Niartha lifted the child and laid her into her son's arms. "And you have made me a grandmother," she whispered, and kissed them all three, in turn. "What are you going to call her?"

She learned, then, that through all the terrible events that had befallen Maura, the girl had clung to the fading memory of her mother. She had now only a vague recollection of her face, last seen in anguish as Maura was dragged from her by her captors, and she had turned to face those vicious men. But her name was Fritha. "Our baby is called Fritha," they said, and Ricberht held his little family close.

"Fritha," echoed Niartha and Ulla, nodding with quiet satisfaction.

"Now let them both rest," Niartha said. "We have food and drink for you. Then you can take Ulla home, and go and celebrate in the hall." As he ate, she asked what had taken him so long to arrive.

His face darkened, and he tore quite savagely at the crust of bread. "It was Eorpwald."

"Oh, no! What did he want?"

"He came to take some pieces as gifts for tomorrow's feast.

I asked him what he would trade, and he said he would decide when he had seen what I had. I had just put some things out, when the girl arrived to tell me about the baby, so I asked if he could call back in the morning. He said it was not convenient. What could I do? I don't trust him, so I stayed watching his hands, when I was really longing to clear up and empty the kiln. In the end he took four things and offered me one gold piece. I told him it had cost me five of them to make the work. Randulf backed me up..."

"Randulf! Did Eorpwald see him?" cried Ulla, horrified. "I mean, of course he did, but what did he do?"

"Nothing. He sort of stared at him. Then he gave me six pieces, without a word more, shoved the things into his bag, and we thought he was going to leave. Then Eorpwald told me he was surprised that anyone would marry me. He was even more surprised that I could father a child. He was sneering, so I could have hit him. I nearly did, but I suddenly realized he wasn't worth it. He stared at me to see what I would do; then he laughed and walked off. I slammed the door behind him. Then Randulf and I cleared up, and I've shut up the workshop till after Yule. Randulf is fine, Ulla. Let me take you back home now."

They thanked her sincerely for her help and care that day, and she promised to see them before the feast on the next night. It was not the easiest of times for Ulla, having lost her only child, but she was a woman of spirit, Niartha knew, and she embraced her warmly.

"Come in quietly tonight," she reminded Ricberht. "Or stay at the hall overnight, if you get too merry!"

17

Raedwald took the unusual step of calling a special moot of the elders, holding it in his small anteroom, while the women organised the decorating of the hall and that night's feast.

"There is a matter outstanding," he told them, "and I wish it to be settled, so that we may all enjoy the next few days wholeheartedly." He told them his purpose, offered them mulled ale and, in full agreement, they waited, so that Eorpwald, Randulf, Arnulf and Ricberht could be summoned.

As demanded by the king, Aelfric told what he had witnessed that midsummer night, eighteen months before. Arnulf was asked for his agreement to that account.

Then the king ordered Randulf to strip off his tunic, to show his scarred and withered arm. He stood before them, head hanging, but Raedwald bade him look up, proud. "You have done more with your other arm and restored some strength to this," the king told him. "Nothing to be ashamed of, man!"

Then Ricberht told of what Randulf could do to help him in the jewellery workshop.

"Nevertheless," stated Raedwald, "I have lost my swordsmith. I think no-one else will make another Beorhtfyr. If war comes again, I will need to find another strong man. Maybe this can be Arnulf, or maybe Beorn. Perhaps Randulf can advise his brother, but he will not be able to show him. Time alone will tell. So now we will award the compensation due to Randulf."

Eorpwald, led by Aelfric, stood before the king, who held, to his surprise, not only the ivory wand of the Wuffings, but also a great stone, surmounted by a bronze stag. Eorpwald could not take his eyes off it as Raedwald made his pronouncement. He even felt a thrill of fear.

"I judge," the king said, "that this offence is at least the same as binding a man unlawfully. Randulf can no longer ply his craft, and his worth as a smith has been diminished. Therefore the penalty is to pay the sum of one hundred shillings, or that weight in gold. To be paid immediately," he informed his son. "Ricberht will know the value."

Eorpwald flashed Ricberht an evil glance, but the court sat impassively, while he lifted his bag and counted out some gold pieces. Raedwald looked questioningly at the goldsmith.

"May I fetch my balance-scales, my lord?" asked Ricberht. While he hurried off to get them, they waited again, in silence, as the minutes passed. On his return, Ricberht set the small scales on the table at Raedwald's side, checking that it stood firm and level to the eye. He placed some weights in one small tray and laid Eorpwald's offerings in the other. "Ten more, I think, lord," he advised. Eorpwald obliged with a scowl. "That is fair, lord king."

Raedwald took the pieces, poured them into a leather drawstring bag and handed it to Randulf, who held it in his big left hand, and gazed in awe at them. He collected himself enough to say, "I thank you, lord king." Then he turned to Eorpwald to utter the words that acknowledged the payment. "The debt is paid," he said, but he did not thank him.

"One thing more," said Raedwald. "At our last meeting on this subject, I decreed that Ricberht is owed compensation for the disruption of his wedding feast. Twenty more shillings are due."

Eorpwald positively snarled. He had hoped his father would forget what he had said. He drew out more pieces, and slapped them onto Ricberht's hand.

"The debt is paid," said Ricberht, and bowed to the king in thanks and surprise.

"The hearing is over," said the king, and the smiths surged off in gleeful comradeship. They could be heard calling for drink as they passed through the hall. Raedwald returned the sceptre and wand to his carved, oaken chest, and clipped the key to his belt. Eorpwald watched wordlessly. It was the same key his mother used to hold. Now Raedwald had no woman, he thought, not without an angry satisfaction, as he left the chamber.

"No drink in the hall until tonight," they were all told. "Unless you are the king!" People were putting up swags of ivy, branches of holly, and great bunches of mistletoe. The floor would then be swept and the tables arranged: silver dishes for the king (and his son they supposed), and special wooden platters instead of bread to hold the delicacies on offer tonight. Outside, the bakehouse smelled delicious, and so did the spit-roasts, turned by slaves below open-sided shelters. There was too much to cook at the ordinary hearths, though every woman was making something good. The men were kept busy, fetching, lifting, carrying. Some tried to disappear, to finish off some gift for the evening's ceremony, but the three smiths sat at Randulf's hearth and drank in glee. Ulla had dried her eyes, overcome as she was with the compensation, and set off to take the news to Niartha.

"Just an excuse to see the baby," Arnulf laughed. "Will Maura make it to the feast tonight? Or must she be confined? She *is* a mother, after all!" They laid plans to use the litter last employed to carry poor old Garmund, and promised to be at Niartha's in good time.

"Everyone can wet the baby's head!" Randulf said. "Thor only knows who'll be in a fit state to get them home. You'd better stay here the night. I mean it! Ulla will be only too pleased."

THE MOTHERS' NIGHT

Ricberht went home in time to prepare his womenfolk for the night ahead. Maura was thrilled, and, while rather more cautious, Niartha said she should be safe enough, provided she rested now, did not try to dance, and drank only milk, for Fritha's sake, as well as her own. When she got tired, they would retreat to Ulla's house. Arnulf and his brother were laying out extra bedding, right then, Ricberht told them. Niartha packed a large basket, with padding for mother and child, and some draughts in case of need.

They had made honey-cakes and whipped some cream, so did not come empty-handed, and there were nuts and dried fruits, as well. With the men carrying the litter, they set off well before dusk so as to lay out their offerings, and see the babe was fed and settled in a stout basket, before the feast started. Niartha planned to keep mother and child close, and in sight, all evening.

On this night, the women were given places at tables, beside their menfolk, and the servants would feast after. A boar's head was carried in, and amid the cheering and singing to welcome it, Fritha awoke and cried. Ricberht picked her up, and was then made to carry her proudly round the hall. As he passed Raedwald and Eorpwald on the dais, the king beckoned Ricberht to come to him. Ricberht brought the child, and the king smiled as she gripped his little finger. He stroked her head gently.

"I think you've got a little redhead here," he said. "Look how her hair glows in the torchlight!" He released his finger, felt in the purse at his waist, and put a gold piece into the tiny hand. "May the gods smile on you, little one. What is her name? Fritha? That's the same as Frig, isn't it? Or is it Freya? Whichever, she is named well, for a goddess." Ricberht bowed low, smiled and thanked the king. He and Eorpwald ignored each other, and the baby was carried back to her delighted mother.

After the eating came the giving of gifts. Each woman received something, as the king saw to it that even widows who had also lost their children were honoured tonight, while husbands, sons and grandsons brought out their gifts. Combs of ivory or bone, beautifully carved, wooden boxes, pins, brooches, pendants, woven shawls, fine head-cloths, all were proudly shown off. Then the *scop* lifted his harp and sang a chant to honour goddesses and brave women from old tales. As he fell silent, the piper began to play, some tables were taken down to clear a space, up and around the long hearth in the centre of the hall, and dancing began. Drink continued to flow.

As the singing became more raucous, and the dancing wilder, Niartha touched Maura's arm, and inclined her head toward the door. They rose up, Niartha's new gold chain swinging from her neck, and Maura's morning-gift necklace shining at her breast. Ricberht had not made a mother's gift, fearing to tempt the fates, but had promised to make Maura something special for Yule, in four days' time. He took them back to Ulla's house, with that kind woman, and returned to share another drink with his friends. They even toasted the new father, for all to join in.

Ricberht saw Eorpwald sitting beside his father, watching them as they drank and laughed. How glad he was that the baby was a girl. If it had been a boy, it would inevitably end up under Eorpwald's command, or at the very least being trained by him, and he knew all about Eorpwald's spite. The thought of his child with the red-gold hair made him beam with delight, and he went to fetch another tray of drinks.

Eorpwald thought it was a lot of fuss over a girl. Himself, he would want a son. And that son will one day be king, he thought, as I shall. And I shall find another smith or two, make no mistake. He failed to raise his goblet. Then he got his father's permission to leave the table, and went to join the dance. He seized the hand of Aelfric's daughter. Perhaps he could get lucky tonight.

Aelfric, however, was watching, as a good father would.

PAULINUS

Today we celebrated the mass for Christ's birth, Anno Domini DCXXIV, in the new church, close by Edwin's hall at Yefrin.

In the beginning was the Word, and the Word was with God, and the Word was God.

The same was in the beginning with God.

All things were made by him: and without him was not anything made that was made.

In him was life: and the life was the light of men. And the light shineth in darkness; and the darkness comprehended it not.

There was a man sent from God, whose name was John. The same came for a witness, to bear witness of the Light, that all men through him might believe. He was not that Light, but was sent to bear witness of that Light.

That was the true Light, which lighteth every man that cometh into the world. He was in the world, and the world was made by him, and the world knew him not. He came into his own, and his own received him not.

But as many as received him, to them he gave the power to become the sons of God, even to them that believe on his name: which were born, not of blood, nor of the will of the flesh, nor of the will of man, but of God.

And the Word was made flesh and dwelt among us. And we beheld his glory, the glory as of the only begotten of the Father, full of grace and truth.

In the Name of the Father, and of the Son, and of the Holy Ghost.

Amen

18

Yet another year passed, more or less uneventfully, and the same feasts were celebrated, in the same, traditional ways. As usual, by the evening of Yule, everyone in the village was stuffed with food and drink, tired out and glad to sit quietly beside their own hearths.

That morning had coincided with the celebration of the birth of Christ, six hundred and twenty-four years before, and the church was as beautifully dressed as the hall. Onna had sent one of the monks he was sheltering for the winter, and he had a hard journey through falling snow, together with the horse-carls Onna had provided to guide him. He arrived, his cowl and garments white and sodden, and had to be warmed and dried out. He insisted on holding a midnight mass and obviously expected the baptised king to attend. Unwilling to cause problems, Raedwald did so, and quite enjoyed the gentle story, he told Niartha next day, though he felt awkward under the gaze of the monk when he knelt to take the bread and wine. It was a long time since the High King had bent his knee to anyone, and he had neglected this god, although permitting others to worship him.

He did not like all the mild meekness of this Christ. Raedwald's old gods admired courage and the strength to fight. All this talk of being saved went against his grain – surely a man had a duty to save himself, and his dependants? Raedwald had saved Edwin, hadn't he? He had saved Niartha, too. Not to mention the hundreds of men who followed him to battle and came back safe. Those who had not were in Valhalla, for sure, feasting with the gods. Surely one would soon tire of singing 'alleluia' for eternity!

Still, no point in stirring up trouble. Like their king, the people practised his policy of 'live and let live,' and they all rubbed along together pretty well, not just at Raedwaldsham, but throughout Raedwald's wide domains. So on Christmas morning he joined the Christians again in the church, and listened to the monk intoning prayers and songs in that alien tongue. For a moment he wondered about his youngest son, Sigeberht. He would, no doubt, be participating in the same rite, in the same language, all those many miles away. Should he send for him? No, best not. Eorpwald would only mock his brother.

What could he do about that young man? He was not well-liked, except among a few rowdy youths, nor was he willing to ingratiate himself. He seemed to think he had the right to do exactly what he chose. Perhaps they should go on a journey together in the spring, to visit the lesser kings, and exert some sway where they encountered problems. Yes, that would be good for the lad. Kings were still elected, or at least approved by the elders of their people, not automatically because they were their fathers' sons. Men like Aelfric were not afraid to let Eorpwald's misdoings come to light.

Take that Mothers' Night a year ago: Aelfric had caught the prince kissing the girl at the door of the public hall – her father's own territory – and Eorpwald's hand had loosened her dress. Aelfric had taken his daughter home and rebuked her, but begged Raedwald to admonish his son. It was to be hoped that not too many people were aware. "Why could you not turn to the dancing girls, like everyone else?" Raedwald demanded of his son. There had been no trouble since, so perhaps that is just what Eorpwald had done. He must think about finding the lad a wife.

Suddenly Raedwald needed to talk to Niartha. He donned his cloak, called for his horse and rode out along the track. The moon gleamed with an eerie blue light on the snow, and the hoofprints stretched black behind him. What a perfect night. He felt no superstitious fear as he entered the trees. He actually smiled to himself as he wondered if the Christians' god were protecting him. He passed the little hut where Brand had lived for about three years now. Smoke was sifting through the roof, and he saw the same grey fingers rising like mist above Niartha's thatch, twenty yards further on. She had left the torches burning at her door, and he knew he would be welcome at her blazing hearth. He tied his horse to the beam by the fence, and raised her latch, calling softly as he did so.

Niartha rose to meet him, joy in her face, and came into his embrace. They laughed as she drew back, shivering, and he flung his cloak on a peg at the door, and drew her again into his arms, kissing her until she cried out and led him to her warm bed. It was very late before they slept.

It was, therefore, unfortunate that Eorpwald chose the

103

next morning to ride out hunting. It was a bright dawn, frost over the snow, and the wind was keen. The troop of young thanes and horse carls thudded down the track towards the great forest, hounds yelping at their horses' feet. They swept across the glade near the oak, and were cantering past Niartha's house, when Eorpwald reined in, skidding to a halt, so that his followers pulled up in sudden disorder.

"What is it?" they asked each other, looking this way and that. One man dismounted and went to Eorpwald's horse, to see if was lame.

"Is that not my father's horse? There! Tied to the fence?" It certainly was. But, so what? Everyone knew of the king's visits here. All, that is, except one man…his son.

In a sudden fury, he flung himself from his horse, tossed the reins to the man standing beside it, and marched to the door, raising his fist to beat on it. A voice cried out sharply. "Stop!" But it was too late. Aroused by the noise of their approach, Raedwald opened the door, to find Eorpwald's fist almost in his face.

The king was wearing a loose robe, his hair dishevelled, and his feet bare. Behind him was Niartha, her face crumpled with sleep, and she, too, was wearing only a shift. She took a startled look at the two men, and retreated into her inner room.

" Have you come for your breakfast?" asked Raedwald.

"Of course not, father! What are you doing here? As if I could not see!" shouted Eorpwald.   The king pulled his son inside and shut the door. "What I do is of no concern to you, boy," he growled. "Now get off hunting, if that is what you are doing."

"It is my concern if you are being ensnared by that witch-woman!"

"Niartha is no witch," began the king, but Eorpwald interrupted him.

"She poisoned my mother!"

"That is not true, and we proved it, as you know. Now leave this alone, boy! By Thunor! Be silent! Now get out of here. I will speak to you tonight."

"If she does not lure you here, instead," leered Eorpwald. The king's fist flew out and struck his son, firmly on the jaw, so that he staggered back, falling against the door. He held a hand to his bleeding mouth.

Raedwald yanked the young man to his feet, pulled open the door, and propelled him through it, with a mighty shove so that he sprawled in the snow. The door closed firmly behind him and a hush fell on the hunting band. Eorpwald's horse bent its head and blew at him. In silence, he remounted and turned away from the house. "Let's go hunting, then," he said grimly, holding his woollen scarf to his face. Even the hounds seemed subdued.

NIARTHA

I am deeply perturbed. Neither Raedwald nor I have given thought to his son's dislike of me. The king has never brought me forward in company or at an assembly, but nor have we tried hard to conceal his visits to me. There has been no need. The people know that Raedwald enjoys the company of women. He is, after all, a man, and a king, to take where he chooses. If he chooses me, it is because he is bolder than other men. I do not boast of it, and the women seem to respect my seclusion.

Now Eorpwald has discovered us. He is as jealous and malicious as ever. I fear how he will take vengeance for the blow his father gave him.

I told Raedwald of my fear, afraid that he might mock me, but he knows his son, and told me that he would keep a watch on the atheling. He even went to Brand, and got him to come back to stay at the house, until we felt that I was safe. I wonder if I shall ever feel truly safe again.

I have told Ricberht and Maura what happened this morning, and she offered to come home with me. I think she will do better, however, looking after her baby, in the little house near the smithy. Ricberht will be close at hand, and the other smiths nearby. Ricberht gave me the *fylfot* brooch he always wears for protection and promised to make another for himself that very day. This time, he said, it would be a Thor's Hammer. Before I came away, he scratched Woden's runes at his doorposts and told Brand to do the same when we got home.

I wonder to myself, as I sit spinning by my hearth, are the gods punishing me for loving Raedwald as now I do? I have never forgotten my Wulf, lying on the cold, northern headland near where he was killed. I had so little time with him, and I was so young. For years we had been separated and, though he had taught me how to love a man, we had lain together so very few times, and I never had the chance after I had found him again. He feels dear to me still,

106

but far away and long ago. Loyal, kind, brave Gurth had protected me, but was not for me. Only Raedwald has shown me so much kindness, brought me here so that my son might flourish, kept faith with his queen, until her death, and brings me so much happiness.

How will he reconcile his son to our love? If Eorpwald will not accept this, what can Raedwald do? And how will he protect me and my son, whom Eorpwald hates?

19

Eorpwald did not come home that night. The hunt killed two wild boar, and he sent the troop back to Raedwaldsham, and rode, with two companions, to Helmingham, to see his twin cousins. He blamed a low branch for his split and swollen mouth, and said his father had sent him to ask after their health. If they thought this was odd, having seen the High King between Mothers' Night and Yule, they did not show it. They fed him for a couple of nights and then said they were going to join Raedwald's deerhunt, obviously expecting Eorpwald to know all about it. So he had to join in.

A royal hart was brought to bay, below a low cliff of crag in a hawthorn thicket, and Raedwald awarded the head to the Helming twins, together with one of the huge haunches of the beast. The king had noticed his son's presence in the chase, but ignored him. Now, as the men were setting about the cutting of the deer's hide from the carcass, he beckoned Eorpwald to ride beside him. They returned home without a word having been passed between them. That evening, Raedwald had their food brought to his anteroom, giving Aelfric orders that they were not to be disturbed. They would serve themselves with food from the large platters, and there was wine in plenty.

So no-one heard what the king said to the sullen prince. He looked no less sullen when he came out into the hall, but had a crestfallen air. He took himself off to his usual bed in the dead queen's house. When Raedwald appeared, he was rubbing his hands jovially, and calling for the harper. People relaxed.

Once the month of Hretha came, and the cold lessened its grip, Raedwald did what he had suggested to Niartha and began a tour of his kingdoms. Where he could and if the winds permitted, he took ship, pausing to stay at the halls and burghs round the great, curving coast, riding inland where the ways were passable after the winter. He distributed gifts to those who served him well, obeying his laws, bringing wealth from good harvests, guarding the lands. If there was a dispute, he listened and gave judgement. He would sit on the carved folding-stool he carried with him, the stone sceptre cushioned on his right knee, and administer whatever justice was needed. It might be death; it might be the payment of compensation; it might be a simple command to make peace. Eorpwald was required to stand and listen, so that he might learn.

From the borders of the East Saxons, through the territories of the Eastern Angles, into Lindsey and to the shores of the Humber they went. They met with Edwin in Deira. He told Raedwald that his queen was thinking about accepting Christian baptism. "Let her, why not?" said Raedwald.

Edwin was surprised, but listened as Raedwald described how his relaxed attitude to the new religion had brought few problems.

"It is only where the new regime has been enforced," said Raedwald, "that the folk feel oppressed. Look at Kent. Eadbald – he calls himself Aethelwald now –oh, you know that already – you married his sister, didn't you? Anyway he has lost a great many people, because of his insistence on conversion. It seems to me, that if a king converts, then trouble follows."

"But you, yourself were baptised," said Edwin.

"True enough, though I hardly ever go to the Christian mass. I have left my people free to choose. My own son, here-" he indicated the listening Eorpwald, "has not been baptised."

"Nor will I ever be!" said Eorpwald. Raedwald hushed him, gently enough.

"A wise man is wary of saying 'never'," he smiled. Edwin nodded in agreement, but avoided Raedwald's eyes.

The reports Edwin gave of his activities in his huge kingdom were enough to convince Raedwald how right he had been to support the younger man. Edwin had, with Raedwald's help, it was true, overcome resistance from the Britons, and from Aethelfrith's northern Anglians, so that his realm spread from east to west, and now included the two large islands in the western sea, protecting his lands if need be from the Irish Celts. He trusted, he said, that one day a woman and her babe would walk in safety from coast to coast, under his protection.

Raedwald laughed cheerfully at this and said he did not doubt it. "Come to see us, when you have time," he said. "You will always be welcome at Raedwaldsham – that is what they call it now.

I've been there so long! Eh, lad?" he said to Eorpwald. "We'd like a visit from the next High King!"

Edwin's face reddened, and he waved his hand dismissively.

"Who else will they choose when I am gone?" Raedwald beamed. "There's none to hold a candle to your deeds. Be ready when they ask you! And keep an eye on that bishop of yours, that Paulinus, or he'll have you on your knees all day, and you'll forget the thrill of a good battle! Let him talk to the women. That's all he's fit for."

Next day they parted with friendly embraces, and promises to see each other in maybe a year or two. Edwin had always admired Raedwald. He was not entirely sure about his mentor's relaxed attitude to the question of Christianity, but he had a point about a king exerting too much pressure on his people. He would go on thinking about it, he decided.

What Raedwald had said about his becoming High King – well, that was certainly something to think of. Raedwald had not mentioned who might be his heir to the lands of the Eastern Angles, and the prince was not a prepossessing character. If Edwin were to become High King, he, himself, would hold sway over all the lands that were now Raedwald's. He wondered what Eorpwald might make of that.

In truth, the idea had jolted Eorpwald. He had known, since childhood, that Edwin was a brave fighter, and a staunch ally. Though Raedwald had left Eorpwald behind at the battle of the River Idle, he had taken his second son with him on other northern forays, in support of Edwin, and here was a man to admire. He was certainly a likely choice as a future High King. How could Eorpwald, himself, find such glory? It seemed that there was no-one left to fight back home, though their western boundary with the Mercians still provided a few clashes. Perhaps he could suggest a trip to Wedresfield on the way home. Maybe he could go by himself, if Raedwald did not wish to go there.

When he asked, Raedwald made it clear that he did *not* wish to go there. Eorpwald persisted in his request to be allowed to make a visit on his own.

"I could see that all is well there," he urged. "And you have shown me what to do, if there is a situation that needs seeing to."

Raedwald had never set foot in the hall at Wedresfeld since the day he rejected Niartha, then his new wife, who had betrayed him with his brother. The king who took the throne there, after Niartha's father had died, was Aescgar, now a very old man. It was likely he would welcome a strengthening of alliance against the Mercians. Or, indeed, he might even be persuaded to join them, if Raedwald did not show him support. Perhaps it might even be necessary for Eorpwald to threaten a show of strength.

Eorpwald needed to be allowed to prove himself. Raedwald let his son go, taking twelve thanes and a number of horse-carls with him. They parted at the port of Sheringham, so that Eorpwald could ride on the good road at the edge of the fens, and Raedwald could sail straight home to the Deben, and to Niartha, now again his beloved. He had been away too long. It would soon be Midsummer, and without his son around, he could bring Niartha to the feast.

EORPWALD

As he rode, Eorpwald sang aloud, a riding song, a song for a warrior. It was his favourite rune poem, about the horse, a magnificent creature, who makes his owner proud, who is a valuable treasure to own. Your steed can carry you speedily to great adventures, in far-off lands, to meet new folk and find joy in strange places. Eorpwald felt free, at last, in a way he had not, ever since he left the Danish court.

They rode from dawn till dusk, with hardly a break, and arrived at a bridge-side inn, not far from Wedresfeld. The keeper was perplexed at what to do to accommodate them all, but it was a fine night, and the horse-carls were content to doss down in the barn on some early hay, even if their horses chewed the bedding all night. The thanes slept, four to a bed in three crammed rooms. Apparently they were lucky there were any beds left, as this was a busy trade route from coast to fen, and onward to the great towns further south. They were well fed and the ale was good.

Eorpwald came late to the bed he was sharing. His cheerful singing had soon found him a cheerful girl, willing to show him her favours. He took her to the field of hay-stooks, laid some flat, and then tossed her down on top of them. He left a piece of silver with her, and promised to return that way. He never did, but she did not lose sleep over him. It was just another good romp.

Eorpwald sent three thanes ahead, just as Raedwald used to do, to herald his approach, and was welcomed duly at the hall of Aescgar. The old man rose to greet the son of the High King, and had wine poured for him. They talked amicably about Raedwald's health, and Aescgar's. The king asked the young man to describe the battles he had been in, but was soon nodding off. The hall steward came to the rescue, and took the thanes to find their mid-day meal. When they were refreshed, he brought the elders to meet them, and the king was livelier after a short sleep. He was over seventy, after all.

Eorpwald looked eagerly around the hall to see if there was anything younger and tastier. It seemed that the women were kept well away from strangers. Over the meal that night, he heard that the Mercians were proving to be a problem along the border. They occasionally raided for cattle, had even taken slaves. He asked what retaliation they had made, and they looked a bit shame-faced, as they admitted their warriors were few, not well-trained, and most of them too young or too old. They tried to keep the peace, by trading on terms that were all too often in the Mercians' favour.

"Why have you not asked for Raedwald's help?" asked Eorpwald, impatiently. This was just the sort of situation in which the High King would intervene. He would have to be told.

"We did not feel sure that he would wish to come," they told him. When he asked why, they, in their turn, asked if he knew of the relationship between Raedwald and Wedresfeld.

"I know nothing. Tell me now," he insisted. So they told him about the marriage of their princess to Raedwald, when he was not yet king. They told him how she loved Raedwald's brother, and how Raedwald cast her off and exiled Prince Eni ("Wulf, they called him") to the far north. They told how the princess was outcast after her father died, and how their queen's brother, Aescgar, took the throne, in spite of the strong claim of the old king's brother, Edgar.

"What was the name of this princess?" demanded Eorpwald. It was Niartha.

BEORHTFYR

Only the king's hand may release the sword from its sheath. When the swordsmith is summoned to hone the blade, it is in the king's presence. He kneels to the task as if in homage as much to the blade as to the king.

Once it is honed to its lethal sharpness, the steel is polished with care, and declines into its darkness, its brightness quenched.

Now, in the king's time of need, he grasps the gem-bright, golden hilt. The glorious scabbard hangs unheeded at his side. The blade hisses into the light and he raises the sword, silver to the sky.

Its power is released by the might of his arm. His power is released, as his flashing blade ignites the wrath of warriors. They follow the blazing bright fire, hearts glowing with courage, wrath awakened. Where this sword leads, swift steeds will stamp upon the earth.

This is the sword of the king. Its battle-song rings out. It inflames the hearts of the heroes. It drinks deeply of the blood of battling men. It deals death to the daunted.

NIARTHA

Raedwald decided, as Eorpwald had, apparently, rightly predicted, to pursue the matter of the trading rights. He also, he told me, felt it would do no harm to mend a few fences with Aescgar and his people. I understood this. He took only thirty men, and only Beorn from among the smiths. So it was from Beorn that we at Raedwaldsham heard the story of what happened.

When the men of Wedresfeld clashed with their rival traders at the mart just across the border into the next kingdom, Raedwald's troop galloped up, putting the fear of all the gods into the local population. He did not kill anyone, but seized two men and waited.

Sure enough, the neighbouring king, Ulfric, sent a messenger to demand their return. When he found out it was Raedwald who challenged him, he sent for help among the neighbouring domains, but came immediately to the border in a cocksure display of bravado. Raedwald not only disarmed Ulfric, he also disabused him. The long-standing trading agreement was no longer to be broken. Wedresfeld would be protected.

Raedwald turned his horse, signalling his troop to leave what could hardly be called a battlefield, when one of Ulfric's men hurled his spear angrily into the knot of men. It struck Raedwald. Eorpwald's sword came out, as he rode the man down and severed his neck. A short, grim, bloody fight ensued, with men killed on both sides – Ulfric was one of them, killed by Beorhtfyr, no less, in the hand of Raedwald - before each side withdrew.

Raedwald was not killed, had fought, even with the flung angon lodged in his thigh. This had to be painfully withdrawn, and he was carried home, across the breadth of his kingdom, on a litter. By the time they got there, he was in a fever. By the time Aelfric sent for me, Raedwald was delirious.

I used every art I know. Bindings, poultices, herbal drinks, not even the Nine Herb Charm, nothing worked. We tried to cool the fiery body; then we tried to warm him when he shivered; he flinched even from my touch. Only I could get him to swallow the liquids. In the end, after two days, I used infusions of willow-bark to sedate him and alleviate the pain, but I knew he was dying.

I told Aelfric to summon the elders. I found out later how he advised them to send messages throughout the whole wide realm, that the kings should prepare themselves to come when summoned, to the funeral of their Bretwalda, their High King.

When Aelfric sent for Ricberht to support me, my son told me the great hall was full, but hushed. I stayed beside Raedwald, eating a little when made to do so, drinking sips from the wine I was trying to administer to the king, to see if it would revive him.

My arm cradled the king's neck and head as he lay on a woollen blanket, clad only in a linen tunic, and covered with his great bear-skin. In the end, I put aside the little cup and laid my head beside Raedwald's on the pillow I had never shared. It was to my bed he came, never I to his. Tears blurred my sight. He will never come to me again.

He stirred, and turned his head, his eyes bright in an ashen face. He said my name. He knew me! I bent over him, and Aelfric and Ricberht started forward, but I stopped them. I smiled at my lover and stroked his greying hair. I whispered quiet words to him, too quiet for the others to hear, gently kissed his brow and his lips, and the strain left his face. He gazed at me and his lips moved soundlessly. He shook in a kind of convulsion, with a soft groan, and his gaze became fixed. My face was the last thing he saw. I laid my head on his chest and wept.

When Aelfric put out his hand to close the king's eyes, I forestalled him. I wanted my hand to be the last to touch him. Ricberht tried to get me to leave, but I would not go. I was the one to lay out Raedwald's body, clothed it simply, wrapped in his cloak, for temporary burial in a flimsy coffin, until the funeral was prepared. Others might see to the ceremonial; I would care for the man I had grown to love.

I feel now as if all my life will be lived in the past.

20

Only later that night did Niartha think to ask where Eorpwald was all these last days. Beorn had told them that before Raedwald left Wedresfeld, he had insisted that his son stay there to sort out any repercussions, and to get the folk of the neighbouring settlements organised into a better state of resistance against the Mercians. The king was in pain, but had suffered wounds before, and had no idea of how deadly this one was.

So Eorpwald was with Aescgar when news came of his father's imminent death. He encountered the later message as he rode desperately back home. To find that his father already lay in the churchyard made him furious, but Aelfric explained how they had followed the normal practice. No funeral had yet taken place. Did he want his father buried with Christian rites? Or should they be preparing a mound up on the hoo?

Naturally, Eorpwald wanted nothing to do with the monks he so despised, so the time-honoured rituals would take place. While the warriors and kings of Raedwald's lands assembled, over the next ten days, the *ceorls* began to dig the huge pit in the sandy ridge above the river. 'Seawitch', Raedwald's ship, was dragged up from the stream, hauled over tree-trunk rollers by slaves and horses, ready to be lowered into the pit. The mast and oars were removed, and the carpenters made a roofed shelter to form a special burial chamber in the heart of the great vessel.

Aelfric and the elders met to discuss what should be laid in the chamber with the king. There was some disagreement, but eventually the prince was persuaded that his father must lie in great state, as High King, and in the presence of men of such significance as the kings of Kent, Essex, the Middle Saxons, East Anglia, Lindsey and Edwin of Northumbria. He must also be allowed to take his greatest treasures with him, to face Woden, in the great hall of Asgard, with honour as a hero worthy of respect.

This man, Raedwald, was Lord of the Feast: his harp, the

board game with its fine pieces, the huge cauldron that hung from the roof of his hall, bronze bowls, the vast silver dish, the mighty drinking horns – all these reminded his people of the king's generosity as he had rewarded his followers.

He was their Warrior-King, the Battle-Leader: his helmet, shield, spears and sword must lie beside him. No, they argued with Eorpwald, Raedwald's hand was the last to wield Beorhtfyr. So too must lie the ivory wand of the Wuffings, argued Aelfric. He and Eorpwald nearly came to blows over this. But the elders won. Eorpwald had not yet been proclaimed heir to the Wuffing kingdom, and he might not be elected king. So the wand lay beside the man whose name meant 'Wise Ruler' or 'Wielder of Justice,' as did the royal sceptre, its stag gleaming in the dimness of the chamber.

When the body of the king was prepared, he was clothed in fine garments, and wore the emblems of the power he held as High King: the shoulder-clasps, the great gold buckle, the purse and, of course, he wore his sword-belt, though Beorhtfyr itself lay beside him, his right hand resting on the hilt. His magnificent helmet stood at his left shoulder, as inscrutable in its death as it had been in the wearing. Here lay the Bretwalda, Ruler of Wide Realms.

What surprised the gathered company as they gazed for the last time on their mighty leader was the offering that lay beside the right shoulder of the king. A quiet figure, clothed in the white robes of a monk, had stepped forward, unstopped by the guard of thanes, and placed a stack of silver bowls, marked with Coptic-style crosses and two spoons, marked with the names of Saulos and Paulos – Christian emblems, in the grave of the Anglian High King. Even when his cowl slipped from his head, as he ducked out from the low roof of the chamber, he was not recognized, until he moved over to where Niartha stood with the other women, and spoke quietly to her. It was Sigeberht, who allowed her to clasp him warmly. Paulinus, who accompanied Edwin from the north, had persuaded Edwin to send word to Raedwald's youngest son. He knew Eorpwald would not have done so. Even now, Sigeberht ignored his brother and joined Paulinus, standing well back from the proceedings.

Raedwald had not been given the last rites of the church, and was presumably not destined for Paulinus's heaven, but Sigeberht knew where the gifts, given at Raedwald's baptism twenty-one years ago, were kept in the wall of the church his father had built. Perhaps, even now, God would have mercy on Raedwald's soul. He watched as a priest in a boarskin robe, fearsome head and tusks gleaming, placed runes scratched on birch-bark on the body of his father; Sigeberht crossed himself, as did several others, for protection against what he now saw as daemonic practice. Soon the Christians moved away, down to the track below the hoo.

The final wall of the chamber was closed, leaving only one small oil-lamp burning within. Niartha had placed it there to light her lover's ship on its journey to Valhalla. Eorpwald watched her grimly, held fast by the need for dignified behaviour. How dared she approach the king as he lay there in his splendour? He did not notice as she dropped a small field-flower on Raedwald's breast, unseen among the jewels. No-one noticed a small ladybird crawl under the cloth of a thin pillow-case beneath the king's head.

Ricberht put his arm around her and wiped her tears. He was stunned to see the things he had wrought for Raedwald, surrounding his king as he took 'Seawitch' on her last voyage on the dark seas of death, ready to meet whatever gods came to greet him. The sword would rust, the wood, leather and metal crumble away, the bronze would dim but the great stone would hold its hardness, jewels would gleam and the gold would be shining fresh in a thousand years, if any eyes should ever see these things again.

The warriors rode around the ship, as the *scop* sang the song of the noble king. As the people moved, weeping, back towards the royal hall, four miles away along the hoo, they spoke the words that would be echoed at the feast that night: how generous was their king, how brave in battle, how protective of his people, how loyal to his friends. Men began to fill in the ship with the sandy soil, piling the mound higher over the next few days, and turfing it over. No man would dare to approach it except in awe, so great was Raedwald's monument.

The mounds of the kings of the Wuffings made a statement of power, visible to all who rounded the bend of the Deben River. Perhaps it was just as important to those kings to lie in sight of the river, which had helped to make their kingdom great.

21

Niartha could not face going to the feast. She begged to be allowed to stay at Ricberht's little house to look after Fritha, and Maura willingly agreed. The child was almost eighteen months old, at the stage where they have no fear and no sense, needing constant watching, and more than likely to tire their nurse out before they are ready to sleep. With the long, late evenings, it was hard to persuade her to stay in bed.

They threw corn for Maura's chickens. It was a joy to see the toddler run about after them, though she squawked as loudly as the hen who pecked her. Niartha fed her with a boiled egg and gave her a cup of warm milk. Then she sat Fritha on her knee and played finger-games with her, and sang until the child suddenly produced that last surge of energy they find before finally giving in to sleep. So she walked the little one to and fro on the grass where the people had danced at her parents' wedding. Niartha shrugged off the memory of how that night had ended, but after she had watched Fritha fall asleep, she could not help thinking of Randulf, of Ricberht – and of Eorpwald.

Tonight was for Raedwald, and the speaking and singing would be all in his honour. In two days, the kings would meet, up at Blythburgh, hosted by Onna, to elect the next High King. She hoped it would be Edwin. That would remove the pressures of responsibility for the wider realm from the warriors here at Raedwaldsham. Niartha wept, thinking that it *was* no longer his home. Had he made his voyage yet, she wondered. Was he now feasting in Valhalla, ghostly heroic voices raised in his praise, just as the warm, human voices were raised here... she could hear them faintly as she sat sadly by the door in the summer sunset.

After the kings departed, in four days' time, the Wuffings would foregather to choose their king. She dreaded the likely outcome. Aelfric was an excellent counsellor, elder and hall steward, but he was not a battle-leader. The twins and their dim half-brother at Helmingham, Aethelric, were unlikely candidates, being able with the sword, but less able in their judgement. She hoped people would perceive Eorpwald in the same light, but Raedwald had given him opportunities to broaden his experience, even beyond what he had done for his favourite nephew, Onna.

Would Onna seek to put himself forward against his cousin, she wondered. He was reputed to be an upright man, brave and loyal. He was undoubtedly wiser than Eorpwald, but he had held himself a little remote, willing to support Raedwald, in his jurisdiction, but perhaps too willing to give ear to the monks, who avoided the Deben in favour of the Blyth. How she wished it might be Onna they chose.

She was not surprised, however, to learn the outcome of both these elections.

Edwin became High King and returned with Paulinus and a number of his liegemen to Northumbria. Later, though they heard news of him sooner than they might have expected, they learned that he had been baptised, with all his people, and was actively promoting the Christian religion. How long would he leave the Eastern Angles in peace?

Peace? Under Eorpwald? There was no such thing. There was even a death in the Wuffing village on the night of the election

Anyone who held a vote was also eligible for selection, if enough men deemed him worthy. The warriors were assembled, though only those with blood-ties to the Wuffings could have a voice, or those to whom the power to vote had been granted by a previous king, or who held a position that granted them the right. Arnulf and Randulf had the right by blood, and Beorn, too. Aelfric, of course, like all the elders. One or two of the older warriors had won Raedwald's respect and been given the voice, even though they came from different stock. Some men of the Helmings and the Blythings had a vote, by tenuous ancestral claims. Where necessary, the scop was consulted to confirm a claim, as he had the words of the old sagas in his head, and sang them regularly at the feasts.

When Ricberht stepped forward to put his counter into his chosen basket, like all the rest, Eorpwald made a furious challenge.

"How can this man be allowed to vote? He is not a Wuffing. He has no father that is known of!"

"I am the king's jewel-smith," asserted Ricberht. "That gives me the right…"

"You *were* the smith!" yelled Eorpwald. "Now you are nothing! You and your cronies!" He waved his fist at the brothers and Beorn, standing beside Ricberht.

"You have no jurisdiction here, yet, atheling," Aelfric admonished him. "There is no man here to do the work of these men. And unless you become king, they have the right to do the work and the right to vote that this work brings."

Enough voices were raised in their support that Eorpwald had to subside, or lose too much favour among the warriors, younger thanes, his fellow-huntsmen, many of whom had received gifts in the last few days. A good smith always had a following, so greatly were they respected.

Onna calmed things down, in his typical fashion, and asked Eorpwald to say how he would make a good king for his people.

"I shall fight, of course," was the first thought he uttered. "Those Mercians are asking for trouble. They can have it!" There were a few cheers, but also some groaning. The Mercians were far enough away, across the wide fenlands, and were reputed to be rather slow in regaining spirit. After Edwin had shown his strength, things had gone very quiet for a while.

"Why stir up trouble needlessly?" asked one old man.

"Pipe down, grandpa," said Eorpwald. Some laughed, others demanded more respect.

"You seem to me," said Onna, "to be doing a good job of dividing the people here. Did you learn nothing from your father of good judgement?" Eorpwald scowled.

"Well-spoken," said Aelfric. "We need more of the peace that Raedwald brought to us."

"What about the Christians?" asked someone else. "We have lived together well enough. Shall we go on in the same way?"

"Why should we? They have no teeth. Some even refuse to fight! We need to get the strength of the old gods behind us!" Eorpwald answered.

"Are you saying your father was wrong?" asked Onna. There came a sudden silence.

"Yes!" shouted Eorpwald. "We have drifted along, like an old ship bumping the bottom of a creek! Now is the time to set sail and go into the deep sea! We need to fight the waves! Where is our old spirit?"

Hubbub ensued, so that it took many minutes before order could be restored.

Aelfric collected the baskets of slivers of wood, and took three men with him to the anteroom to count them.

The horns, goblets and beakers were filled again by the time they emerged, and Eorpwald and his crowd of friends were drinking merrily. Aelfric raised his hand for quiet, and gave the numbers of those who had received votes. One or two men had attracted the odd vote, probably out of spite against another, or out of indecision. Things were going to be tight between Onna and Eorpwald. In the end, it was the larger community, closer to the Wuffing hall, which won. Eorpwald was declared king. Onna bowed to him and gripped his hand. Tomorrow would see the crowning, and all must come to pay homage. Tonight was for spreading the news, and in Eorpwald's case, for celebrating it.

Ricberht and the other smiths drank a health, but did not say to whom. Then they slipped away, all of them to Niartha's house, where all their wives had gathered to wait. Not one of them felt like celebrating, and they were even too sick at heart to drown their sorrows. They left Niartha with Brand to look after her, and set off through the shadowy wood, back toward their houses near the smithies. There, Beorn and Ricberht took their folk indoors, while Randulf and Ulla walked in the moonlight to their home in the village.

They had nearly made it, when there erupted from the hall a drunken rout. Aelfric had succeeded in putting an end to the proceedings, but only after the drink ran out. Eorpwald and his group literally bumped into Randulf.

"Look who it is! The one-armed smith!" Jeering and shoving, they swung him round by his good left arm. Even if he had been able to wield a sword, Randulf was not wearing one, nor could he grip with his right hand the knife at the left side of his belt.

"Leave him alone, you bullies," screamed Ulla, but her voice was drowned by their scornful cries. She frantically beat at the nearest man, trying to protect her husband. She grabbed his hair and pulled on it till it tore in her grasp. He bellowed and pushed her off. She fell, straight onto the knife in the hand of another man. That man was Eorpwald. Blood from her mouth gushed all over his jerkin, and he yelped in disgust, withdrew his blade and watched her fall, Randulf dropping to his knees beside her.

As other people came from the hall, and noticed something was amiss, Eorpwald's crew grabbed him and melted into the darkness. Ulla died where she lay, and Randulf howled an oath of vengeance.

The uproar lasted through the night. Randulf had to be dragged from Ulla's body, broken to the point where he became incoherent. Arnulf carried first Randulf then Ulla to Beorn's house, to be watched over, while he found Ricberht and went to tell Niartha.

The young thanes swore that the woman had attacked them and that she fell onto Eorpwald's knife by some weird chance. No-one could believe that they would attack a defenceless, one-armed man, surely, and certainly not a woman! Anyway, everyone knew Randulf had a grudge against Eorpwald. Besides, to accuse the king was absurd: he would swear to protect his people, never harm them! Under the eyes of the elders, their bluster died.

Where was Eorpwald? He had retreated to his mother's old house, too upset by Ulla's death to answer questions, they said. Who had the right to question him? He knew Randulf would blame him. Those smiths were bound to stir up trouble.

The elders listened. They would certainly question Randulf in the morning. Why, they wanted to know, was Eorpwald carrying an unsheathed knife? But they had just come from feasting, they had taken a lot of drink...no reason could be given. Eorpwald had definitely not drawn it for a fight. If anyone was fighting, it was Randulf!

Aelfric dismissed them all to their houses, though hardly a soul slept. In the morning, he talked to Randulf, but made no sense of what had happened. It sounded like a drunken brawl, even though Randulf was convinced it was intentional: after all, they had seized him, hadn't they? He demanded that Eorpwald be brought to account.

Again, the elders met. They decided that they must let Ulla's burial take place as a priority. Then they would summon Eorpwald to a hearing, and decide if compensation were due. He was not yet king, and the code of law held good. Someone would have to take charge of Randulf, crazed as he was with grief and fury.

Only then, after all this, would they see to the throning of the man elected king. There was no mood of celebration in the village.

22

Ulla was buried in the churchyard by a hastily-summoned monk, lodged at the Alde burgh following Raedwald's funeral; she had, after all been baptised. Her simple coffin, from Borgil's workshop, lay in the church for what was left of the night. To it in the morning came Randulf, literally supported by the strong arms of his brother, and with the other smiths and their wives. The folk of the village either joined in the requiem mass, or clustered, voices hushed, outside the church to watch the burial. Niartha came, and entered the church with the family. She had been with Randulf all night, and was hollow-eyed with sorrow and fatigue. She sat at the back of the church and listened to the monk as he intoned prayers, read from his book and intoned some sort of chant. No word was understood, except by the initiated, but it was mysteriously soothing.

Aelfric came to her, as she stood sadly beside the open grave, ready to drop earth upon the coffin, like the other folk, so that Nerthus, the Earth Mother, would take her to her breast. Aelfric begged Niartha to take Randulf to her house.

"He needs to be out of the village for some while, but especially today," he said. "Is this possible?"

They whispered to Ricberht, who consulted with Arnulf, and the word went round. As the little party stood desolately, looking down at the coffin, the family moved around the bowed figure of Randulf, and quietly led him away. Arnulf had his cart nearby, and the women clambered aboard, hauled Randulf into their midst, and trundled off towards the oak, the men riding horseback beside them.

When the elders questioned Eorpwald, he told them nothing new, repeating the tale of Ulla's wild behaviour. He said he had been cutting an apple, when she fell onto his knife. He said Randulf was drunk. With no new, let alone truthful, witnesses of the event, they had to accept this version of events. No compensation could be justified.

If Eorpwald noticed the absence of the smiths from his

throning later that afternoon, he made no comment. If he wished to make them swear the oath of allegiance, he could make a special issue of it. The same procedure was followed at his throning as had been performed for his father so many years before, beginning with the ceremony of admittance at the door of the hall. The boar-headed priest who had officiated at the ship-burial now sought the voices of the warriors in support of the new king. Some men shouted the name of Eorpwald firmly enough to be noticed, others spoke it, but none refuted it. The old men remembered much more joy at Raedwald's name.

The priest signed the brow of the kneeling man with the *fylfot* and invoked the strength and protection of the gods to ensure the prosperity of the new king and of his people. A few men could be seen surreptitiously crossing themselves.

Then, with Eorpwald seated on the throne-stool, he took the only piece of regalia left from among the pieces used at Raedwald's throning – a simple circlet of gold, which he lifted above Eorpwald's head as he stood behind him. He placed it onto the king's forehead, and pronounced him king. The warriors stamped their feet, clapped their hands and gave a cheer.

Aelfric moved forward and laid Eorpwald's sword, unsheathed across the king's knees.

"May this weapon earn a name to equal that of Beorhtfyr, lord king," he said. He bent onto one knee and laid his head and hand on the sword, in the act of fealty, then arose to take his place near the front of the dais, as, one by one, the thanes came silently and performed the same act.

The first, unhappy task Aelfric performed for King Eorpwald was to tell him that the feast was not yet quite ready to be brought into the hall. As he saw the frown appear, he murmured quietly that the women had been up baking all night, and had been to Ulla's funeral in the morning.

"But the drink is prepared, lord," he said. So the trestles were brought in, and more torches lit, cauldrons hung over the hearth and, once the king had received the jewelled goblet full of wine, the horns were passed. Bowls and dishes followed. It was not, assuredly, as grand a feast as that for the High King's funeral, but it was sufficient to placate Eorpwald.

The events of the day (and of the previous night) had left the people exhausted, but no-one could leave until the king gave the sign. Eventually, even Eorpwald sagged against the table, and Aelfric asked permission for the feast to end. Eorpwald waved his hand, knocking over the dregs of his wine as he did so. Aelfric signalled to two thanes, and they hauled the king up and took him to what had been his father's room at the end of the hall-building. Aelfric saw to the locking up of the treasure chest, transferring the key from his own belt, where it had been since Raedwald's last, tragic, battle-excursion, to the belt he had just removed from Eorpwald's unresisting body. He blew out the candle and dropped the thick ox-hide to curtain the door. He passed a weary hand over his brow and left the guards to listen to the snoring king. His footsteps shuffled through the rushes on the floor of the empty hall.

When he stood in the forecourt, he could hear no sound in the village. An owl shrieked in the trees beside the trackway. There was no-one to see the tears that fell on the cheeks of the old man, as he retreated towards his little porch-room. As he laid the beam across and locked down the latch, he rested his head on the oaken door of the hall and wept for his great king.

NIARTHA

Arnulf and Beorn have gone home, very late. The moon is high. Brand took Ricberht, Maura and the babe to his own little cottage a while ago. They will lay down trestle boards with sacks of soft hay and bracken and Maura says they will be fine there for one night. Randulf sits by my hearth. He has said little all day, and has been silent for some hours now.

With the others gone, I put fresh bedding in the little room for him. He makes no attempt to move. In the end, I sit on a folded blanket on the floor beside his stool and hand him a beaker of mead. He takes it absently, holding it for a few minutes, then drinks it down. It makes him cough, then he begins to cry. I put an arm round his shoulders and he slides to the floor beside me, weeping. All he can say is Ulla's name. I say nothing. What is there left to say? Eventually he falls silent, drooped across my knees, and I see that he is asleep. I give him a few moments and then extricate myself cautiously. I bring a couple more blankets and skins for pillows and covers, deaden the fire and blow out the candle. Nothing can do poor Randulf more good tonight than sleep.

I lie awake, in spite of my weariness. Will Randulf be willing to stay with me and Brand for the time being, at least? He needs someone to look after him. Perhaps he and Brand might live in Brand's house? But Ricberht is not happy for me to be alone, nor does he want to move away from his smithy.

The thought of Eorpwald is enough to drive sleep away further. Raedwald recognized the threat his son poses to me, and knew how hostile he is to Ricberht. But we have lost Raedwald, and once more my tears spill for him.

What is going to happen to the smiths now? Eorpwald will surely have missed them at the throning. If they refuse to pledge allegiance, they will be outcast or even killed. I toss on my bed in anguish, until I have to get up and go outside to calm myself, before the chill of midnight sends me back to my bed. Randulf has not stirred

I cover my head and wait for oblivion. Terrible things have happened to people in the past and they have survived. I should know – who better? But surely there is just so much the gods can ask of us?

EORPWALD

Eorpwald opened his eyes in the new bed. It was dark, with no window-space in the room, though he could hear voices. He sat up, holding a hand to his aching head, and suddenly recalled the main event of the previous day.

"I am king!" he thought, and swung his legs to the ground. To be honest, the day had started like this so many times before, that he wondered how he felt about getting up. He needed a drink. Attempting to stand, he realized that, if he really *were* king, he could get a slave to fetch it for him. No need to go to the hall! He could lie in bed until he decided what to do. He gave a yell, and winced at his own noise. A head appeared cautiously round the door curtain.

"What can I do for you, lord?" said the guard.

"Send a slave with a flagon of wine!" The head vanished.

In a couple of minutes, a voice asked permission to enter, and a boy came in, carrying a wooden tray, with a candle, the required flagon and a goblet. There were also some pieces of honeyed oatcake. Eorpwald took the drink and dunked one of the cakes. The boy stood at the wall, waiting.

"What do you want?" asked Eorpwald.

"I am here to serve you, lord," said the boy, with a startled look. "Shall I bring your clothes?" He looked around the room. The only chests had been Raedwald's, and one of them apparently contained treasure, never, of course, seen by a slave-boy.

"Send Aelfric to me," demanded Eorpwald. The boy vanished. Aelfric must have been very close by, for he arrived with surprising haste.

"Lord king?" he enquired. "Is all well?"

"No! Why are my clothes not here? My chest? My weapons?"

"You did not ask for them, my lord. Last night..." Aelfric's words tailed off.

"Well get them now!" snapped Eorpwald.

"I will see to it straight away, king." The stuff had to be brought across from the old house, and room made for them. When they went to shift Raedwald's clothes, Eorpwald stopped them.

"Wait! Let us see if any of the things are fit for me to wear." There were a few wry glances, as the broad shoulders and chest of Raedwald had needed large tunics, which swamped the wiry frame of his son. His shoes might do, and even the leggings if tightly wrapped, and the cloaks, especially the thick, red one he wore in winter. Woven of dense treble yarn, still impregnated with the grease of the sheep, it was both soft and fairly waterproof. It was a little long but could be shortened easily enough.

"Give the rest to the villagers," said Eorpwald, magnanimously. "Take these things to be washed." He pulled off the garments he had fallen into bed with the night before, plunged his head into a bowl of water and swilled his face, his armpits and his privates, before pulling on a thin, sleeveless undertunic, a pair of brown trousers, and a rust-coloured, linen overtunic, clasped at the shoulders. A slave wound strips of brightly-coloured woven braid around the leggings and slid the king's feet into his soft-leather, summer boots. He was about to clip the buckle to his belt, when a slave stepped forward to do it for him. Eorpwald noticed the great key suspended from the belt and raised his eyebrows at Aelfric who stood by. The hall steward nodded.

"It is yours, now, lord king," he said. "Until you find a queen for your people." He cuffed the boy, who had giggled nervously.

"Shall I need a cloak?" queried Eorpwald.

"Perhaps a short one, when the king goes outside? There is a wind from the sea, and it brings a sea-fret this near the coast in summer." Eorpwald knew that, perfectly well, thought Aelfric.

"Have this one ready," the new king commanded, grandly. "And find the brooch with the green stone that goes with it."

"The pin is broken, lord king," said his slave. "Shall I take it to the jewel-smith?"

With a jolt, Eorpwald remembered everything. Ulla's death, the questioning he had undergone, the delay to his feast. Now he remembered those who had not attended the throning. They must be dealt with.

"I will eat now," he informed Aelfric. "When I have done, I will see all the king's smiths. Have them brought ready. Under guard," he added as an afterthought. "And summon all the elders first. And that priest."

23

Idunna came, screaming, up the track, to find Niartha. Maura heard her and rushed out of Brand's house, followed by Ricberht and Brand. They were all clad merely in tunics, but flung themselves after her as she beat on Niartha's door.

"They have taken Beorn!" she gasped. "And Arnulf!"

"Who? Who has taken them? Where?" Niartha pulled her inside and they clustered round her while she sobbed for breath and told them what she had seen.

"It must be Eorpwald," said Ricberht.

"Yes, the king, they said, the king!" Idunna wept.

"You must get away," Niartha told her son, seizing him by the shoulders. "You and Randulf. They will come for you here when they find your houses empty. You have to go!"

"Where? I can't leave Maura. Or the baby! Who will look after you?"

"They will be safer with me, if Eorpwald decides to punish you. Brand is here. Now, get some clothes on! I'll put some food in a bag. Maura, hurry up, get him a cloak from Brand's place. Go!"

They stared at her for a second, trying to make sense, then fled. She remembered Randulf, who sat by the dead fire, totally confused by the clamour and confusion. He seemed to take in that he was to 'go with Ricberht', but did not ask where or why. Niartha and Gilda, her house-girl, grabbed pieces of dried meat, the loaves they had not eaten yesterday, a jar of dried fruit and some flagons of mead, stoppered with wood and wax. She pushed in a firestone, remembering in a flash how she had once been in need of one. Then Niartha stuffed some clothing into another sack, and rolled each of the bundles inside a blanket. Round these she tied hides. Never had she thought to be doing this again, and she choked back grief at the memories.

Brand had tied the bundles to the two horses, and Ricberht was clasping his wife, his face hidden in her hair, when they heard hooves. It was too late even to hide behind the house, but to their relief they saw Borgil, charging towards them.

"Come with me now!" he panted, red-faced. "Get into the trees! They are not far behind! I bring word from Aelfric!"

Brand practically threw the two men into their saddles and Borgil urged the little troop deep into the trackless forest. In seconds the sound of their retreat faded, so that only the bracken rustled in the morning breeze.

Niartha had had no time to bid her son farewell, nor to reassure Randulf. She lifted Maura and drew her indoors.

"Where is Fritha?" she asked. Maura's tears broke out afresh.

"I'll fetch her," said Brand.

"Take Idunna with you! She can hide at yours until it is safe. Keep out of sight, Idunna! I will come to you as soon as I can. Hurry back with the child, Brand!" It took fierce words in the next few minutes, but Niartha calmed Maura sufficiently not to frighten her child.

"Now," she told them all. "When they come, we must say the smiths have gone to the wick today. Brand, you go outside and chop wood – we need some, anyway, and you can keep watch. Borgil will come back and tell us what Aelfric is thinking. I just hope he keeps out of sight meantime. Now, take Fritha to get some eggs. We have to look as if everything is normal."

When the thanes arrived they found a busy householder, making pancakes on a griddle outside her door, her servant spreading blankets on the bushes to air, a little girl sitting on her mother's knee, her finger pointing toward them in cheerful excitement. Brand lifted his long-handled chopper to his shoulder and straightened his aching back.

He greeted them civilly. "Good day!" They reined in rapidly, and their horses breathed heavily, snorting and stamping.

"Ricberht is to come with us! And Randulf. Where are they?" One man made as if to push past Niartha to get inside her house, but was stopped by her calm reply.

"They have gone to the wick for supplies."

"But the king wants them!"

"If he had sent for them earlier, you would have caught them." What an unhappy word, she thought, but did not let it show in her face. "As it is, they left at sunrise. They will be back well before sundown. Will the king still need them by then? Do you wish to wait?" She could have bitten her tongue, as it was the last thing they wanted. She almost felt Maura flinch beside her. Fritha was wriggling, wanting to get down. She loved Ricberht's old horse, and she wanted to get to these shining mounts, their harness ornamented with gilded fittings. Brand put down his chopper and lifted her from Maura, taking her to pat the nose of the leader's horse. There was no chance that he would let her get near the legs of these restless steeds.

"No," the leader, a young man called Plegmund, decided. "We will tell Eorpwald – tell the king – what has happened. You make sure the smiths come to the hall tonight, or there will be trouble." He pulled the horse's head round and cantered off, down the track towards the village, his fellows strung out behind him.

"Brand," Niartha said after a moment's quiet, "will you go and fetch Idunna? She must be frantic."

They sat and drank a warm concoction of sweet marjoram, which Niartha said would soothe them. Idunna told how Beorn had been seized from his bed, with Idunna lying naked beside him. Luckily she had left her son at his grandmother's that night. They let Beorn grab a tunic, but he had no time even to put on shoes. Arnulf was taken from next-door, at the same time, but he was up and dressed. His forge was left open and who knew who might get in there and take things?

"What is going to happen? What does the king want with my Beorn?" Idunna wept helplessly.

Niartha and Brand told her how the other two smiths had got away into the forest, and how Borgil had words for them from Aelfric. Surely he would come back to tell them?

Meanwhile, things had to appear normal – whatever that was. Perhaps, Niartha suggested gently, it would be best for Idunna to go to her mother's. There were brothers there to protect her, and she could be with her little son. They decided to wait until midday for Borgil to reappear, and then Brand could ride to the village with Idunna behind him, and bring whatever news he could. He could secure the forge, and bring some things for Maura, but try to keep away from the hall. If Eorpwald had forgotten him, so much the better.

At the hottest part of the day, they heard rustling from the verge of the forest, and Borgil called softly to Brand, was given a signal that all was clear, and he tied his horse behind the house, with a bucket of water and a switch of hay. He sank onto the grass and wiped his sweating brow on his sleeve, before downing a stoup of ale in one, long pull.

"I've got them to the coast," he said. Maura gave a startled cry, but he patted her arm. "It's what Aelfric told me to do," he said. "The trader was there, and he can take them north. Aelfric is going to say that he sent them there yesterday, after the funeral, to bring news of our king's election to King Edwin. He will say that is what Edwin wanted."

"Oh, no!" Niartha gasped, putting her hand to her mouth in sudden dismay. "I told Eorpwald's men that Ricberht had taken Randulf to the market. Now he will have two stories! He will know we are lying!"

"Just pretend they didn't want to upset you by going away, so they lied to you," he said.

"But Ricberht never lies to me!" Maura wept.

"Well, you'll have to say that he has this time," said Niartha, grimly. "Now, remember, Idunna, you don't know anything about all this. You've been at your mother's since the men took Beorn. Borgil, you'd better ride round through the forest. We don't want them to know you have been this way. Brand, you take Idunna back through the trees on this side of the village and let her slip through to her mother's from the back of the forge. Try not to be seen, but just behave as usual, if you do meet anyone."

"Let us have news, Idunna," begged Maura. "Send Borgil, unless Beorn is free to come. Or Arnulf." At the mention of these names, her tears threatened again, so Niartha made her get busy, feeding them all, before they were left alone to wait.

It was dusk before Brand reappeared, laden with a roll of clothes and bedding.

"I saw Aelfric!" he reported. "Eorpwald was mighty angry that he had sent the smiths away. He's got the other two in the lock-up and says he will deal with them tomorrow. Nobody knows what's in his mind. Aelfric had a word with Arnulf when they locked him up, and he came to the forge. Arnulf was really fretting about leaving it open."

"Aelfric is a good man," said Niartha. "There is no-one else to manage Eorpwald. Not now that Raedwald has gone." Her voice faded.

"Well, but there might be," said Brand. "Aelfric has truly sent Ricberht to Edwin, with the news of what Eorpwald is like. He hopes the High King will keep an eye on what goes on here."

"But it's so far away!" exclaimed Maura, clutching her sleepy daughter to her. "When will Ricberht come back?"

"We don't know, though King Edwin might send him back straight away. But the other thing I've got to tell you is that the ship will put in at the Blyth on the way north, and Aelfric has asked Ricberht to beg Onna to visit here as soon as may be. He's always been able to manage Eorpwald before."

"True, but Eorpwald was not then king of the Wuffings," said Niartha.

They sat by the hearth as night drew in and Fritha fell asleep. Their thoughts were with Ricberht, and the forlorn figure of Randulf; they feared for Beorn and Arnulf, who were, perhaps, unaware of what had happened that day and afraid of what tomorrow might bring.

The elders had been very disgruntled at having most of the day wasted, waiting in the hall. The priest had actually taken himself off, he was so disgusted. What was the reason that the two smiths were being held, they demanded. Where were their fellows? One or two of the old men were quietly put in the picture by Aelfric. Others he could not be sure of: they had sons who were among Eorpwald's drinking companions. As word got round the village, there were several who were beginning to wonder if they had made the right man king.

Next day Eorpwald decided he would rather go hunting than deal with the smiths. It was Ricberht he was really after, and the others were less important. They could wait. He rode out, horns blaring, staghounds yelling, and the people watched them go, standing mutely at their doors.

When men had settled to their work and the women were chattering in the bakehouse, Aelfric visited the lock-up. It was a small, wooden shed in the corner of the forecourt compound. It was guarded by one *ceorl*, and Idunna stood beside him. She had brought food and drink for her two menfolk, and had the good sense to share it with the guard, so he let her call through the narrow, horizontal slit in the door, and push food through it. Aelfric dismissed him, opened the door and let the sunshine stream into the smelly little hole. Idunna went to clasp her husband, but the two were fouled from having to sit in the mire of their own excrement. Aelfric called two slaves over to bring buckets of water, rakes and clean straw. He made Idunna run for fresh clothing and, while she was gone, he told them all he knew.

"What is he waiting for? Why are we here? If it's about the act of allegiance, he only has to give us the chance!" To be told that a day's hunting was more important was infuriating. "If that is the little he thinks of us king's smiths, then we'd be better off out of it. Can't you let us go, like Ricberht?" Arnulf demanded, but Aelfric shook his head, regretfully.

"I've risked a lot to do just this," he replied. "But be patient. Perhaps Onna can intervene."

"And perhaps he'll find us both dead by the time he comes," muttered Beorn. But they thanked Aelfric for his kindness and did not resist when he shut the door on them again. At least they had food, water, blankets and a bucket to see them through the night.

One of Eorpwald's men killed a fine, red stag after a long chase. Naturally, they let the king take the credit. Its antlers would grace the wall of the hall, and there was a good supply of meat. The hunters enjoyed their success, drinking well into the night and sleeping well into the next morning.

The king was surprised to be aroused by his hall steward with the news that the king of the Blythings had sailed round the coast by night, and was awaiting his cousin's greeting in the hall. No, he had not sent a herald. Onna had come, himself.

NIARTHA

At night, I left the house, quietly, fearing lest Brand should be wakened by the creak of the door, but he slept soundly. I had tried to stifle my feelings all day, for the sake of Idunna and of Maura and the little one. Now I wept for the sudden going of my son, and my fear for him and his fellows. I wept, too, for Randulf and the death of my friend, Ulla. And I had not yet wept all my tears for the loss of Raedwald. Perhaps I never would.

I moved through the dewy grass to the fallen trunk beyond the track and sat on it, wrapped in my cloak. The memory of the times Raedwald had come to me there and put his arms around me left me bent double with grief, and I cried until I was exhausted.

When I looked up and dried my face, the full moon lit the grass, and a white hind and her faun stood outside my house. I watched as they grazed, and then a swooping bat startled them, so they leapt away to the darkness of the trees beyond the little midden. Brand stirred, as I came through the door, but I hushed him and he sank back, relaxed. I took myself to bed and found sufficient peace to sleep.

Today I was summoned to the hall. I took Brand with me, but left Maura, telling her to hide in Brand's house for the day. I wondered if we would ever feel safe enough for her to go to her own home, though now I was glad to have her near.

Aelfric caught me by the arm as I arrived at the door of the hall and told me that Onna had come. My heart lifted, and I smiled at the old steward.

"Good work!" I whispered, and moved into the big room. Onna was seated, with three of his thanes, on the guests' dais opposite Raedwald's high seat. No. Of course it was Eorpwald's now. He sat, one leg thrown over the low arm, and Aelfric moved up the hall to join him. Below the king's dais stood Arnulf and Beorn, guarded and hands tied in front of them.

I wanted to go to them, but was escorted to a place below

Onna's seat, where I bowed to each king, my hand to my heart, as was the custom. I stood and waited.

"What is this tale I heard about your son going to the market-wick yesterday?" demanded Eorpwald. I thought quickly.

"It was the day before, king," I said. "But he has not yet returned. I am sorry. Something must have delayed him. When he comes home..."

"You know perfectly well that he is not coming home."

"What do you mean, lord? Why is he not coming home? What have you – what has happened to him?" I hoped I was convincing. I was not supposed to know about the message to Edwin. I looked anxiously from one man to another. "Please, tell me. Have you hurt him?" I begged Eorpwald.

Onna spoke. "Be calm, Niartha. Your son is safe. I saw him two nights ago, sailing north to take news of the Wuffings' new king to Edwin. He did not wish to hurt you or his wife so did not tell you his plan." The tale was a sham, but Onna's smooth words seemed to be enough to convince Eorpwald that Ricberht had concealed his departure from us womenfolk.

Onna surprised most of us again, when he announced that Aelfric had done the right thing in sending news of Eorpwald's crowning to the High King as fast as could be. The trading ship was about to leave and the opportunity would have been missed. "I would have wished for my chief elders to do the same," Onna said.

"Now tell us, cousin, what you would do to men who did not come in fealty to your throne," said Eorpwald, glaring angrily at the prisoners.

"Before you answer, lord," I told Onna, "you should know that all those men were in mourning for the wife of one of them, whose funeral was held that same day. She had been killed by the king," I added, before Eorpwald leapt to his feet, waving his sword to silence me. I was appalled at my own temerity. At Onna's gesture, one of his thanes placed a stool for me to sit on. I did not wait for Eorpwald's permission, but sank onto it, shaking. Of course, I realized, Onna knew about this from Ricberht, but would not say so.

Somehow, Aelfric found his voice, to tell Onna that what I said was true, though Ulla's death seemed to be a terrible accident. Eorpwald sat glowering while Onna questioned Arnulf. He could not be seen to quarrel with his guest.

"Cousin," Onna said at last. "Have you given these men

the chance to offer fealty to you, or have they been in mourning?" He looked significantly at their bound wrists. "Which is the bereaved husband?" He seemed surprised that Randulf should have been sent as an envoy, but Aelfric told him that the man could best be spared, being crippled in one arm. Eorpwald was obviously not keen to have that tale retold, so he ordered the ropes removed.

"Are you willing to swear allegiance to this man as your elected king?" asked Onna. For an endless moment I feared that Arnulf might refuse. Perhaps Aelfric had managed to talk some sense into him, I wondered, if he had had the chance. Arnulf said gruffly that he would swear. Beorn ducked his head in agreement.

"Call your elders, cousin," advised Onna. They assembled. We watched as Eorpwald got Aelfric to place the coronet on his brow, and place his sword across his knees. Each in turn, Arnulf and Beorn bent the knee and touched the sword with head and hand. Their faces were set, grimly.

"I hope I shall be able to bear witness again, when the other smiths return," said Onna, smoothly. "What a pleasing day's work. Shall we ride to Helmingham, cousin? They have a consignment of new wine. I would like to hear your opinion." He took the king's arm, whipped the coronet off and tossed it to Aelfric. I swear he winked at the old man as they moved away, leaving the rest of us agape.

Arnulf and Beorn went for a quick dip in the river and then joined Brand and me as we went to fetch Idunna and her son. You could hear her screams of joy all over the village. With the king out of the way, the hall was soon full of happy drinkers. Brand and I went home to tell Maura the good news. She decided to go home next day. I wish I had stopped her.

24

It took ten days, stopping to trade, but to Ricberht's delight, the skipper wanted to put in at the Cocket River. There had been a shortage of pleasure since he had fled the Deben, unable to so much as kiss his baby daughter, nor his mother. At the Blyth he had been able to pass word to king Onna about the events of the day of Eorpwald's throning, which he hoped might help the cause of Arnulf and Beorn, if Onna could get there in time. That king had seemed remarkably calm and willing to help his cousin's people.

The sea voyage was as interesting and as uncomfortable as the one he remembered from his youth. This shipmaster was Lukas Lukasson, son of the old sailor whom Ricberht had known as a boy, and who had shipped him and his mother from Bernicia to the Deben, so many years before.

At the Cocket, he found that Raedwald had been right about the fisherfolk. They had recovered from the shock of Gurth's death at the battle of the River Idle. Bertha, as strong-minded as ever, persuaded her people to choose Wilhelm, her adopted son, as headman. About eight years older than Ricberht, he was a strong, quiet man, well able to see to the management of fishing on the coast, and of trade with the burgh upstream and beyond. He could fight, Ricberht knew, because he had enviously watched Gurth teaching Wilhelm the use of sword, shield and spear before he was able to join in. But Wilhelm preferred to fish, hunt and ride.

He and the other dwellers in the hamlet asked fondly after Niartha. Ricberht spoke little of their fears, but told them of Raedwald's death, and that they had a new king.

"I am on my way to find the High King, to tell him," he told them.

"Who is the High King, then?" they asked. News had not reached here yet. He told them about Edwin, and found the king had won their liking and respect.

"He seems a fair man," said old Bertha. "Not one for making

up his mind in a hurry, but he seems to be putting this country to rights, or nearly so." They talked long into the night.

Randulf still did not have much to say, but sat, listening, and nodding at what Ricberht recounted. On the ship, when he was not being sea-sick, he had stood, gripping the gunwale and staring out at the waves flashing in sunlight or invisible in the darkness. It seemed to calm him.

Ricberht told Bertha privately what had happened to Ulla, and all the pent-up fury he felt towards Eorpwald. She listened, and said nothing for a while. Then she said that she hoped he would have the chance to let Edwin know the full story.

"Things are not right at your place, lad, " she said in her lilting, northern voice which reminded him of Maura's. "I think the High King will want to see you right."

"I hope so," Ricberht sighed.

To his amazement, Randulf said he wanted to go no further. "I am no use to a king, now," he said. "You have Aelfric's token and you can tell the tale. Edwin knows you for a fine smith. Stay with him, if you can't get back home."

Ricberht protested that Randulf was still of use to *him*, and that he was definitely going home to Maura, Fritha and Niartha, whatever Edwin said.

"I'll come back here, and see how things are with you," he promised Randulf. He felt glad that he had told Bertha the story. She would look after the grief-stricken man. Nor would Eorpwald find him here.

That second night, Bertha told Ricberht the story of Niartha's time in the hamlet. It was time he learnt of his mother's courage, she felt, and of her lover. He needed to know of Raedwald's justice, and even of the betrayer who had been Ricberht's father. At last Ricberht had the chance to understand some of his mother's silences and to find his true self. He hugged Bertha, gratefully. Some day he would find a way to reassure his mother that he knew everything, and that it was all perfectly all right.

Next day he took a tearful farewell, not least of Randulf. Wilhelm and a small band of huntsmen rode with him upstream, through the great forest, and passed him on to another troop at a boundary to a valley far inland. These men told him that King Edwin was at Yefrin, and they would be there next day. He put into the hand of one of the King's Messengers the little bag which Aelfric had given him, containing the token by which one of the Wuffings could be recognized. The man rode off into the darkness. Edwin would be expecting him, he told Ricberht.

25

Ricberht realized that Edwin's men guarded the roads well. Several times they were stopped, and identified themselves, showing a small, flat board of wood, marked with a runic symbol, which designated a message from Wilhelm's people, he was told. There was obviously a system in place to ensure that travellers gave an account of themselves. In each instance, they were then greeted, allowed to pass and offered hospitality at a sort of guard-post, when night approached.

With the sun high overhead, they rode around a bend into a wide valley, between high hills like the mounds of giants. They were stopped again, and word was passed onward before they were allowed to proceed. Ricberht would never forget his first sight of Yefrin. Beside the roadway extended a vast sweep of land, where a huge, double palisade enclosed a great sweep of land, holding sheep, cattle and horses. Riding past this, he saw a hall, outstretched, its size rivalling that of King Raedwald, with outer buildings extending beyond it. This majestic building was surrounded by many others, for housing the people, for foodstores and for workshops. Beyond these, there was an extraordinary structure, shaped like a wedge cut from a round loaf, with tiered seating, a platform before the lowest benches, contained within a fence. This must be an enclosure for a moot, thought Ricberht. Further on he could see more buildings. One had a golden cross, fixed to an end gable. It must be a church, he thought. His escort had told him that this was not Edwin's main stronghold, but a stopping place amidst his extensive lands, and a centre for men to come to bring tribute and settle disputes. Whatever must his headquarters be like? Ricberht marvelled.

The troop rode in and their horses were taken to a paddock beyond the gate. The men were given food and drink at a guest-house beside the hall and took the chance to wash the dust from their hands and faces, before being summoned to make their reports. Their weapons were, of course, left at the door, and the steward, a tall, grey-haired man, richly dressed, led Ricberht up through the main room of the hall, leaving the others to join their fellows. It was impossible for Ricberht not to gape at the scale of this building. The rafters towered into darkness, but the place was lit with torches, leaning from iron brackets. At least two open doors allowed some light to pass, but were so deeply overhung by eaves that they kept out some draughts and much light. Woven hangings glowed on the walls, interspersed with wolf-skins and the antlered heads of huge stags. Shields, gold-studded, glinted in the torchlight. Around the walls were platforms on which were extra benches and trestles. Ricberht imagined servants running along these to bring food and drink to the feasting tables, or perhaps some parade of warriors, or a royal procession. Their footsteps were soft on rushes, but he noticed that wood had been laid for the floor.

The steward thumped with his staff, outside a doorway, curtained with the hide of what must have been the hugest ox in the land. A voice said, "Come in!" Pulling back the curtain, the steward beckoned Ricberht to go in, and then withdrew, dropping the leather behind him. Ricberht moved into a fairly small chamber, perhaps the size of Raedwald's anteroom. Raedwald's no longer, his thought flickered.

Edwin sat on a cushioned seat, its arms gilded, though this was not his throne. In his hand he held the little bag with Aelfric's token lying upon it. He was simply dressed, wearing one great ring, but no other jewels.

"This has reached me with remarkable speed," he said. "I have been here only a few days, myself. Is all well in Raedwaldsham?"

Ricberht bent his knee and bowed his head. "I have to tell you, lord," he said, "we have a new king. It is Eorpwald." He stopped and looked up to see if Edwin knew the name. He gave no sign of it, but, seeing Ricberht's hesitation, Edwin bade him sit. Ricberht's jaw dropped. Sit? In the presence of the new High King? Again he paused, and Edwin nudged a stool with his foot and gestured towards it. Ricberht sat, and tried to collect his wits.

In the end, with some prompting and searching questions, Edwin got the story. In fact, he had, of course, met Eorpwald with Raedwald, knew more of him from conversations with Onna, had seen his hostility toward the Christian priests, and had hoped the Wuffings would choose more wisely. Hearing of the death of the swordsmith's wife was disturbing. He wondered why they had not

145

then delayed the throning, but Eorpwald had already been elected. He seemed to recall that there was a problem between Eorpwald and at least one of his father's smiths. He asked for, and received frank answers from the young man Aelfric had sent to him.

"Is it safe for you to return home?" he asked after a lengthy pause for thought.

"I do not know, lord," replied Ricberht. "If word comes about what has happened to Arnulf and Beorn, I shall know what to expect. But I must return. My wife will be afraid, and my mother. I do not know if I shall still be the king's goldsmith. If not, I think we must leave." He sat, head down, fidgeting on his stool in distress.

"I will send for information," said Edwin. "You must stay here until my Messenger returns. I shall employ you here until then. It will take about three weeks, at least. Then we can decide. Either I shall keep you here – do not be anxious! I will have the womenfolk brought to you, if needs be. Or you shall return with my next message to King Eorpwald. It seems," he said, half to himself, "as if I must keep an eye on that young man."

Ricberht stood and bowed again, thanking the king. "May I ask, lord..." he said, hesitantly, "may I ask that word be sent to my home, to let them know that all will be well?"

"See Ecgric, my steward," Edwin advised him. "He will let the Messenger take your words as well as mine. Do it now. The man will leave at dawn. Send Ecgric to me."

As Ricberht left the room, a servant immediately approached and escorted him back to the steward. Ricberht gave him Edwin's words, and he strode off to do as the king bade.

Ricberht took off the Thor's hammer he had made to wear as protection and wrapped it in a piece of cloth he tore from one of his undertunics. When the messenger found him, he promised to put it in the hands of Maura or of Niartha. Yes, of course he would remember the names. Was he not Messenger to the High King? He would tell them that Ricberht was safe and hoped to be home in a few weeks.

Ricberht lay awake, going over in his mind all that had been said that day. He trusted Edwin. Surely all would be well. In spite of his homesickness, he fell asleep at last.

26

Onna stayed for several days, ostensibly to celebrate Eorpwald's kingship. He also took the chance to talk to some of his old friends, and to visit Helmingham, where his mother's brother had ruled for so long. He was very old and frail now. So much death, he thought. He found himself thinking of the words of the Christian priests, if only he could remember them: "A time to be born and a time to die... a time to weep and a time to laugh...a time to love and a time to hate... a time of war and a time of peace." There was something, too, about how "a man should rejoice, and do good in his life," and he wished Eorpwald could find it in his heart to think such thoughts.

He wondered how the two sad men who had come to him at Blythburgh might be faring, and how King Edwin would deal with the Eorpwald problem. Edwin was not renowned for prompt action, but seemed to be a just man. No doubt news would reach them soon enough. Meanwhile, he bade farewell, first of all to Aelfric (with whom he held private words, late at night) and then, more openly, to his cousin, Eorpwald, inviting him to visit whenever he chose, bringing as many as twelve thanes with him if he wished, and promising to return soon.

Arnulf and Beorn occupied themselves, making ploughshares, spear-heads, daggers and *seaxes* – whatever the villagers needed, in fact. They kept away from the hall, and out of the king's sight. Soon Idunna was pregnant again, and was glad to have Beorn at home in the evenings, to play with his robust and adventurous little son. Whenever she could, she walked the couple of hundred yards to Maura's house, always sure of a warm welcome, while the two toddlers rolled in the grass and threw cleavers at each other.

It felt like half a year to Maura, but was actually only about five weeks after Ricberht's departure, when Brand came running to tell them that a King's Messenger had arrived at the hall. Then he rushed off to fetch Niartha, and told them all to wait at Arnulf's place, while he found out what news he could.

To his surprise, as he hovered near the door of the hall, about an hour later, Aelfric left the hall in the company of the man Edwin had sent. The old steward immediately hailed Brand and asked him to take the Messenger to Maura or Niartha.

The man would say nothing, until he was brought to Arnulf's door to be met by anxious faces and eager questions.

"I bring this token," he announced and handed to Niartha the tiny cloth-wrapped parcel, containing Ricberht's hammer-of-Thor amulet. "Your son is well, staying at Yefrin until the king allows him to leave. Then he hopes to be here in a few more weeks." He bowed and, message delivered, he turned to go. Of course, they gave him food and drink and made him sit while he told them when Ricberht had reached Edwin's hall and how he had looked. How was Randulf?

The man knew nothing of Randulf, for Ricberht had sent no word of his companion.

"He was alone when I saw him. He came with one of our escort troops. Nobody else."

Their hearts sank. Anything could have happened in all these weeks. Suddenly Niartha asked, "Do you know where Ricberht landed in Edwin's kingdom? Where was he escorted from?"

The man thought, then said he had been met at the head of the Cocket valley.

"Then I know where Randulf is!" exclaimed Niartha. "Ricberht will have taken him to Bertha! She will care for him. Clever boy!" she beamed. Arnulf nodded slowly.

"Let us hope you are right," he agreed.

Maura and Niartha sent loving messages back, and expressed their belief that all seemed calm at Raedwaldsham. Aelfric took the man away, with more words for the High King so far away in the north. The rest of them hugged each other in delight. Surely, now that all was well, Ricberht would soon be home.

Once again, Niartha asked Maura if she would like to come to the oak with her, as she would be alone for a few more weeks still, before her husband returned. But the girl said she was content. Idunna was near, and the village only a little further, where she could exchange provisions.

"Come to see me every day, if you like," she begged Niartha. "I wish we had more room so you could stay!"

"I have to look after my goats," smiled Niartha.

"And the tickens!" squeaked Fritha.

"Yes, come and see the tickens tomorrow, and you shall have some eggs!"

"We'll be there by noon," promised Maura. But she did not come.

Once again, they had not taken Eorpwald into account. Preoccupied by Onna's visit, and dealing with requests from the shipmen anxious to make the most of what was left of the summer travelling months, he had put Ricberht out of his mind. Now this messenger had come. He said he brought the good wishes of the High King. Why, he now wondered, could Ricberht not have returned with them? He sent for Aelfric. Had anything been said about the two smiths? Aelfric said that Ricberht had sent a message to his wife and mother, but he knew nothing more, and was dismissed to go about his duties.

Eorpwald brooded, sitting over his wine-cup as the day waned. He felt dissatisfied, but could not think what to do. Then he rose from his seat and called three of his thanes to him.

"Bring your swords," he told them.

A few minutes later, they arrived at Arnulf's forge and tied the horses to the rail outside. Beorn appeared at the door, saw who it was, retreated for a second, while he hissed a warning, and then came outside, bending his head respectfully as he did so. Arnulf appeared, rather more slowly, and also bowed to the king.

"Is there something I can do for you, lord king?" he enquired at length. Eorpwald seemed to come to a decision, and moved up close to the big man. For a moment Arnulf thought he was going to attack, as his hand went to his sword, but Eorpwald was merely gesturing towards his weapon, lifting it at his belt.

"I need a new sword." The two smiths looked at each other, then back at the king. "Can you do this?" His voice held a challenge.

"Yes, king," said Arnulf, "but it will take longer than usual. I may need to get my brother's advice. We have made many a seax, but never a sword fit for a king."

"Surely you have watched him at work?"

"Lord, that is true. But to get the mix right for the steel, to do the twisting-"

"If you cannot do it, I will find a smith who can, and you can go elsewhere for work!" shouted Eorpwald.

"We will do it, lord king," said Arnulf.

"And the scabbard, too," demanded the king.

"The jewel-smith..." began Arnulf, but Beorn stopped him.

"I can do the work, once the sword is finished, of course," he said. "Brand and I can sort it out." They had watched Ricberht often enough, he thought. And Borgil would help.

"You may take the measure of this sword," said Eorpwald, "but I need it an inch longer, and a little heavier. The grip of the hilt can be broader, too." He removed the blade from its sheath to demonstrate. "Measure it now. I cannot leave this here."

Beorn hastened off, to return with some cord, which he used to get the right lengths. He had to measure the king's hand, which he did rather nervously, keeping his eyes fixed on the cord. As Arnulf took the sword, he could tell it was too light and short for a full-grown man. He balanced it in his grip, then handed it back, deferentially, to the king.

"Do I have permission to go to the wick for ore, charcoal and leather, lord?" he asked.

"Very well. Be there at first light tomorrow." Eorpwald turned to leave, but Arnulf had to ask a question, which Raedwald would never have left him to ask.

"What would you wish me to trade with?" he asked the new king. Eorpwald seemed surprised.

"Ask Aelfric to arrange it," he said carelessly, thrusting the blade into its old sheath. As he swung his horse's head round, he saw Idunna standing at her door, no doubt worrying what he was doing at the forge.

The thought of her fear brought a surge of satisfaction. He led his men further along the track, even though it was growing dark. He arrived at Niartha's house as the moonlight strengthened in the clearing, rode right up to her door and beat on it with his fist, leaning from his horse, so that she leapt back in fright as she opened it to find the bulk of his horse close upon her. She drew back to reveal Brand, sword drawn behind her.

Quickly she collected herself and Brand put up his weapon, as she greeted Eorpwald, with what calmness she could find. She offered him a drink and a welcome in her house, but he declined.

"I wish only to hear what the High King's Messenger has said to you," he stated. "I would have expected you to bring me word, not have to come for it myself."

"Did he not see you, lord king?" she said, surprised. "We simply heard from my son that he is well and will come home when Edwin – when the High King – permits it."

"Why did your son not come, himself? Why is Edwin keeping him? His first loyalty is to me!"

If Niartha's first thought was that loyalty was something to be earned, she did not say so.

"Perhaps he needs my son's skills," she ventured.

"He is needed here. I have work for the smiths. And when you next get word to him, you may tell him that. He will need to prove himself to me."

"Surely he must have the High King's permission, lord?" Niartha dared to comment, but Eorpwald jabbed fiercely at his horse's belly, and cantered off into the gathering darkness, followed by the three men.

"Whatever was that all about?" she said to Brand. He shrugged and shook his head.

"Should I go to the village?" he asked. Niartha said she thought it was not necessary until the morning. She was bitterly to regret that decision.

EORPWALD

Maura had heard the horses pass her little house, and could see the light at Arnulf's forge. Fritha was fast asleep, so she left her in her cot and ran over the dew-wet grass to ask if all was well. The two smiths explained Eorpwald's visit, and said they would consult with Borgil next day. They would also see if Aelfric could get word north again, as they needed help if they were to satisfy the king.

They locked up the forge and called good night to Maura, as she ran back along the verge of the track. Before she had gone halfway, they had reached their own houses and shut the doors. Suddenly Maura heard hooves thudding on the track, coming from the forest.

She became aware of the blackness of the night, and began to run blindly towards her house. As she did so, the moon shone out brightly, breaking from a cloud, and in her yellow dress she glowed in its light. Eorpwald saw her, not knowing who she was, simply that here was a woman, running like a deer, slim as a flower, and his for the picking. He sped towards her, and his men followed. They played the same game they had done with Sigeberht all those years ago, encircling her as they rode, ignoring her pleading cries.

Then the king grabbed her, hauling her before him onto the horse, hand clutched to her breast, still riding round and round. Then he drew rein. He flung her to the ground, tossing his cloak from his shoulders in the same movement, and pinned her where she lay, half-winded. He called to the men to help him hold her, ripped off his belt with the sword falling to the grass, loosened the drawstring of his breeches, and fell on her, tearing at her garments till she lay exposed. One of the men, Plegmund, put his hand over her mouth to muffle her screams, as they held her arms above her head, while the king rutted. When his head sank to her breast he tasted milk. Only then did he look at her.

"The smith's woman," he breathed. She tried to twist away

from him, only to have her face gripped tightly so that his spittle wet her as he hissed. "A pity your husband did not stay to mind you! He will want to know how you leave your house at night! But then, what does one expect from such as you?" He slapped her face. "I am the king. I have the right to take what is mine… and you are mine tonight. If you tell anyone of this, I will return, and I will let each of these men take his fill of you. Now get back to that brat of yours!" He pulled himself out of her, and now she could feel his moisture as the night air touched her body. He stood over her, re-dressing himself. She curled into a ball as he lifted his sword, but he just laughed, and rolled her suddenly from the cloak. She crawled away, in helpless tears, and heard the hoofbeats as they rode off toward the hall.

She used the water meant for the next morning to lave herself wherever the king had touched her, welcoming its chill. She tried to stifle her sobs lest Fritha should wake. She would burn every item of her clothing next day. Meanwhile, she fell onto the bed she had shared so joyfully with Ricberht, rolled herself into a blanket, and lay weeping until dawn.

NIARTHA

Brand went early this morning to Arnulf's forge to find out what Eorpwald's words meant. They were going to send for Borgil and the four men would talk over how they could share their skills to make a sword for this new king of theirs. Brand was going to tell them of Eorpwald's visit to my house, last night.

When the afternoon was well advanced, and still Maura had not appeared, I felt sure that something was wrong. Perhaps the child was sick. So I packed some eggs into soft fleece in my basket and walked through the trees. I still half-think I hear Raedwald riding towards me. Then the thought of Eorpwald's visit chased away such dreams.

I found Maura inside, door closed so that I had to knock at it to be admitted. Immediately, I knew something was very wrong, but nothing would persuade Maura to say what was troubling her. Only when Fritha fell asleep did my son's wife finally begin to cry. I was sitting, so appalled at what she told me that I could not find words, and the girl broke down even more, thinking that I was blaming her.

"I could not stop them! It was not my fault!" she pleaded, holding my skirts as she knelt beside me. "Now he will come again and they will all do it to me... he said they would if I told anyone!" She fell to the ground, sobbing.

I sank down beside her to cradle her until she fell quiet.

The first thing was to take Maura and Fritha to my house, and to ask Brand to come to stay with us again. He may yet have to know, I told Maura. At first, I privately resolved to tell Arnulf (but not Beorn in case Idunna let it slip in the village), and also wondered whether to tell Aelfric. I shall have to get him to try to arrange for Ricberht's return, but without letting my son know what has happened.

Oh, ye gods! Who knows what Ricberht might not do, if he learns of this rape? Perhaps it would be safest, after all, to keep it just between Maura and myself. For the time being I will say nothing to a living soul. I will guard my whole family, and not let the king come near them.

I persuaded Maura to bundle up clothing, Fritha's bedding, any food that might waste and anything she valued. I went to get Brand, telling the men that Maura was lonely, not feeling well and needed help with the child. They accepted this readily enough, and Arnulf lent us his cart again, to carry all the things.

I learned from Brand that Beorn had returned from the Gipping wick with enough ore to begin work on the sword. They plan to begin tomorrow. Arnulf saw Aelfric, who persuaded Eorpwald to part with enough silver to make the trades they needed. Had the man learned nothing from his father? That was the question they all asked. I know the answer. Eorpwald has very little of his father in him.

Maura was glad enough to allow Brand to play with little Fritha, and take her to see her beloved 'tickens', while we folded their things into a chest and put her treasured necklace into a jar on a high shelf.

"Let Fritha sleep in my room tonight," I suggested, and to my relief, she did not object. In fact, I put them both to bed early, as Fritha was soon tired out, and I knew Maura had not slept last night. Brand had struck up a relationship with Gilda, my servant, and I knew they shared a nook beside the back door of the house. I suppose they have had plenty of time to get together, and she is discreet enough, though I can hear muffled giggling in the darkness. She will make a good enough wife for Brand, but I shall miss her when the time comes. I suppose if he gets her with child that will…

Suddenly I am wide awake. What if Eorpwald has left a child in Maura? It is many weeks since Ricberht left her, and who knows how many more until he returns? A child would be impossible to hide, and I will not have my son thinking she has betrayed him! If any man else had done this rape, he would be forced to pay a costly price in compensation. But this is the king, himself. As yet we have to learn that he has a sense of justice.

I will watch for the signs. If need be, I will see to it that she loses such a child. She need never know how, nor her husband. Nor will Eorpwald, I think grimly. It will be necessary to hasten the weaning of Fritha now. With those small sharp teeth of hers, I think Maura will need little persuading. I shall encourage Fritha in her eagerness to be 'a big girl now'. I have to know, even before Maura does, if I am to abort the thing unborn, unshaped, unwanted, before it becomes a child.

27

True to his word, Edwin saw to it that Ricberht was introduced to his smiths. One of them, named Grimbald, had been with Edwin when he came to Raedwald's funeral. He was pleased to see the man, he told Ricberht, who had made that stag for the stone; he was quietly approving of the way Ricberht shared the credit for the making, with his fellows. If he could work with others, he told the newcomer, then perhaps he would like to work on a new shield for the king?

"That was the first work I ever did, for my king – a shield!" burst out Ricberht, eagerly.

"Was that the one buried with the old High King? It stood close behind his head in the chamber they built in the great ship."

Ricberht was delighted that Grimbald had noticed it. They began to make comparisons, putting forward ideas, so that soon they were talking like old friends. Grimbald took Ricberht to meet the other smiths, describing what skill he had, and how he might help with the shield. The goldsmith was a young lad whose father had died a few weeks before and he had ideas, he told Ricberht, but was not sure how to go about developing them. They went off to his workshop, emerging only when the horn blew to call them in to eat.

From that night Ricberht stayed in Grimbald's house, and moved between the various smithies to lend a hand as required. Lying in bed each night, he never lost his anxious wish to be with Maura and his own people again, but now there was the mingled satisfaction that he was once more working for a king, with men who valued the scope of his crafting. He wondered if Eorpwald would release him so that he could bring his wife and child to the north. What about Niartha? His mind closed and he slept.

The King's Messenger did not return as quickly as might be hoped. The weather turned stormy, with strong and adverse winds, so that he was forced to turn in and wait, once at Sheringham, near the great bight of shallow water that led to the fens, then again into the mouth of the Humber River, where he knew there was a large settlement a few miles off the north bank. Eventually he had taken horse after horse, in the king's name, and made his way to Yefrin, four weeks after leaving Raedwaldsham.

"All is well," he reported first to the king, and later to Ricberht, who encountered him in the hall that night. "Your womenfolk will be glad to see your return, no doubt."

After supper, Ricberht asked Ecgric, the steward, if he might be allowed to seek the king's permission to leave for home, now that the new shield was almost finished. He waited while Ecgric went to speak to the king. He was summoned from his bench to approach Edwin on his high seat.

"I trust you will stay to see the shield offered for my approval," Edwin told him, smiling. "It is only fair that you should be rewarded with the rest. I hear that you have been much involved in the design and making." He paused with an enquiring look.

"If you wish it, lord king," said Ricberht, warm with pleasure.

"Then you will stay a few more days. Then, no doubt you wish to return to the Cocket?"

Was there nothing this man did not know? Ricberht nodded his reply. "If I may take that road, lord," he asked. "I will meet my friends there again, and wait for a trader to the south."

"Ecgric will provide an escort, after the feast for the shield. I shall be sorry to lose such a smith," said the king. Now was surely the moment to ask if he might move back with his family, but Ricberht did not. There would be time enough to seek this favour, after he had talked to his wife. Ricberht bowed low and went back to the hearth. Grimbald pushed a drinking horn into his hand.

"Time to catch up! You are a round behind the rest of us!" Ricberht took a great swig and passed the horn along. When he told them that he was staying to see the shield presented to the High King, there were shouts of gladness.

Next day was spent fitting the gold-plated dragon-head clasps around the twisted leather of the rim. Like Raedwald's, Edwin's shield had a mighty central boss, several ornamental strips, which also served to bind the coloured leather covering the shield, and totemic creatures to represent the strength and glory of the new High King. It would be kept, wrapped in a fine cloth, under Grimbald's bed that night, and they would not let it out of sight until the night of the feast.

To Ricberht's surprise, the Christian priest, Paulinus, was called upon to bless the feast. Apparently the queen, Aethelberga, was in favour of Christianity. Daughter of the saintly King Aethelbert of Kent, and sister of Eadbald (once Eorpwald's wild friend) she had been very encouraging to her brother in his surprising conversion. Paulinus had gone to Canterbury during Raedwald's time and had been much involved. Now Pope Boniface wanted Paulinus to make sure of Edwin's conversion, by getting his wife to put pressure on the king. No-one had ever been able to hurry Edwin into a decision, and he had seen how Raedwald kept the peace in East Anglia. It was going to need something momentous to jolt Edwin into action.

For now, the king courteously bowed his head as the tall, white-clad Roman priest gave thanks to his God for the food and for the skilful work of men's hands, he said. Ricberht looked down at his hands. He had washed them for the feast, but they were scarred, burned and deeply engrained with the sooty colours of the metals. He could not see what any god would want with them. It was the pictures in his mind he thought were god-given, but he had had those long before he heard of Christ. He picked up his piece of venison and began to tear eagerly at the meat. Cheerful voices rang in the hall.

Of course, Edwin approved of the shield. He praised all his smiths by name, including Ricberht. At that name Paulinus, sitting at the table just below the royal dais, looked around, startled, though Ricberht did not notice. Ricberht was surprised in his turn when, as he finally rose from the table, he found the tall man approaching him. Paulinus was tall and dark, olive-skinned, and with a nose as hooked as an eagle's. He put a hand on Ricberht's shoulder and took his other in greeting.

"I did not expect to see you here, my son," he said. Ricberht could only incline his head, thinking as he so often had in the past, 'I am no man's son.' But now he knew the truth of that, and for a second he objected to being called this priest's son. They weren't supposed to have children were they? But immediately he remembered this was a common form of address. He realised that Paulinus had asked him a question.

"Forgive me," he said. "I was surprised. Did you ask what I was doing here?" Paulinus smiled, and drew him to a corner where they could converse more easily. Gradually Paulinus elicited the story of Ulla's death, Eorpwald's throning, Ricberht's escape to the north.

"Is it safe for you to go back?" he asked.

"It seems so, lord," said Ricberht.

"I am no lord, not yet, though I have been promised a bishopric, and that will make me a lord of the church. Call me 'father', as my people do, until that time comes." He saw Ricberht frown a little. "My given name is Paulinus – you may use that, if you wish. It is what Raedwald always called me."

"Well, Paulinus. We have received word that all is well at Raedwaldsham. I have King Edwin's approval to leave here when an escort can take me to the coast. I long to see my wife again."

"Your wife?" Of course, Paulinus would not have got to hear of Maura when he came for Raedwald's burial. Ricberht told him they had a child.

"And your mother? I saw her attending Raedwald's funeral. It seemed she had an important part to play." Ricberht simply nodded his assent.

"So this Eorpwald. Will he be a good king?" asked the man who would soon be a bishop. Ricberht wondered what sort of power that would give him.

"The elders decided he was strong and well-travelled. He knew his father's kingdoms and should grow in wisdom as years pass. I hope those all prove true. But he is not another Raedwald. He does not seem to realize he has a duty to his people. It will be good for us if the new High King keeps an eye upon him," Ricberht commented. Paulinus sat in thought for a moment.

"I shall pray that all will be well," he said. He stood up, and made the sign of blessing on Ricberht's head. "I also pray that you and yours may find safety and peace by joining the church of Christ." Ricberht bent his head. He was wondering how Christ would protect anyone from Eorpwald.

Next day was the last he spent at Yefrin. King Edwin was riding south to his palace near the Derwent River, outside the growing town of Eofric. Some thanes were being sent to the burghs on the eastern coasts of his realm and Ricberht would go with one group to find a ship to the south. First he would spend time with Bertha and Wilhelm. He hoped he could persuade Randulf to come home with him. There seemed no chance of sending a message to Maura. He had been away for over two months, and had many more days of travel yet to come.

PAULINUS

I have read to Edwin, the High King, the words of the letter written to him by our Holy Father, Pope Boniface:

"...We presume that Your Majesty has heard in fuller detail, as from a neighbouring territory, how our Redeemer in His mercy has brought light to our excellent son, Eadbald and the nations subject to him. We therefore trust that Heaven's mercy will grant this wonderful gift to you as it has to him, more especially as we understand that your gracious Queen and true partner is already endowed with the gift of eternal life through the regeneration of Holy Baptism. In this letter we affectionately urge Your Majesties to renounce idol-worship, reject the mummery of shrines and the deceitful flattery of omens, and believe in God the Father Almighty, and in His Son Jesus Christ, and in the Holy Spirit. This Faith will free you from Satan's bondage, and through the liberative power of the holy and undivided Trinity you will inherit eternal life...

"We impart to you the blessing of your protector, blessed Peter, Prince of the Apostles. With it we send you a tunic with a golden ornament, and a cloak from Ancyra, asking Your Majesty to accept these gifts with the same goodwill as that with which we send them."

Be it so, Lord Jesus.

I will lift up mine eyes unto the hills, from whence cometh my help.

My help cometh from the Lord, which made heaven and earth.

He will not suffer thy foot to be moved: he that keepeth Israel shall neither slumber nor sleep.

The Lord is thy keeper: the Lord is thy shade upon thy right hand.

The sun shall not smite thee by day, nor the moon by night.

The Lord shall preserve thee from all evil: he shall preserve thy soul.

The Lord shall preserve thy going out and thy coming in from this time forth, and even for evermore.

Amen

NIARTHA

Fritha has weaned herself very quickly, fascinated at being given milk, just like the frisky baby kids in their little paddock next to our house. She looks at us over the rim of her little wooden cup, takes her mouth away and bleats at us, milk dripping down her chin. Occasionally she still needs a comforting cuddle at night, but Maura's milk has dried up, and now she says her breasts are tender. I can tell this is not the milk fever, and I know she has not had her monthly bleeding. This morning she was sick, for the second time. I have decided to take action. I have told Maura I have something to stop her retching, and that she has probably eaten something disagreeable. It seems as though Maura has given no thought to the consequences of the rape, though the deed itself has left her too afraid to go into the village, or indeed, no further than my herb-garden. She seems to think that children may be born only out of love.

I have made an infusion of saffron and pennyroyal, flavoured with mint for her to drink, and said she may have the stomach ache for a few more days, but she should not be sick again. She is relieved not to be feeding Fritha.

Brand will take the little one to the forge today. The pair of them love to watch the work. When Brand is needed to help Arnulf, they put Fritha on a stool ouside the door and tell her everything they are doing. She says she will be a 'smiff' herself one day, and joins in their laughter. They have made two attempts at the welding and twisting iron for the king's sword, but wish they had Randulf to tell them when the mix is right. They dread Eorpwald becoming impatient.

Gilda and I go about the usual tasks of sweeping, washing and weeding, but I suggest to Maura that she sits outside the front door on my bench. I give her the drink, and though she says it is strange, she sips at it readily. In the warmth of the afternoon, I hear Maura give a little moan, and she clasps her belly. I come to reassure her that this is part of the stomach treatment, and she tries to smile. Soon she gasps again.

"It is like the monthly cramps," she says, "but fiercer. More like –" she stops and stares at me. "Am I having another baby? How could I when Ricberht..." Again she stops and grips my arm. "Is it what Eorpwald did? Tell me!" she begs.

I sit beside her. "It is probably only a bad monthly," I reassure her. "It could be because of weaning Fritha. Things change in a woman's body at these times. I doubt if we shall see a baby. Are you bleeding?"

We go inside, and sure enough, there is blood. We find pads of wool wrapped in old cloth, and I get her to sit down again. Then there come some wrenching pains. In a while, I change the pads, without showing her how the last one had a large clot of blood and tissue, trailing mucus. She must pass enough blood for the womb to clear, so I let her lie on her bed for an hour or two.

I go to prepare another drink made from oak bark boiled in milk that I know will stem the courses of her blood. The pains begin to ease, so I let her drink this down. If needed, she may have more at bed-time. She has not felt sick again, nor is she running a fever. I leave her to sleep until her child comes home, full of babble and excitement.

I sit outside, thanking the gods for sparing Ricberht the finding of Eorpwald's child got upon his wife. I wonder if she will be able to stop herself from telling him what the king did. I am sitting, head on my hands, when Brand carries Fritha home. She has been pretending he is her horse, and is whipping him with a few blades of grass, as he jiggles her up and down.

"Is the little mother better?" he asks, and I am glad to be able to say that she is, while at the same time grabbing Fritha to stop her from running in and jumping on her mother.

"I haven't got the eggs yet," I tell her, and she runs off to find Gilda and do her favourite job.

Brand comes and squats down beside me. He knows very well when all is not right, but this secret is too important to share. I tell him I have a headache and have just taken a willow-bark drink, and this seems to satisfy him. How many more lies must I tell?

He has brought some meat-balls from Idunna, and we shall have them with mashed turnip and sliced carrots. Life will go on.

28

Randulf came out with the fisher-folk to greet Ricberht. One of the boys, checking a fish-trap up the river saw a lone rider on the riverbank path, and ran home to tell his headman, Wilhelm, just as he was supposed to do. He was too young to know Ricberht, but saw immediately that he would be welcome.

"Is there news?" Ricberht asked eagerly, but Randulf shook his head. He knew his friend wanted only news of home. "Are you…" he nearly said 'better' but tried to find another word for what he needed to know. Bertha covered his awkwardness.

"Randulf is feeling much stronger now," she smiled. "I'm thinking we should keep him here. He is very useful to have around the place!"

"Well," said Ricberht, "he can stay if he wants to. But I am going home on the next ship south. I know all was well at home about six weeks ago. The King's Messenger told me so. He saw Arnulf and Beorn working – he thinks it was on a sword." He glanced sideways at Randulf and was relieved to see eagerness in his eyes. "And I have been busy, too! I helped to make a new shield for the High King! What do you think of that?"

Bertha flapped her apron at them. "Come on inside! You can eat and drink while you talk, can't you?"

"She doesn't change, " grinned Wilhelm. "She's as bossy as ever! You'd not think I was headman here now!" But he put his arm round Bertha's ample girth. He still loved the woman who had fostered him since he was about eight years old. "So, tell us about the king's hall. I hear it's a fine place…"

It was late that night, lying in their beds after a convivial evening, that Randulf said that he definitely wanted to go home.

"It was no way to leave things," he said. "I know we were not safe, but if Eorpwald has calmed down, and if we are to work for him, then I wish to be there. I think I will ask Arnulf to take me in. I just don't fancy being in the house without her, you know… Ulla." His voice trailed off.

"I am sure she would say that is the best thing to do," said Ricberht. "It will suit everyone well, to have you two together." And be safer, he thought. "It will be good to have your company on the ship," he added. "I wonder how long it will be before a trader calls in here."

They had time to help with harvesting the second hay crop, the corn and the apples from the little cluster of trees Ricberht could remember climbing as a child. If Randulf had had the full strength of two arms, he might even have suggested taking horse and trying their luck, but that was not a good choice without a troop of men to support them. Part of that way would lie through Mercian territory, and they had heard enough to know how small would be their chances of survival.

So they waited with growing impatience. At last, a sail was sighted, off Cocket Island. Men, women and children clustered at the quayside, stoutly rebuilt by Wilhelm. Goods were exchanged, including those from the burgh just upstream, so it took two days of noisy barter. Sailors were fed and allowed to doss down in the little hall after depleting a barrel of ale.

They agreed to take the two smiths as far south as they were going, but who knew if it would be all the way to the Deben? If there was trading to be done there from somewhere like Sheringham, then, yes, they would go. Wait and see. And another couple of pairs of hands would not go amiss.

"Make that three hands, eh?" They roared with drunken laughter, and Ricberht stiffened, ready to defend his friend. Randulf just joined in the laughter, seized the joker in his left grip, and dunked his head in the cauldron of warm water standing on the cold ashes of the hearth until he came up spluttering. Then Randulf just sat down again and smiled. Now they were all friends.

Next morning, on an early tide, they put out to sea. The villagers stood on the headland, waving and yelling 'Farewell!' Loud enough, thought Bertha, to waken the dead. But the man who lay deep in the ground beside them did not rouse.

The ship surged over the waves. Ricberht wrapped himself in his cloak as the fresh north wind caught them. They should make good time, and he found the movement exhilarating, as he stood below the high-necked prow. Randulf, however, soon succumbed to sickness, hanging over the side, midships, as he knelt on the stacked oars, with spray intermittently smacking his face. He did not complain when they put in that night, nor the one after.

On the fourth day they reached Sheringham, paid for their passage and went on shore to find a lodging, so that Randulf could recover. The shipmaster told them to find out after breakfast if he was going further south with a new cargo. Randulf pleaded with Ricberht, insisting he could sit a horse and manage it; anything except take to the water again.

"At least we are in our own lands again," he wheedled. "You have the gold Edwin gave you for the work on his shield, so we can buy two nags, even if we can't borrow them. That poor old fellow of yours needs replacing soon, in any case."

"True enough," admitted Ricberht. "I worry about using him now, myself. Very well. I'll get our things together in the morning, while you go out and find horses. Don't be long, though. We need to tell the skipper." They rolled out their bedding and lay down, feeling the floor heaving under them as if they were still on board. In the morning they ate thick slices of bacon, with warm bread and a jug of ale, then separated as planned.

So many people passed in and out of this port that it was not difficult to find a pair of horses left by travellers, and at a good bargain, together with their tack. Randulf returned a surprisingly heavy bag of Edwin's treasure to Ricberht and they lifted their baggage rolls out to their steeds. Ricberht took one look and gave a shout of laughter, causing the horses to wag their heads up and down and skitter about.

"You certainly didn't pick them for their beauty," he gasped. "We'll call them Blot and Splash – just look at those markings!" He calmed his beast and got the baggage tied firmly, then did the same for Randulf's. "Did you try to ride them?" he asked.

"No!" Randulf's tone was sufficiently firm for Ricberht to realize that his friend had preferred to make the attempt with no other onlookers.

"Right!" He led Splash to the mounting-stone and steadied him while Randulf swung himself onto the broad back. "Whoa, boy! He seems quiet enough, doesn't he? Can you manage him?" He watched while his friend walked the horse, turned it and brought it to a halt. Then he mounted and did the same.

They trotted along to the quayside and wished the shipmen a safe voyage.

"We'll see you at the Deben one day!" the sailors called.

166

"Not if we see you first!" came the shouts, and the two smiths rode off, laughing.

They had to travel south, over rolling hills, through heath and forest or go round the coast, with marshes and river-mouths to cross. They opted for the first, so before they left the port town they stocked up with food and drink, found a fletcher's to buy arrows, and put new strings to their bows. They would have to spend at least one night on the way, and might even have to lie in the open, if they found no settlement by nightfall.

Randulf hoped there would be a moon to help them see. He did not fancy encountering a wild animal in pitch darkness, and there were likely to be many of those in the wild country that lay between them and the gentler lands near home.

They picked their way through some marshes, onto slightly higher ground then over these low wolds, crossing the odd stream and one larger river. Here they paused to water the horses and devour some cheese and bread, before moving on. Ricberht did not want to put Randulf's riding skills to the test. His horse was amenable, but if a strong grip were to be necessary, he might get into trouble. Nor did he wish to tire the animals overmuch. So they walked the beasts steadily, only occasionally breaking into a trot where the ground was level. They saw the occasional bird of prey, and the odd deer, but no sign of anything more dangerous. As dusk descended, they stopped at a tiny settlement where some alders grew beside the ford of a river. There were only three small houses, but they were greeted warmly and given a bed each, with two of the families. In return for the kind hospitality, they shared news of the new High King, and were delighted to hear that these folk had heard of Raedwaldsham, though they had only the vaguest idea that it was 'a long ways to the south of here.'

So, south they went next day, winding up and down little valleys onto lower, flatter, marshier ground. That night they had to camp beside a clump of willows at a place where two rivers met. It seemed wise to wait until morning to pick their route, so Randulf made a fire, while Ricberht flung two hides over the drooping branches, and laid their bedrolls on the grass. It was too late to try to fish, so they made do with some dried meat, raw carrot and more cheese. At least they still had some ale. The horses moved slowly as far as their tethers would permit, munching on the grass, and reaching into the river to drink. The men lay in companionable silence, staring out from their rough shelter. How fortunate they were to have dry, warm weather, they agreed. The stars came out, but they were asleep before the moon of late summer lifted over the trees.

With dawn a mere hint of pink light, they were startled awake by the shrilling of the horses, and the stamping of their feet. They leapt from their shelter, each man grabbing the weapon placed ready to hand. A wild boar had approached from bushes nearby and stood still, eyes fixed on the horses rearing and tossing in their fear. Ricberht gave a hunting signal to Randulf with his hand, and while Randulf crouched, spear at the ready in the left hand that still lacked strength, Ricberht slithered as quietly as he could in the deep shadow of the willows, circling till he could see the side of the stout beast. With all his force, he flung his spear, lodging it behind a foreleg. He dived back as the shrieking creature turned frantically in a circle; he swiftly picked up his bow, fitted an arrow and shot into the great neck. As the boar twisted, the spear caught in some brambles, held fast, and, turning, the beast impaled itself even deeper. Its cries ceased, it twitched and lay dead.

Randulf ran over to the horses and gentled them into stillness. Then he came over to his friend. "For a goldsmith, you make a good hunter," he said, clapping him on the back.

"The gods were smiling," said Ricberht, breathing heavily. "Hey! At least we can carry some meat home, if we get going! We should get there this evening, surely." He thought how delighted Maura would be to see how much food they had brought, not to mention seeing him again. He could wait no longer, he felt. They stirred up the fire, and in the growing light, they ate even more bread and cheese, drank water, and got out their knives to cut off some meat. Randulf found it difficult. His left hand was clumsy against the thick, hairy hide of the boar, and his right could not get a firm grip on the heavy leg.

"I'll see to this. You get the bedrolls wrapped in those hides," suggested Ricberht. One hide made a roughly-tied sack, holding haunches of meat, though they had to leave the head. Ricberht stuck it on a willow stump, to honour the gods of the place. As the sun rose, they were off, moving upstream a little until they found a place to cross the river. It could not have been as much as three hours later, when Randulf gave a cry.

"This is Debenham!" he shouted. "See? Those are the rushy hollows where the river rises! The homestead is round the next corner, I think!" It was true. They gladly accepted some ham and beer from the basket- maker, but did not wish to linger. Helmingham was only a few miles away, and from there they might glean news of home.

By midday, they were sitting in the hall of the Helmings. Randulf was better-known here than Ricberht, but many of the warriors here had seen his work, and they were again given cups of mead and slices from a roasting ox in return for a hasty recounting of their journey north.

No, there was no news of Eorpwald. On the whole, the men of Helmingham thought that was good news in itself. They knew what a quarrelsome fellow he could be.

"Your womenfolk will be glad to see you," they teased the two travellers. Ricberht saw his friend's face fall, and covered for him hastily. This home-coming was not going to be as easy for Randulf as it would be for him and his lovely Maura.

"We must be off," he urged. "This meat will lose its freshness."

"So will you!" they hollered. One of them blew his horn as they departed. The horses trotted off into the trees. In the late afternoon of the first day of the Harvest month, they rode over Wuffa's ford and up the track to their village.

NIARTHA

I shall never forget the joy on Ricberht's face when he rode up to my house after all those weeks away. Maura was sitting on the bench when she heard him, and stood up ready to dive indoors, until she saw who it was. Her shout brought me to her, and then Fritha raced out, so that I seized her before she darted under the horse's hooves.

Ricberht practically fell from the saddle, and caught Maura up in his arms, twirling her round and around, while he kissed her till they both drew breath. Then it was Fritha's turn, as he exclaimed at how big she had grown, and how she was a big girl, not his baby any more.

"I *are* your baby!" she insisted, squeezing his cheeks and kissing his nose. He hugged them both tightly, then turned to me and came into my embrace so that I, too, could hug him in relief.

He made Gilda take the bundle of meat to be cooked at the bakehouse, with enough left over for the smokehouse and the salting. We would be sharing it with our friends in the village, of course.

We spent hours questioning him. I was delighted to hear how our old friends in the north had welcomed him, and how they had given Randulf the time to grieve and the solace he needed. We exclaimed in wonder at what he told us of Edwin and his hall. We asked why it had taken so long for him to come home, when the Messenger had gone back north so many weeks before. He told us about Paulinus, about the way Edwin was ridding his people of lawless men, escorting folk from place to place, until all could travel freely. We ate roast meat, with herbs and vegetables and the sweet pulp of early apples from the tree in my garden. I broke out a flask of wine, from the little store I had been given by Raedwald.

Gilda put the sleeping child into her cot, and we sat in the twilight for a while. Ricberht told how he had left Randulf at his brother's house, and that this seemed likely to be a permanent arrangement, by mutual consent. I am pleased. Randulf will be kept busy with work he can do, and need not return to the empty house, no longer ringing with Ulla's voice, laughing or chiding.

My son and his wife must now have time of their own. Tonight they will stay here, so I beckon to Gilda and go inside to my bed. Fritha is sleeping with Gilda tonight.

When she has seemed to wish it, I have talked several times with Maura, since I took the creature from her. We agree that Ricberht must not be put into danger, by any act of retaliation against the king. She does not want to tell Ricberht what happened with Eorpwald, but is afraid one of the thanes may speak of it. She was not sure who the men were, who had pinned her down. I think that, if they had wished to brag of it, they would surely have done so by now, and this is what I have said to her. None of Eorpwald's cronies has given a sign, when I have encountered any of them, and nor has Eorpwald.

True, I have kept out of his way, but still go to the village, as normal. Maura has kept away, even from Idunna, though we have made a point of inviting her to come here very often. It is a good place for children to play here, at the edge of the forest, and I do not think she has found Maura's absence puzzling.

Tonight, Ricberht will want to take Maura, as a man should, who desires his woman. I hope she can give herself to him as openly and willingly as she ever has. The thought of Raedwald's love fills my mind, and I roll restlessly, till my limbs relax.

29

When Ricberht turned to his wife to love her as he had yearned to do for so long, she pressed close to him, kissing his chest so that her hair tumbled over them both and he could not see her face. She caressed him so that he could hardly contain himself, and he rolled her onto her back, stroking the softness of her inner thighs, then entered the moist warmth of her body, sating his urgent need, and lay gasping, sprawled heavily over her. He moved to ease her, and found she was crying.

" What is it, my love? Did I hurt you? Forgive me." He kissed her lips and smoothed her forehead.

"No," she whispered. "It is not that. I am foolish. I - it has been so long, and I have needed you so much!" She did not mean her sexual need, but that was, naturally how he took her words.

"Now you have me, and I shall be here whenever you need me again," he laughed quietly. "There, now, hug me, and I will be here when you wake. I shall not let you go till I have made you content." She lay, pillowed within his arms, and let the grief slide away as she felt the warmth of his love. Perhaps all would be well. Perhaps this love would get another child.

The rooster sounded his dawn cry, and this time Maura roused her husband, kissing his body, and being kissed, until they lay, pulsing together, breathing happily.

"I shall take you home to our house before tonight," Ricberht told her. "Arnulf said you have been here for weeks. Why, was not all well with you? Or was it Fritha, or my mother?"

"I felt lonely. I know Idunna was there, but she has her mother and all the family. Niartha wanted us to come, and I was glad."

"But there was nothing amiss?" he urged.

"No. It is quiet here, and Fritha can play, and there is Gilda and Brand to keep her amused."

"Brand? Is he staying here again? Were you scared?"

"No, no!" she cried, " he is here sometimes, but then he has had to help in the forge. The king..." she nearly faltered. "The king wants a new sword. It is good you have come home. He says it is a test of the smiths' skill. If he does not approve, they will have to leave."

"So that is what Arnulf meant last night. He said he could do with some advice, but it would wait a day or two." He swung his legs over the wooden side of the bed, leant back to kiss her one more time, pulled on a tunic and went to find water and the sharp knife he used to shave himself with. If Eorpwald wanted a new sword, then it would be the best sword they could make. They would not waste another day.

Over breakfast, to Fritha's fury, he told Niartha that he would go to the forge to see that Arnulf had all the help he needed, and he would set up his workshop, ready to decorate the hilt and the scabbard.

"I shall come back to fetch you tonight," he told his daughter, who was red-faced with anger and pounding any bit of his body she could reach. "Ouch! Mind where you are hitting a man," he gasped and held her from him. Gilda took her away, protesting that she wanted her father: he had to stay!

"Come and see the new chicks," said Gilda.

"I really think you will have to take some home to keep," said Niartha. "That way she will accept the change. You can have the next kid, too, if it's a nanny."

Ricberht left them planning how he would make pens for the creatures. As if this sword was not going to take up weeks of work! Perhaps one of Idunna's brothers would fence in a paddock beside the house in return for a new *seax*. He must remember to ask.

"Be packed up before dark!" he told them. "I'll borrow Arnulf's cart." He went to untie his horse, and they waved from the door as he rode off on Blot. Everyone had had a good laugh at the name, and the ugly, gentle horse.

"Was everything all right?" asked Niartha gently. She put an arm round Maura's shoulders, looking into her face.

"Yes," came the quiet reply. "I told him I had needed him, and we loved each other." Tears threatened to well up, so Niartha squeezed her briskly.

"Clever girl, " she said. "Well done. Now let's make sure we keep him safe. Come with me now – we have washing to do and

173

packing up, too. I will find a covered basket for the chicks later on. I am sure Borgil will have a box you can keep them in until they grow. Tell Fritha she can take five chicks home. That will stop her bawling!" The day passed swiftly for Ricberht's womenfolk.

At the forge, too, there was much discussion. Borgil had formed the wooden handgrip, ready to be plated with gold and held to the tang of the sword. What was needed was the shape of the bronze form for the pommel, and the metal guards on the hilt – and these had to be plated and ornamented. Randulf managed to scrawl charcoal sketches, left-handed, on a piece of pale calfskin but, when he grew frustrated at the inelegant shapes he had produced, he gestured to Ricberht to make a finer curve here, or a smaller projection there. At length he said it was right, and Beorn set to work on the bronze, while Arnulf consulted Randulf about the complex twisting of the rods to form the central core of the blade. What he had done so far was not entirely wasted. Straight iron rods were interspersed with the twists, to form a pattern when hammered, and later the outer rods would be forged, to form the cutting edge of the blade. The measurements, the cutting and welding needed the combined efforts of both Brand and Arnulf and would occupy many days. The sword must be held straight as it cooled between each welding. Last would come the final shaping, polishing and the honing to the finest degree of sharpness.

"Let us hope Eorpwald holds his patience," said Randulf. "We have to let the hall steward know we are back in the village. The king must be told."

Next day, Eorpwald came, just before noon, accompanied by three young thanes. He saw Randulf working the bellows for his brother, while Beorn poured molten bronze into the mould he had carved yesterday. Arnulf and Brand were twisting a bundle of rods, one end gripped in a vice fixed to the workbench, the other in a grip, held and turned by the force of their own fists. They could not stop, or the metal would cool, so went on working, unable to bend the knee to the king, or put a hand to the brow in acknowledgement.

"Lord king," grunted Arnulf "as you see, we are working on your sword."

"As I would expect," said the king, unsmiling. "With so many of you now at work, I shall hope to see it done in time for the Harvest feast. That gives you twenty days. On the night of the full moon, I must be holding this sword. I am the king who will feed his folk. Be ready." At least one man was thinking that the feeding was done by the field-workers, the farmers around the village, the cattlemen, the fishermen, the girls who were now merrily picking apples. But, of course, most of it went into the granary and storage barns. It was the king who distributed it. This man had yet to prove himself able to do this fairly, and to reward those who had done him service in their work.

Eorpwald had been looking around, and demanded to know where Ricberht was.

"He is in his workshop, lord," said Randulf. "Shall I fetch him?"

"No. I shall go to see him working." The king turned and left. The smiths drew breaths of deep relief but Randulf left the bellows on their plate and went to the door. He could see the king arriving at the door of Ricberht's smithy.

The goldsmith was laying out his tools on the bench. One lot of gold was in the little furnace, and would soon be ready to pour. Last night he had sat, after supper, carving the shallow, curving mould for the sideplates of the hand-grip. He had already, in his store, sheets of gold for plating the upper and lower guards of hilts, and filigree clips to apply to them, once they were fixed to the wooden grip. This, itself, had to be bound with tape and gold wire. Borgil had brought the shaped wood to him, first thing. He would have to work on the panels for the pommel when Beorn had shaped the bronze. He was planning out the work of several days, when Eorpwald interrupted him.

Perhaps Eorpwald had hoped to catch him out. He certainly seemed surprised to see pieces of gold laid out on the bench, tools in order, and the furnace hot.

"Already hard at work, then," he commented, noncommittally.

Ricberht could not gauge the king's mood. He bowed and picked up the mould.

"Would you like to see one of the forms for the hilt, lord?" he asked. "It will be ready to pour in a few moments. Not too near," he warned as Eorpwald came and leant on the bench. "There will be sparks flying. Your cloak..." he gestured. In any case, he needed to be standing just where Eorpwald had planted himself. "Forgive me. I have to see if the flame is right." He stepped forward a little, so the king gave way. Ricberht peered into the mouth of the kiln, took a long-handled pair of tongs, withdrew the gold in its small ladle, and turned his wrist to pour it into the mould. His skill had ensured that there was very little wastage, but he let the last drops fall into the dish he kept for residue, so that it could be used again. Sure enough, a few sparks flared, but Ricberht ignored even those that touched his hand.

"This must cool," he told the king, "but if you wish to wait, lord, I can show you the shaping. Would you like me to fetch a drink for you and your men? My wife will have some mead ready." He made as if to guide them, but Eorpwald stopped him.

"We know how hospitable your wife is," he said. If his followers smiled, Ricberht did not see. "On this occasion, we will waste no more time. The work is to be done at full moon. As I told your fellows, you have twenty days." He left.

Ricberht meant, but forgot, to ask Maura when she had given the king hospitality. He busied himself with his work, glad to see Randulf, when he came to help. Twenty days should give them time, if they made no mistakes and had no accidents.

Two days later, at the elders' moot, called to organise the bringing-in of the crops and settle the numbers for the feast, one of them, a man called Bedwyn, was primed by Aelfric to say how splendid he thought the king's new sword would be. All agreed that it was good to have them all back. No-one mentioned Randulf's name at all. Bedwyn also commented that it would be useful to have extra farm tools, new scythes and so on, ready for the spring planting. True, for this harvest, these men could not be called to work, if they were to get the splendid sword ready for the feast, but a boy could lead the horse, when they borrowed Arnulf's cart. And then there was Cerdic's wagon… If Eorpwald had had plans to dismiss any or all of the smiths, he kept quiet. Now he would know how much support there was for them, Aelfric thought, and squeezed Bedwyn's arm in thanks, as he smiled inwardly.

Two days before the Harvest Supper, the smiths, Borgil and all the women met, shortly before the workers came in from the fields. They came to Niartha's house, where she had laid out trestles, just as they had on the bonefire night, to feed her guests.

First, they gathered round while Arnulf removed from its sacking the sword, in a wooden scabbard, ornately-carved and impressed with gold. Idunna's mother had made the braid for the ties, which Arnulf now undid. He slid the sword from the sheath, and laid it on the sacking, where it shone, against the shoddy background. The welding had produced patterning as fine as they had seen. Though Randulf detected a certain wavering from the true line, he knew no other eye could see it. He clasped his brother and told him it was fine work.

Ricberht knew that, like the plainer scabbard, this hilt was not as splendid as the one he had given Beorhtfyr, but it had gold, garnets, wirework and filigree. He was proud of it, even if he disliked the king for whom it was made. Surely the king must approve it! They would take it to the hall in the morning to show him. Tonight was theirs to mark the finishing of the task.

Niartha, Maura, Idunna and Gilda carried out trays of food and goblets of drinks. They had survived the first six months of the reign of King Eorpwald. The men were too tired to get rip-roaring drunk. There was the feast to come, and they felt sure the king could find no grounds to dismiss any of them. Then they would show the village how smiths celebrated.

BEORHTFYR

The sword waited once, lying in darkness, newly-wrought, until the hand that made it should set it free.

Then, mastered by the might of the ruler's hand, it waited inside the scabbard's blackness until the sunlight seared the blade. Flung to the fight, its flames flashed, quenched again as its glow faded in the gloom of night.

Now the fire is doused, dark in the pit, deprived of daylight. Courage lies cold. Where is the warrior? Going to his gods.

The sword is watching, dim in the darkness. It may wait a thousand winters. Will the wise hand of the god waken it to work again?

Still in the silence, becalmed as the boat that bears it, living beyond the life of its lord, Beorhtfyr bides its time. The air in the chamber chills.

30

If it were not for Aelfric's intervention, Eorpwald might have found fault with the new sword, at this last minute, to dishonour the smiths and even find a way to outcast whichever man could be said to have produced faulty work.

They brought the sword for approval, when the king came to the hall for his noontide meal. Aelfric saw to it that he was accompanied by a few elders, as the younger men were supervising the bringing-in of the last of the harvest. After Arnulf had unwrapped the work, Ricberht loosened the scabbard and handed the whole lot to the king. The elders applauded at the sight of the bright scabbard and gleaming hilt.

Eorpwald rubbed his thumb over the gilded wood, but none flaked off. He drew off the sheath and laid it on the table before him, and raised up the point of the sword. He tested the hilt a few times, again rubbed his thumb over the grip, but found no uncomfortable roughness. Too smooth, and the sword might swivel in the fist. He stood clear and hefted the blade. All could see from the swing of the weapon that it was the right length and weight and, again, the onlookers cried out to congratulate the smiths.

"May I be sure that this blade will not shatter?" Eorpwald asked.

"As sure as any man may be, lord," said Randulf. "The metal was well-forged, well-worked. It should serve you well." If you ever fight another battle, he thought, masking his feelings.

To everyone's shocked amazement, Eorpwald brought up the sword and brought its edge down onto the table before him. Everyone gasped aloud. The blade cut deep into the soft board, but did not shatter. He extricated it and inspected the edge. It was unchipped.

"I will need to re-hone that edge, king," said Arnulf, levelly. "Just to make sure it is as good as when you took it." His voice was level, uncharged with the contempt he felt for a man who could treat such a fine weapon with such brutality.

"Do that," said Eorpwald, and laid the sword down. "Bring it to the feast tomorrow. I shall expect to see you all there. And your women," he added. He carefully looked at Ricberht. "That includes your mother."

This should have been a gracious invitation, but sounded more like a threat.

However, next evening, they found themselves seated in a position of honour. Eorpwald wished to impress his people with his generosity tonight. It was the first major feast since his throning, for they had felt no inclination to do much at Midsummer, so soon after the death of their great king. Now he must assert himself, as feeder of his people and protector of the needy. He ordered the presentation of the sword to precede the opening of the feast, so that it could hang on the wall behind him, just as Beorhtfyr used to do, catching the torchlight.

The people assembled, when the horn sounded at the door of the hall. Once they were in place, it called again, for silence. Aelfric gave the signal and the three chief smiths stood before the dais, Beorn and Borgil behind them.

Arnulf said nothing, but all three bent the knee, and then he laid the sheathed weapon in the hand of the king. They prayed inwardly to Woden to give him the wisdom not to play any stupid tricks as he had done the morning before.

The revellers clapped their hands and stamped their feet at the sight of the golden scabbard, and Ricberht's heart lifted. When the king released the blade and lifted it, they cheered loudly. The smiths had done well, they felt. Eorpwald thought the cheers were for him. He smiled graciously, handed the sword to Aelfric to be hung on the wall, scabbard gleaming separately below it, and gave the sign for all to be seated. He did not say a word. Aelfric bent to whisper in his ear and the king waved an impatient hand.

The horns were filled, the food brought in and the people gorged themselves. Well over an hour later, the *scop* came to the dais and lifted his harp, and Aelfric thumped on the wooden floor with his staff. Gradually the hall fell silent.

"We shall sing songs to praise Freya for this good harvest," said the king. "But first, I wish to thank those who have served me well." He proceeded to give armbands to the farmers, fishers and shipmen, and horses to three of his thanes. Niartha saw Maura put a hand to her eyes, and knew now the men who had assisted at the rape. Aelfric was given a fine goblet of blue glass, which he promptly filled with wine and drank a *waes hael* to the king. Then the king beckoned the smiths to approach. "These men," he said, loudly, "have made a very handsome sword. When I next fight, it will earn itself a name. Until then, until it proves itself, I shall reward each of them with the title of King's Smith. Take this for your pains." He gave Arnulf a leather pouch, apparently well-stuffed with whatever lay within.

The people applauded wildly again. The smiths bowed and retreated to their table. The bag was of soft hide, its lining the hair of the badger it was made from. The big man tipped out the gold tremisses. Thirty small coins lay on the table before him. Six each. No-one said a word as he tipped them back and tied the bag to his belt. Under cover of raucous singing, they spoke warily.

"He has given us what was already ours," growled Arnulf, "except for Beorn. I am pleased for you, boy." They all nodded in agreement.

"I feel like giving him back the gold," said Ricberht. Again they nodded. It was an insulting amount, shared between them. But they would not risk making such a gesture. Nor would they give the king the satisfaction of seeing how disgusted they were. The women withdrew, when things became unusually rowdy, even for a harvest feast. The smiths drank mightily, all the more when the king left the hall, accompanied by two of the dancing girls. They were carried home by hall-slaves that night and left at their cold hearths for their women to deal with, if they had any. Luckily, Idunna and Maura knew what to expect.

That night Aelfric was stricken suddenly and died just before dawn. He was buried next day in the warriors' burial ground, near Diuma's grave.

Eorpwald appointed one of his cronies, Plegmund, to be the new hall steward. That young man went to Aelfric's house, found his daughter, Guthrun, and demanded the keys and horn, hitherto held by her father. When he ordered her to give him her father's staff, it was too much. She declared it had been buried with her father. Anyway, she did not have it. He could look behind the door, if he wished. That is where it was kept. He did look. He also looked at her.

Perhaps he could do the king a great service, he realized. When he returned to the hall, he requested a private word with the king. As darkness stifled the village, three thanes, one of whom was Plegmund, beat on the girl's door, commanding her to open it in the king's name.

They seized Guthrun and bore her to the hall, where Eorpwald told her she was to be his wife. She fainted. When she came to, she was in his bed, with a guard at the door. At midnight the king came to her. Drunkenly, observed by his men, he tied her wrist to his and bellowed that they were handfast, as all could see. Then he dropped the curtain of hide in their faces and fell on her, as he had longed to do for so long.

Next day he got Plegmund to sound his horn, calling all the folk to the hall. He told them there was to be another feast that night, to celebrate his wedding to Aelfric's daughter. The boar-headed priest was called on, once again, and came in haste. The people were stunned. Apart from what they could perceive to be little more than rape, their precious supplies were about to be depleted.

The poor girl looked at them from eyes bruised with weeping. No-one could help her. She had no other kin. For a moment she caught Maura's gaze and they exchanged a look as intense as it was brief. Not brief enough, however, for Eorpwald to miss it.

After another, subdued feast, the villagers were dismissed, and Guthrun was left to her fate. As a child, a girl would often dream of becoming a queen, so beautiful, so powerful, so much respected by her noble husband. Guthrun's beauty was stained by grief, horror and degradation: she was entirely powerless, it seemed; her husband had respect for no man and certainly for no woman. She wanted to die.

Her wish would be granted.

NIARTHA

We live our lives; we keep our silence when we must; we work, all of us, and hope to escape the notice of our king. Arnulf, Beorn and Ricberht have twice ridden to the western marches of this province, when Eorpwald has been commanded by King Edwin to strengthen the defences and the smiths go to support the warriors with their work. They, too, have fought, on more than one occasion, but have returned safely, Tiw be thanked, with only the odd cut or bruise to show.

At Midsummer, when Eorpwald had been king for about a year, Maura had her second child, another girl. Again, she and Ricberht seemed content. They were going to call her after me, but when they asked, another name came to me, one from nearer the home of Maura's own people. This child had the same thick, dark hair as Maura, and the same vivid blue eyes. I remembered the kindness shown to me once, on my travels with my own child.

"Call her Morwyn," I suggested. I was glad when they agreed; privately, I wished my name to come to the king's attention as little as possible. I saw him in the hall when it was necessary for me to attend a feast, and watched from the shadow of my doorway when he rode out hunting, or towards the coast. Otherwise, I kept away. Maura did the same. But the next day, I was summoned, urgently.

That day, the queen died, giving birth to a still-born son. I was called to assist Idunna's mother, as midwife, with Eorpwald's consent. I had to tell him that he had lost a son. He glared at me so ferociously that I thought he would kill me there and then. I was ready to flee, to take horse and ride – who knew where? Surely, he would seek vengeance. But he turned his back.

Guthrun was not awarded a burial in the royal mounds site. We laid her to rest beside her father, with her baby on her breast. Eorpwald did not attend; he sat drinking in the hall.

When winter came, it was a harsh one. Snow fell in the

Blood Month, so we all made one gigantic fire of wood and bone, on the foreshore of the river below the village, and it was difficult work, cutting the meat and smoking it. Salting left people with sore, chapped and bleeding fingers. My salves were much in demand. It was hard to get the logs lit for Yule, so wet and cold were they, but we celebrated that and, indeed Mothers' Night before it. I remember one disturbing moment when I noticed Eorpwald's eyes on Maura, where she sat, holding Morwyn on her knee, Fritha playing with her baby sister's fingers. Perhaps he had not realised she had another child.

After Yule, the snow fell again, and kept on falling for many days. The roads were impassable, so deep were the drifts, so we had to use our stores, unable to reach the markets. Men made holes in the ice and tried to catch fish, usually without much success. Then the people began to fall sick. In the end, I came to stay at Ricberht's house, where he had built an extra room for just such need. I brought with me as many of my stores of herbal remedies as we could all carry, struggling through the snow so that we arrived with freezing wet clothes and boots. Ricberht carried the boots the few yards to his smithy, and left them where the heat of the kilns would dry them out. Soon, lack of work would leave the kilns cold.

The fever swept through the village, striking folk of all ages. Where a man was needed to fetch firewood, his neighbours helped. When a woman was too ill to rise from her bed, her friends or family would bring in a pot of hot stew, or take a child to be cared for, or even nursed at a breast.

The men went to the yard outside the church and dug a large pit, as deep as they could manage. The dead were laid in it, wrapped in waxed cloth, until we could hold a ceremony for them. They filled it with snow and loose earth, but knew they would have to open it again. There was no chance of a burial up on the hoo or anywhere else until the earth thawed.

Next, three infants died. One woman, ill aready, began to deliver twins, early by three months. It was a nightmare. Neither child was strong enough to feed, even from a willing nurse, and the mother died, bleeding and sobbing, to the sound of their feeble cries. Both babies died inside the day. Then Ricberht came to fetch me, white-faced, to say that Morwyn was ill, and he was worried about Maura. I fled back to the house.

Brand took Fritha home with him on one of the horses. Gilda lived with him now, and she would care well for the child, I knew. Now I turned to the two flushed faces before me. All night I sat up, administering drinks of honey with a fiery spirit Raedwald had brought back from a northern hall a few years before. It made the eyes water, but seemed to relieve Maura's cough. She drank willow-bark water to stop her body from aching, with liquid of sweet marjoram and masterwort. The dried leaves of these plants I soaked in warm water, and laid them on her chest, binding them to her. I did the same for the baby. Eventually the willow drink seemed to take effect, and at last Maura slept.

It is hard to get a child to swallow what is distasteful, so Ricberht helped to hold Morwyn firmly, and I poured tiny scoops of liquid down her throat when she mewled in protest. I used sweet marjoram with the honey, thinking the spirit might be too strong for her. Maura had been too ill to feed her child, so I gave Morwyn sips of goat's milk as often as I could. By midnight, the little one was too weak to swallow. She lay limply on the pillow I held on my knee. Her face was pale and her breathing was harsh. I gently rubbed a liniment of watermint and comfrey onto her tiny chest and back, hoping to revive her. Again I tried to drop honey and willow-bark, this time with added drops of a distillation from the corn-flower, onto the back of her throat, anything to try to help her cough and clear her chest.

All this time, Ricberht stayed beside us. He tended the fire, brought warm soup for us to sip, fetched water to cool the head of his sleeping wife. Anxiously he whispered to me, as he watched the child grow weaker, until, at last, I knew there was nothing more I could do. He held the little one, cradling her and weeping, until she drew her last breath. I took the little body and wrapped it in the cloak Maura had made for her. Then I laid her in her cradle and sat beside my son, stroking his bowed head and sharing his grief.

At daybreak, Maura awoke, and I managed to make sure that she was much better, fever reduced, sore throat eased and her limbs not aching as they had for the past two days, before she asked for her child. I had to tell her, and Ricberht pleaded with her to believe that I had tried everything. I had to get him to give her another sedative drink, and eventually she fell into a calmer state, but lay weeping.

I had to persuade them that it was best to leave Fritha with Gilda and Brand until Maura was stronger. Ricberht went to get Beorn to help him bury the poor baby. He came back to his wife, blue with cold, and I left them together.

Indeed I was needed in other houses, even though I was

tired out from sleeplessness and sorrow. I feared we might lose more, but in the end only another man and two women died. This was a great deal for our little village to bear, and we would have to find a way to support those left needy.

In this, you would expect the king to take the lead. We have Eorpwald for our king. For many days he has never left the hall. He sits and drinks with his companions, calling for food, more logs, even for dancing girls, while his people lie sick and dying around him and we cannot yet bury them.

PAULINUS

Too many years ago, in Raedwald's kingdom, I extracted a vow from Edwin, before he knew who I was, that he would heed the advice of anyone who saved him from his predicament and give him the throne he sought. Then I laid my right hand on his head, telling him to remember this sign, when next it was made, and then to keep his promise and I left him, sitting in darkness.

I have come to the king again, just now, and laid my right hand upon his head, asking Edwin if he remembered this sign. I thought he would faint with fear and shock, but I raised him and spoke to him as mildly as I could. I reminded him that God has given him his kingdom, saving him from his enemies. Now he must keep his word and accept the Christian faith. God will reward faithful service with an everlasting crown in heaven.

At last the king has agreed to become a Christian: it is what he wants, and what he should rightly do, to keep his vow. First he wishes to consult his companions and the elders of his people, in the hope that they will also be baptised. He is having a church built, here in Eofric, dedicated to Peter the Apostle, as I know the Holy Father wishes, and will be baptised there. I hope to persuade him to build a finer building in due course. Now I will seek to save his soul.

Praise ye the Lord. I will praise the Lord with my whole heart, in the assembly of the upright, and in the congregation.

The works of the Lord are great, sought out by all them that have pleasure therein.

His work is honourable and glorious: and his righteousness endureth forever.

He hath made his wonderful works to be remembered: the Lord is gracious and full of compassion.

He hath given meat unto them that fear him: he will ever be mindful of his covenant.

He hath showed his people the power of his works, that he may give them the heritage of the heathen.

The works of his hands are verity and judgement; all his commandments are sure.

They stand fast for ever and ever, and are done in truth and uprightness. He sent redemption unto his people: he hath commanded his covenant for ever: holy and reverend is his name.

The fear of the Lord is the beginning of wisdom: a good understanding have all they that do his commandments: his praise endureth for ever.

Amen

EORPWALD

In a break in the weather, towards the end of the month of Hretha, a King's Messenger arrived from King Edwin, insisting that Eorpwald should attend the High King at Eofric, immediately. He was the same Messenger who had carried Ricberht's token to them and readily talked to him that evening.

They heard how the children of Edwin and his queen, Aethelberga, had been baptised shortly after the last Eostre, or Easter-tide, AD DCXXVI, as the Christians called it now. She had given birth to a daughter on Easter Day itself, and by some miracle, Edwin had survived an assassination attempt that same day. The king was now being hard-pressed by Paulinus to foreswear the old gods and their traditions, but remained undecided, the man said. Paulinus had been very busy baptising men, women and children, even tiny babies in the rivers at Yefrin and at Eofric; but until the High King was baptised himself, the monk would not be satisfied. The lands were certainly more peaceful now, and escorts were not needed, even for the roads winding through the high hills. Edwin was a good king, but many people said he was a ditherer, and they would feel more settled, if he made up his mind about the new religion, one way or another. Perhaps they did not now need a warlike god.

When they asked him if he knew why Edwin had called Eorpwald, the Messenger shook his head. Even if he knew, he was bound by silence in the service of his king. Ricberht and his friends could hardly believe the High King would need advice from such a man as Eorpwald. They actually said so, hoping the Messenger might tell Edwin what was going on in this distant part of his wide realm. As Bretwalda, he might have power to put things right.

The next day, Eorpwald left, taking many thanes with him, but not one smith. It was left to the villagers to bury their dead when the ground softened. They found ways to comfort the bereaved and provide for the needy.

Eorpwald learned that he was not the only one to be

summoned. Onna came to Eofric, as did many of the princes under Edwin's sway. The king welcomed them, housed them and fed them, while all were gathering. He assembled them in a great hall not far from the old town and told them he was about to be baptised, on 12th April (as he called it, a term strange to those who still called it Eostre) DCXXVII. They would observe this sacrament and, a few days later, they would be baptised themselves, led by his queen.

He cited Eadbald (baptised as Aethelbert) of Kent – Eorpwald barely concealed a sneer – and mentioned other kings of various lands in Britain and Europe who were reaping the benefits of a close association with the church: its learning and its riches. Then he invited Paulinus, now a bishop, to preach to them of the spiritual beneftits, not least of which was eternal life in bliss.

They sat for two hours, listening to the bishop. At the evening meal, Edwin invited comments and listened while this one or that asked the same old questions: what could Christ offer them that Woden could not? Where was the strength? Did the Christians ever fight? We have our own life after death, in Valhalla.

Onna and one or two others mentioned the everlasting damnation they would face, if they rejected this three-fold god. Talk of the fiery pit of the Christians' version of Hell was daunting. If the Christians are right, then we are guilty of idolatry and witchcraft, they urged. Edwin referred to the new skills the monks brought, with written words, spreading peaceful messages. This was the kind of life he was giving his people. Then he made his pronouncement. All his provinces would accept this Christian religion, will ye, nill ye.

Duly baptised, the kings returned to their people. On his return, Eorpwald called the elders to a moot and informed them of the edict of the High King, and of his own baptism. Edwin's own Chief Priest of Woden had seen the light, he told them, and had ridden off forthwith to destroy his own shrine and the idols within it. Their own church would stand, but Woden's altar was to be removed and burnt. Immediately. Onna was going to send a Christian priest to them.

That night, Eorpwald lay, tossing restlessly on his lonely bed, reminded angrily of the death of his wife, and of the son she should have born. Suddenly he sat up in the darkness. It was that woman's fault! That Niartha – the one who had killed his mother. She must have seen to it that his son did not take breath. He would seize her tomorrow and charge her with their deaths. Then, as he lay down again, he had another idea.

Words he had heard in Edwin's hall-moot came into his mind. *'We are guilty of witchcraft.'*

Niartha was a witch. He could prove it. If he showed Edwin how he was ridding this province of evil practices, the High King would surely reward him. His own father, King Raedwald, had been baptised, and it had meant little to him. Eorpwald's vows at baptism had kept him his kingdom. He would hesitate at nothing, if it kept him in favour with the High King.

31

At dawn, a troop of men rode to Niartha's house at the oak, only to find it empty. They broke the door down to discover this, and left the place in disarray. Brand and Gilda heard the commotion, and he made the girl take Fritha, who was visiting them as she often did, and run into the forest to hide. Fritha thought this was great fun, running in her nightrobe, and Gilda took her deep into the trees, and kept her busy gathering fir-cones in a glade.

Brand put his sword beside the door and was looking out when the troop approached.

"Where is the witch?" Plegmund demanded. Brand simply gazed at him though his blood ran cold.

"I know nothing of any witch," he replied as calmly as he could. Two men dismounted and came toward him, swords drawn. Brand stepped back and took up his own weapon. "What is all this?" he shouted angrily. "There are no witches here. You may search if you wish, but this is my house! I will tell the king, if you..." Raucous laughter. "The king has sent us, man! He wants the witch. Niartha! Now tell us where she is." Brand thought, frantically.

"I do not know. She was here yesterday, until the king came home. Then she went to the village. Perhaps someone is ill. She may have been called to one of the farms. Yes! That's it! The ferryman, up under the hoo! His back is bad. She's been taking salves for his wife to rub him with. Wish it was me!" He leered, getting the sort of response he would expect. "Anyway, try there!" Brand prayed to all the gods there were that they would believe him. After a brief consultation, the leader jerked his head, and the two men left Brand at his door, swung up onto their horses, and they all rode on towards the hoo, away from the village.

Brand watched them disappear round the curve of the track, and ran as fast as he could towards Ricberht's house. When Gilda returned after waiting a whole hour, Fritha was demanding food, and the cottage was empty, the door swinging open. Something must be seriously wrong, she thought. Should she stay here, or go to the village? In the end, she stayed where Brand would find her, believing that Fritha was safer with her than in the village, if there were trouble. Hearing the voices and hoofbeats of the returning troop, she lifted the child and ran again into the forest before the angry men came galloping up the track.

They did not pause, only yelled something about 'lies' and 'back', so even little Fritha could tell something was wrong. She began to whimper, and Gilda muffled her cries in her lap, hugging the child to her, ready to cry, herself. Whatever was going on?

Brand, meanwhile, had beaten on Ricberht's door, afraid to shout too loud, in case they were observed from the village, further down the slope. Ricberht held his sword, as he opened the door, and pulled Brand hastily inside. His shout of furious alarm, when he heard what was said, brought Maura and Niartha from their beds, cloaks pulled hastily over thin nightrobes. Maura screamed in fear, and her husband hushed her. Niartha had sunk down onto a stool and stared up at the two men, white-faced.

"It is Eorpwald," she murmured. "I always knew he hated me, though only Woden could tell why. He will not let go now, until he has destroyed me." She stood up and faced her son. "You must get away from here. Now! Take Maura, fetch Fritha and leave. Go to Onna. He will protect you. Just go!" She was physically pushing Ricberht. He held her firmly and made her look into his eyes.

"If I go, you will come with us! Get ready, now, both of you." Niartha shook her head, angrily.

"If you are found with me, he will kill you, too." Strange, how they all knew that *that* was Eorpwald's threat. "You go now, and keep your family safe! Now!" She was beating at him with her fists, so that Brand came and took her into his arms. She was sobbing with rage.

The two men looked at each other. Brand said, "She is right. Niartha is right. You must go, but not towards the hoo." He told them how he had sent Eorpwald's men on a fool's errand. "We have half an hour, at the most. We have to find Fritha." Again, he told them briefly how she was safe with Gilda. "Take three horses. Go through the forest and over the heath. Go to Onna. He will hide you. He may be able to save Niartha. But go!"

Ricberht and Maura scrambled into some clothes, Niartha rolling bundles together, and filling a basket with bread, cheese, two flagons of ale and a sealed jar of milk for Fritha. As usual, she pushed in a firestone. Brand tied the packs to one of the horses he brought from behind the smithies. Ricberht ran to his smithy to grab his secret hoard. His hand fell on the rock crystal that Raedwald had given him so long ago, and he thrust it into the sack with the pieces of gold and silver he had squirrelled away, just as Diuma had done. There was no time even to cast an eye of regret as he left his beloved workshop.

Maura and Ricberht clung to Niartha, unable to find words in their fear and despair, until she kissed them one last time and forced them to let her go.

"Ride round the long way," Brand urged them. "If you hear the horsemen, then go deep into the forest. I will run home to find Fritha and Gilda. Niartha, go to Arnulf's. Just go!" He let her grab her dress and skirts, and pushed her towards the blacksmith's house, as Ricberht, leading the laden horse, guided Maura through the trees. She was not used to riding, and he hoped she would manage to hold Fritha in front of her. Brand rushed off towards his own cottage.

When he heard hooves, he dived for cover in some bracken at the side of the trackway. After they passed, he raised his head. Thank the gods they did not have Gilda with them. Then his heart pounded with fear at the thought that they might have caught her at home. He ran on.

He smelled the smoke, before he saw the flame. Furious at being sent on a fool's errand, Eorpwald's men had set fire to both houses, Niartha's and his own. He stood at the palisade and bellowed in wrath, fear and grief. When he took breath, he heard Gilda calling from the trees, and yelled at her that he was here. She tore over the grass to fling herself into his arms, and Fritha scampered after her. Both were shrieking in terror of the flames, and relief at his coming. He drew them away from the houses, now fully alight, crackling from the intense heat. Then he had to clutch at Fritha's robe as she tried to run to get her beloved 'tickens'.

"Hold her," he begged Gilda. "I will let the animals free." As he opened the the little wicker gate, and the animals fled from the heat of the fire, Ricberht and Maura rode from under the trees, and drew up beside them, stricken at the sight of the blazing houses.

"Take her," ordered Brand, picking up Fritha and passing her up to Maura, who clutched her, both of them sobbing as they comforted each other. "There is nothing you can do here," he told Ricberht. "Just get away safely. If you can, you must find a way to let us know where you are. I will get news to you." His face darkened.

They all knew what the news would be. He stood, one arm round Gilda, and they turned away, back into the trees, heading north to find Onna. All were in despair, from Fritha, bewailing the loss of her pets, to Ricberht, who had lost everything. Except, he told himself, as he rode almost blindly, except his wife and child. He would keep them safe, as his mother had implored.

But he would forever feel that he had betrayed her.

32

In fact it took Eorpwald six whole days to find Niartha. Randulf had the wit to go to the hall to complain of the theft of his horse and that of his brother. They did not mention Ricberht at all. The king's troop had reported how Niartha was nowhere between the village and the hoo. Now it looked as if she may have ridden off before they went hunting for her. Eorpwald sent men to the coast, thinking she might have taken ship with the trader who had brought him and Onna from Edwin's moot. That shipman had left. Others Eorpwald sent to the Gipping wick, ordering them to search every house and every ship. This took three days. The people were not very helpful.

By this time, it was clear that her son had vanished, too. How could they have known of his intention to proclaim her a witch? Eorpwald fumed, in frustration. He had conceived the idea at midnight, and she was gone by dawn. She must have foreknowledge! That proved her supernatural powers. More facts to prove she was a witch! Now all he had to do was find her.

He even sent a messenger to Wedresfeld, in case she had thought of returning there.

So where was Niartha all this time? The villagers were appalled at the burning of her house and of Brand's. One woman, Helga, whose child Niartha had saved in last winter's sickness, came to the smithy, weeping in distress, afraid that Niartha had been burnt to death. Gilda and Brand, whom Arnulf had taken into his house, decided to trust her. When the troopers came to search Ricberht's house and the smithies, they smuggled Niartha out of the back, and she hid in Helga's tiny store-room, hidden even from the husband and child, until she could return, at night to the smithy. Arnulf revealed a secret space in the loft of the roof, in the darkness at the back of his forge, where, just as Ricberht did, he hid some of his tools and metals, especially bronze. Here Niartha could make a bed and lie out of sight, now that the forge had been searched. You could see the trackway clearly from the door of the smithy, so they could give her warning. She spent three more nights and days in this way.

Niartha began to wonder how long she could bear to live her life like this. She must find a way of getting to a ship, or Eorpwald might just as well take her and do as he pleased. She had lost her son, his family so dear to her, her house and all her herbs and cures. What was here for her now? She lay down in the smokey little space and Arnulf withdrew the ladder and went home, shutting her in. Alone in the utter darkness she wept in despair. Gilda came at dawn to tell her that the entire village was summoned to the hall. Brand was fearful lest more fires were set, and advised Niartha to hide, deep in the forest until nightfall.

"I have brought you some food and drink," said Gilda. An hour later, Niartha sat beneath a great beech tree, listening to the birdsong, and realizing that she had not been alone like this, or in such danger, for more than thirty years. If Ricberht did not return, with help from Onna, she would surely die, either at Eorpwald's hands, or because, two years short of fifty, her body could not survive the cold and hardship as it had done before.

Thinking what Eorpwald had to gain from declaring she was a witch, she now saw his intent. Of course, he would ingratiate himself with zealous, new Christians, by pursuing those whom they perceived as evil. He would get the approval of Edwin and of Paulinus, now a powerful lord of his church, if he sacrificed her as a devil.

She saw the old gods disappearing from the lands they used to inhabit. No greenwood spirit was going to rise from these woodlands to protect her. No misty seagod would suddenly conjure a ship from the watery depths. No wind from the heath would take shape and bear her away, as if on some winged dragon, through the air. She had felt no fear of monsters as she passed by marsh and grindle-stream. She had no faith in the new god, however many persons he had. Nothing could save her.

Niartha sat on, as if rooted, like the tree itself. She had eaten and drunk what Gilda provided, but had no inclination to return to the dark hole, to hide. She wrapped her cloak around her against the damp mist rising from the river not far away. Darkness fingered its way through the trees, broken by occasional gleams from the harvest moon. The people, she thought sadly, had been deprived of their feast, as Eorpwald had ignored it, and there was no queen to

197

remind him of his duty to the people. She grieved for Guthrun and for Aelfric, and thought of all those, now lost, who had befriended her. At the thought of Raedwald she wept again, and at the thought of Wulf. Finally she slept.

Brand found her, as he searched the forest when daylight dawned. It was a mercy, he told her, that she had been out here, as Eorpwald had held his folk in the hall, while the entire village was searched again. They had not been released until dawn. As far as they could tell, no damage had been done, even to Ricberht's property. Surely the king must give up, soon.

They were wrong. The smiths were being watched carefully, and Brand had been followed by the hunters, men expert at following a spoor. As he bent to raise Niartha to her feet, they rushed him. One man speared him, and they dragged him off, flinging him into a tangle of brambles to die.

Niartha was seized, her hands tied behind her back, and she was flung over the leader's horse, where he gripped her painfully by her bound wrists and cantered off through the trees, back to the village. She was unconscious by the time they dismounted at the door of the hall. She fell to the ground and lay motionless.

"Is she dead, you fools?" Plegmund said angrily. "The king needed her alive." He bent to touch her, discovered she was breathing and made two men carry her inside. They put her down on a deerskin rug beside the hearth, none too gently. She would have to be roused before the king saw her. When he saw Gilda running into the hall, Plegmund gripped her by the arm and told her to see to her mistress. He slit the ropes from Niartha's hands, and let the girl fetch water to wash Niartha's soiled face and hands, and some mead to revive the witch.

When she opened her eyes, Niartha was totally confused. She became aware of Gilda's face bending over her, eyes full of concern and pity. For a moment she thought they were at home. Then she remembered. No home. Only darkness. Then there was Brand. At the memory, she sat up and clasped Gilda to her. Gilda made her sip the mead, and she recognised where she was. Gilda begged, in a hurried whisper, to know where was Brand, but Niartha could only shake her head and weep. The last thing Niartha had seen was her loyal friend being dragged away, pierced by a spear.

"Tell Randulf to search the woods," she managed to breathe, before the girl was pushed aside by Plegmund. Even then, Gilda tried to stay with her former mistress, but she was sent away.

Two hunters hauled Niartha to her feet, but allowed her to stagger to a bench beside the hearth. She pulled her clothes around her into some sort of order, and one of the men threw her the cloak that had dropped beside the horse. She shook the dirt from its folds with as much strength as she could muster. Her headcloth had vanished, so she ran her fingers through her hair and tried to fling it back over her shoulders. Now she realized how Gilda had roused her by tenderly washing her face and hands. Niartha shook with grief at the thought of the terrible discovery awaiting the girl.

Plegmund thrust the cup of mead at her. "Drink this," he said. "You will need strength soon to face the king." Mutely, she took the drink. It was not an act of kindness, merely of necessity. The prisoner had to be strong enough to face the questioner.

"May I have something to eat?" she asked. There was some bread on the table left over from breakfast, and she was allowed to have that. When she asked if Gilda might be allowed to fetch her some leaves of bugloss with hot water to make a restorative, they laughed.

"For sure," scoffed Plegmund. "If you wish the king to know how you wish to practise your craft under his very roof! By all means." He turned to send a man on the errand, when Niartha stopped him, saying there was no need. She straightened her back as she sat before them. She had been a king's daughter. She had been Raedwald's wife – and his lover. She would not let these men demean her any more.

33

Eorpwald waited until the village was holding its breath in suspense. Beorn had found Brand's body and Arnulf had carried him back to the village. The elders had been informed. Some man owed *wergild* for this man's death. But who would claim it? Niartha had set Brand free, many years before. Gilda had lived with him, but they had never formally married. There was no-one to see to it that Brand's death was recompensed. Meantime, his body would lie wrapped in a temporary grave for a funeral. Today, the king had other matters on his mind.

When he finally called the elders into the hall, he was seated on the high seat, with Niartha standing before him to receive his justice. She had chosen Randulf to speak on her behalf and he stood at her right shoulder.

Eorpwald had summoned several villagers, and folk from outlying farmsteads to say, when questioned by Plegmund, how they or their families, or even their cattle, had been poisoned by Niartha's concoctions. The elders listened in dismay and disbelief. Plegmund, on the king's part, told how she had killed Eorpwald's own mother, Raedwald's great queen. Did they not remember? Niartha had allowed Raedwald himself to die. She had also succeeded in killing Guthrun, Eorpwald's beloved queen and deprived this king of an heir, when the child had died with its mother. Her own son had connived at all this. Had he not now fled the land? Or was he fleeing in fear lest his own mother kill another of his children? One was lost last winter, was it not? Like so many others! And the king had every reason to believe that Niartha had foreknowledge of events, which could only have come by supernatural means.

When Niartha was about to drop with fatigue and terror at this onslaught, Randulf begged that she might be seated, and old Bedwyn rose in support. He said it would not help the king if his vicitim (though he chose a more tactful word) were unconscious and unable to hear the judgement of the king. Someone passed her some wine, and she sat, with Randulf supporting her as he stood behind.

By this time it was dusk, and men were coming home from river, field or forest, ready for an evening meal. Eorpwald said the hearing would continue next morning. Niartha was to be held in the lock-up, and, no matter how many voices were raised in protest, he held to his decree. Randulf saw to it that she was given bedding, supper and a bucket for her bodily needs, and she managed to smile at him, as the door was barred and locked down.

Next day Gilda brought clean clothes, and a headdress, all from Idunna. Niartha had no possessions since her house was burnt.

"You look like a queen," the girl whispered to Niartha before the guards took her to the hall. People clustered outside, anxious for any information as men came and went. Only the elders were permitted within.

Randulf now asked for various villagers to be called in turn, to say that Niartha had used no magic, merely her knowledge of the simples she used to make cures. Men told of wounds she had healed. Helga spoke up bravely to tell of the healing of her child. Gilda came and he prompted her to say how the herbs were gathered from verges of fields or even in their own plot. There was nothing unnatural in any of it, Randulf insisted. Then he spoke out, for the first time, of the methods she had used to sew the wound in his right arm, and how her observations of how muscles were used had helped him to regain strength enough for him to do work again. She used only common-sense and practical skills, he insisted.

There were renewed murmurs of approval, and Eorpwald could see how his victim might yet escape. The judgement would be his, but no king ruled safely without the support of his elders. A man was vulnerable who could not rely on loyal backing, both in battle and in his rulings. As Randulf finished speaking, the king leant forward and bade Niartha stand.

"I wish to ask you some questions, myself," he told her, in a firm voice. "You must reply." He asked her if she had not, on occasions, used runes and charms in her work.

"Of course," she replied. "This lore is well established in the customs of our people."

"Did you invoke the power of the gods?"

"Yes. That is what the runes and charms depend upon, as well you know, lord king." It would not hurt to remind him, and others, of what he had professed so often to be the true religion of his people.

"And when the High King tells you that this is a foul and evil practice, and that his lands will now become Christian, what do you say to that?"

"I say that I will obey the wishes of the king of my people. Are you truly a Christian now, lord king?" She stared at him calmly. Suddenly it seemed as if the tables might be turned. Was Eorpwald prepared to stand by his recent baptismal vows? Or would he renege, and uphold the ancient traditions of his people he had hitherto revered?

"It is not for you to question me," he said haughtily. "I have listened to the stories told of this woman, and am ready to advise my people how I wish to proceed in this matter." Now there came an audible sigh of relief, as the people believed that meant Niartha was safe. The elders would surely protect her. However, Eorpwald persisted. "But there is the matter of these regrettable deaths. Some of these folk could well have lived, without her interference. My mother, for instance. And my son."

"The child was dead within the womb!" cried Niartha.

"But how came that womb to be dead?" cried Eorpwald. Suddenly he spoke out loudly.

"This woman is guilty of killing, and I sentence her to death!" He raised his nameless sword, just as Raedwald used to raise the ivory wand of the Wuffings. They all stared at each other, stunned into silence once more.

"The king has spoken," pronounced Plegmund.

Randulf sank beside Niartha on the bench and gripped her hands in despair. She faced the king in silence, waiting to hear how the death would come.

"I shall decide tomorrow what form this justice will take," Eorpwald said. He rose, and so did all present, except the two on the bench, and watched as he left the hall. Niartha was returned to the chilly lock-up, to find a small brazier lit, and a bowl of hot broth. When the door was shut she nearly screamed as something moved by her feet. Gilda had hidden herself below the low bed on the shelf made for the purpose.

"I did not want you to be alone," she said softly, so the guard should not hear. She produced a lanthorn, shielding its light from the doorway, and they ate and warmed themselves. Soon they could hear the man snoring outside, as he leant against the door. In truth, Gilda needed comforting more than Niartha, who had foreseen where Eorpwald's idea of justice would lead, by whatever means. They both felt bereft by the death of Brand, and their tears flowed as they whispered of his loyalty, courage and love.

"I wonder where Fritha is now," Gilda sighed eventually. They remembered her funny ways. How they hoped she and her parents were safe. Niartha made Gilda lie down for a rest. She, herself, would not sleep that night. Once again, it seemed, the gods had abandoned her. Where was Ricberht? Had they made the journey overland to the Blyth? It was easy to get lost on the heath, and there were dangers, as she had warned him many times before.

So few hours were left. She would not waste them in despair. She tried to think only of the people who had loved her, befriended her, and wondered if, even now, Onna might intervene. If any gods were listening, they might take pity.

NIARTHA

But I know that no god, except one, is listening. Eorpwald has a land bereft of all its gods. I felt them drifting in the mist of the forest, to vanish with the warming sun. Only the Earth Mother is left to me now. I am named for her: Nerthus. My mother was given into her keeping at my birth. Now she will take me, too.

I have no tears left. I have nothing left.

The men come for me, angry to find Gilda with me. I shield her from their angry blows. They stand back, abashed, while she straightens my robe and combs my hair, braids it and covers it. She has even pinned on the *fylfot* brooch, which Ricberht gave me, and which I always wear. I thank her, though I have no faith now in its protective powers. She follows me into the hall and no-one stops her.

Eorpwald has brought in a monk who was travelling to find King Onna. The man looks tired and rather bewildered. He is deceived by Eorpwald's apparent eagerness to find out more about the Christian faith. We stand, all of us, while the king questions him about casting out devils and evil spirits.

"And when you find such a one? A witch?" urges Eorpwald. "What then? How do you purge her of such evil?"

"Lord king, such a one, man or woman, cannot be cleansed, unless they forswear their allegiance to the devil," replies the monk. "If they remain obdurate, they must be consumed by fire, so that the evil may not spread." The king regards me thoughtfully. Now I know what my fate will be.

"Ask her, monk. Ask this woman if she will accept the holy rite of baptism."

"If I did so, Eorpwald, it would be of my own free will, not through fear or self-seeking, like you," I say. There is a gasp from those around us, and Eorpwald jerks in anger at my tone and my daring. He pushes the nervous monk to stand in front of me and commands him to ask the question.

"Woman, do you renounce Satan and all his works?" I stand, silent, as I am not sure who or what is this Satan. I only know the Christians fear him.

"Woman, will you allow me to baptise you in the name of the Father, the Son and the Holy Ghost?" When I gently shake my head, he steps close to me, trying to take my hand, but I refuse to let him touch me. "Do you not see your peril?" he asks me quietly. "God will save you, and you will live forever."

I know the poor man is kind, and I know he is trying to save my life as well as my soul. But what kind of life would I live? Eorpwald will hound me to the end of my days. If this is my last day, I do not care.

"I will not," I say, clearly enough for all to hear. There is a groan from some of the elders.

"Then you will burn!" Eorpwald almost shouts triumphantly.

Bedwyn moves forward, shaking. "Lord king, may we not kill her mercifully, before the flames?"

"Be silent, old man," the king waves an arm furiously, so that Plegmund hauls the elder away, weeping. Seeing the wrath on people's faces, the king turns again to the monk. He shakes his strangely shaven head regretfully, but says that the fire must consume the last breath, so that the demon within is destroyed.

Eorpwald takes up his sword. I picture all the hands that made it. But I do not let myself think of my son. Not here. Not now.

"Let the fire be prepared," orders the king. "Let it be built beside the great oak. Where the witch lived, so there she will die. Tell the whole village," he commands. "All are to assemble there at dusk, to see what is the punishment for witchcraft. Evil-doers shall find no mercy."

When the king stands, ready to leave the hall, all have to rise. Under the noise of rustling clothes and moving feet, I hear the king tell Plegmund to keep the monk away from me. He does not want me to have any opportunity to change my mind.

For just a few moments, I feel the warm touch of hands as men whom I have come to like and to respect, whose families I have tended, come up in silent sorrow, not daring to speak before they leave the hall. I am returned to the black cell of the lock-up, alone, though I know Gilda will be close by. I am given food, which I find impossible to swallow. I have no feelings, and hunger is meaningless. I drink, because my mouth and throat are dry.

I wake from a merciful sleep, as the door is opened. The red, low sunset blazes through the trees. The troop of young thanes lead me to a cart, unresisting. It is Arnulf, his face wet with tears, who lifts me up, and seats me on a heap of straw. He says nothing, but as he leans over me he kisses my forehead and presses my shoulder. "We are with you," he says in a low murmur, covering the sound of his voice by stirring the straw with his boot. I squeeze his hand and look into his face so he knows how grateful I am. "Tell them I love them," I whisper, and he gives a tiny nod of the head. He knows.

Surrounded by the riders, I keep my eyes on Arnulf's broad back as we jolt down the track to the open glade, now scarred by the black ash of the burnt-out houses. I see, with sudden choking tears, that some chickens still peck among the plot of herbs, but the goat has gone. I swallow my grief at the loss of all that I had loved.

"This is the place," says the king of the Wuffings, "where the evil witch seduced my great father. Here she poisoned my mother." I hear his words, thinking only that the man is irredeemably deluded. If anyone here is evil, it is Eorpwald in his dangerous pride. "Here she will die."

Arnulf lifts me down from the cart, cradling me in his great arms so that, again, I nearly lose control. He sets me on my feet and Plegmund binds my hands and feet. Two of the thanes lift me onto the great pyre, and tie me to a stake of iron.

'Let Ricberht not hear of this,' I pray to Nerthus. I close my eyes, not wishing to see the face of my enemy, nor of my friends in their distress. There are no more words.

34

Ricberht did not hear of his mother's fate for several weeks. After their hasty flight from Raedwaldsham, he began to think that Blythburgh was too obvious a refuge. Also, he knew Onna was in favour of the new religion, and doubted what might be his reaction to a charge of witchcraft. There were too many monks there, seeking the shelter of a less hostile court than they found further south.

He remembered the route, more or less, that he and Randulf had ridden, about a year ago, and set off, avoiding Helmingham, where too many men knew him. It meant camping in the shelter of gorse bushes one night, and in a filthy barton for a second. Fritha, though dismayed at the frightening separation from her grandmother, was resilient and found great delight in the riding and the places where they stopped. Only when she slept could he and Maura share their fear and anguish, clinging together for warmth and comfort. On the third morning they bathed in a stream and tried to make their appearance less dishevelled, so that they might more easily find passage on a ship to the north Ricberht had his pieces of gold and silver, but if he looked too scruffy, he might be accused of theft.

They had to wait two nights at the portside guesthouse before a ship put in. It would leave for the Humber the next day. Ricberht went to find the horse-dealer. The man laughed when he recognized two of the horses. "You can buy them back, when you come again," he grinned.

Ricberht spent most of the time on board ship trying to stop Fritha clambering over bales of goods and banks of oars. She squealed with glee when the seas sprayed them, but Maura felt too ill to cope with her. When they reached the Humber, she pleaded with her husband to leave the ship. It would be better to wait for a while, in the hope of getting news from the south. Supposing Eorpwald got to hear about the Cocket village! No-one knew they were here, so they were safe. Ricberht was forced to agree.

A few days later, he insisted on moving north again, before

their means of payment ran low. They had nothing they could trade except his precious hoard, and he knew Wilhelm and Bertha would help them to find a place to settle. This time they took the ship of Lukas Lukasson. They reached the Cocket as swiftly as the seas permitted, and the shipman sat in the little hall that night, with leisure at last to share his news over a jug of ale. He said he had heard a tale of a witch being burnt. Down at the Deben, it was. He didn't know any details.

"Is he all right?" he asked, as Ricberht flung himself out of the hall, followed by Maura, in obvious distress.

That night, Ricberht begged Wilhelm and Bertha to shelter his wife and child. He would come back as soon as he might, but he had to go to find out about his mother. Lukas had only one more shipment a few miles north. Then he would return, as soon as winds permitted, to take Ricberht all the way to the Deben, he said. Ricberht seethed with frustration.

He knew they were safe here. Bertha's voice reminded Maura of her mother, and the old woman encouraged her to talk, so that soon Ricberht's wife found friends. Fritha was as happy as could be. There were chickens here. And goats. They would soon begin to build a little house near the one he had lived in all those years ago. That had been built by Gurth, and was now Wilhelm's home. For the first time, he heard Wilhelm's story, and how his father had been shipmaster of Raedwald's *Sea Witch* before he died so horribly.

Ricberht had no way to send word of where he was. As the days passed, he could see that this might be a boon. He wanted Eorpwald to forget him. He choked with grief and fury every time he thought of his mother. Had Eorpwald had her killed in such a horrible way? He forced himself repeatedly to control his feelings. Perhaps it was all lies. Perhaps it was another person who had been burnt to death.

In the first spell of favourable weather, even with a northerly wind, Lukas came, to keep his promise. Ricberht wished to take flight like the great birds that passed over the ship. How effortlessly they flew. He had to bite his tongue at the delays in little ports down the east coast. At last, in the early light of dawn, they turned into the Deben and rowed to the wooden jetty below Ramsholt. He rewarded Lukas handsomely, and urged him to send word to the blacksmith, Arnulf, when he was going north again. The shipman left for the port at the south end of the great river near Prittlewell. It might be many days before the winds were right for a return.

Then Ricberht took his spear and his *seax* and began to walk the miles along the riverbank and into the woods, avoiding the marshy ground where cattle were grazed to heal their sore feet. His own were sore enough by the time he rounded the bend and saw the great mounds of the Wuffing kings. He sat among bushes on a low, craggy outcrop, on the foreshore below the mounds, out of sight of riverboats and passers-by. He did not wish to circle the village before dark. He ate some smoked fish and drank the last of the ale, provided by Lukas. He felt torn by powerful feelings. If only night would come. When it did, it brought rain. He was glad. The sound would muffle any noise he made. There would be guards, of course, but he knew they would shelter under eaves and trees. He picked up his weapons, threw his hood over his head and strode on.

After an hour or two he came to the glade where he had last seen his mother's house and Brand's in flames. It was pitch black, so fortunately he did not see the third area of burnt earth. He moved on, a silent, dark figure, then eventually turned off the track to pass through the fringes of the forest at the back of the forge. His smithy and house stood, lifeless, but he could see and smell the damp smoke rising from Arnulf's house. He moved near to the back wall and put his ear to a crack to hear what voices might be within.

He heard Arnulf's gruff tones as he asked Randulf to pass him another cut of ham. Randulf must have stubbed a toe, for he bumped into something and swore.

Then Arnulf said, quite plainly, "I wish we had news of young Ricberht. If only we knew where he was." Randulf began to reply. Ricberht knew then it was safe, and he ran quickly round to the door, rapping on it, and calling to them that it was he, Ricberht. They were amazed, grabbed at him to pull him inside the door, drag down the beam across it, and thump him in pleasure.

Randulf asked anxiously, "Did anyone see you? Have you talked to anyone in the village?" They were very relieved when he shook his head.

Arnulf refused to talk any more until they had fed him bread and ham and strong beer. Then they put a bench down, so that they could rest their backs on its seat, sitting on the skins on the floor, feet stretched out at various angles round the fire in Arnulf's small hearth. They found the words to tell him what had happened to Niartha, what ploys Eorpwald had used. They comforted their friend as best they could. Arnulf told him that Niartha's last words were of her love for him and his family. They promised to talk more in the morning. Ricberht was worn out with travel, grief and anger.

When he woke, Ricberht was all for going straight to the hall, but they implored him to keep hidden for the time being. Yes, he had every right to take revenge on Eorpwald, but need not rush in madly and lose his own life in the attempt.

"We must set a trap to catch this squirrel," said Randulf. Arnulf said it was more a rat than a squirrel. Ricberht could not think of any creature he detested more than he did Eorpwald. "A snake," he said. They nodded. They should avoid its fangs. Meanwhile, Ricberht had to lie low. Only the brothers must know he was here.

"What about Brand?" asked Ricberht. They had to tell him how Brand had died, trying to save Niartha. "Where are they buried?" he asked, huskily.

The grim truth was that they had buried Brand at the edge of the people's burial-ground, outside the enclosure. He was not a warrior, nor a thane, but the village had turned out to honour him.

"There wasn't a sound," said Randulf softly. "No-one said anything. But each person came and laid some object beside him, anything from a broken cup to a silver knife. You made that one," he told Ricberht. "Then we stood around him and covered him gently. He was a fine man." The others nodded in agreement. "We got roaring drunk that night."

"And what of my mother?" The two brothers glanced at each other and then Arnulf said it was a bad business. Eorpwald had forbidden her to be laid to rest, anywhere on his lands. But a few nights after... well, after the burning... the two of them, with Beorn to keep watch, had swept the remains of burnt ash and bone, putting them into a bronze, hanging bowl. Ricberht gasped. This was what was done for people of high rank – even kings and queens.

"Where did you find this bowl?"

"It was hidden inside the ruins of your mother's house. Did you never see it?" No, he never had, though Bertha had told him how Raedwald had given Niartha such a bowl, he now recalled, filled with rich gifts. How many secrets his mother had kept from him; though he had told her that he loved her for doing so, knowing it was out of her love for him.

"Where does she lie?" he asked, with difficulty.

"Now that's the other part of the story!" said Arnulf. "We took the great bowl and buried it at the edge of the warriors' ground. We thought she was as bold and brave as many a man."

"And a whole lot worthier than some," Randulf added. "We will show you when it is safe to take you there." Ricberht put his face in his hands, and his friends let him weep. Then they passed him another cup of beer, to give him heart.

It was just as well Ricberht had learned to be patient. He had to keep hidden. They dared not risk letting Eorpwald find him, and it was not easy to know who could be trusted. A man's word was no longer the strong bond it had been in the past, not since King Raedwald died.

35

The monk who had tried to persuade Niartha to save herself was called Felix, a name often chosen by those who considered themselves blest. At Eorpwald's command, he spent half a day at the riverside, half a mile from the church, dipping the people in the chilly water. He held a service to give them all a sliver of white bread and a sip of wine, telling them that this was the body and blood of the Christ. Some were bewildered, especially as he read to them in Latin, but the words seemed peaceful enough. Perhaps things would improve now. But the villagers were appalled at the death of their wise-woman and healer. They were also too afraid of their king to disobey him, though many still went on with some of the old ways in secret.

Not everyone in his domain was so ready to take up the new faith, and Eorpwald rode out with a troop of twelve men one morning, to see to a stubborn settlement at Kettlesburgh, beside the young Deben. They encountered a surprisingly strong force, reinforced by men from Framlingham, and were outnumbered by three to one. Eorpwald burnt out the little hamlet nearby and retreated, with only three men. As they fled over the open land beyond the water meadows, one of the men was thrown from his horse, and broke his neck. Eorpwald swore mightly and left him lying there. He and Plegmund rode as fast as they dared toward home.

Then Plegmund's horse went lame. He would have to walk it home, or kill the animal. The damage was not too severe, though the leg felt warm. He must walk. Eorpwald would ride on and send horse-carls with a fresh mount. By this time it was nightfall, and raining. Eorpwald rode on, eventually crossed the ford and turned up the slope towards his village. He passed the forge, and heard laughter coming from the smith's house. He rode towards it, leapt from his horse, and beat at the door with the hilt of his bloodstained sword.

The voices within fell silent. Then Arnulf called from inside for his visitor to identify himself.

"It is I, Eorpwald! Your king, man. Open up!" He heard the beam being lifted, and the big man stood at his threshold. He looked around and realized the king was by himself.

"Where are your men, lord?" he asked. "How come you are alone?" There was a scuffling noise behind him. Eorpwald took a step forward.

"Let me in out of this damnable rain. Send someone to fetch horse-carls and a hall servant. Plegmund needs help. I will rest here until I may return, more properly attended."

Arnulf moved back and allowed the king to enter. He closed the door. Randulf stood at the table and held out a goblet of wine. The king thrust his sword into its scabbard and moved to take the drink. As he did so, he caught sight of a third man, moving from behind the door, *seax* in hand. Before Eorpwald could pull out his blade again, Ricberht was on him. He ripped his curved knife from the king's stomach to his throat.

Arnulf and Ricberht dragged the body back down the track. The rain would soon wash away any blood. They left Eorpwald face down in the ford. They set his horse loose to run where it chose. As they turned to stumble back up to the house, they saw Plegmund leading his horse toward the ford. They leapt on him, releasing the animal to hobble off to drink in the river. Arnulf seized Eorpwald's hall steward by the throat, as he had so often longed to do. He throttled him and left him to lie in the reeds. They stood, dripping with rain and gasping for breath.

In the morning, Bedwyn called a moot, not just of the elders, but of all the people. He held it in the churchyard. In two coffins, hastily provided by Borgil, lay the king and his steward. Bedwyn said they ought to give these two holy burial, but there was no monk, as Felix had now gone back to the land of the Franks, or somesuch. It was obvious, he said, that the king had been murdered. This was not a battle-blow. Nor was Plegmund's death the result of battle.

He proposed to lay them in the holy ground of the churchyard, with words of respect. When a holy man came this way again, he could use the rites of the church, if he saw fit. No-one disagreed. So many of their young men were dead. Only one man came home to tell of the battle they had lost the day before. They interred Eorpwald and his henchman, but few were the words of respect. Arnulf dropped the king's sword onto the coffin. The smiths had hated the making of it; nor had the weapon won any honoured name.

In the hall that night, Arnulf brought Ricberht out of hiding. All but a few greeted him with cries of joy. Gilda fell into his arms, longing for news of Maura and Fritha. Ricberht told his story, from how he had escaped, to the planning of his new house in the fishing village. He told how he had been hiding here for so long. He took a very deep breath and told them he had the right to avenge his mother's death. He told them how he had killed Eorpwald. You could hear the logs settling in the hearth, they were so still. No-one gainsaid him.

"Will you come back here to live amongst us?" Bedwyn asked. Ricberht looked around.

"No," he answered. "I have roots in the north, and will find work for the High King. Choose yourselves a good man, now. He could be a headman, if you choose, or you may take Onna, say, for your king." There were nods, but also cries that Onna had not saved them from Eorpwald's cruelty. This Christ had not brought them peace, whatever the monks said. Next day, they chose Arnulf as their headman, and the village settled to its old ways of live and let live, Christian or not. Edwin, the High King, was far away.

Ricberht took Gilda back to the north, where she settled happily. To his delight he found Maura already swelling with his baby growing inside her. She had so longed to tell him the glad news, and now he would be home when the child was born. She kept forever the secret of Eorpwald's rape and the way Niartha had shielded both Maura (as she thought) and Ricberht from the knowledge of the unwanted child Maura could have borne. Ricberht had taken the life of their enemy, but only the folk at Raedwaldsham knew the truth of Eorpwald's death. At last, Ricberht could build a house beside the Cocket River. He would only leave her, he told Maura, when the High King had work for him.

Then, after three years, came another message. Arnulf had died, a peaceful death, and someone (was it Paulinus?) had encouraged a reluctant Sigeberht to return, claiming his father's throne, although he would usually retreat to a monastery up on the coast, leaving many decisions to his cousin Onna. There was peace, at least for the time being.

Ricberht had made the occasional visit to Yefrin, when King Edwin held court there, and was overcome by the pleasure the great man showed, when Ricberht offered his services. It was good to have his skills honoured once more. He built a jeweller's workshop at the edge of the river. He would teach his son, he thought. He was a sturdy little lad, was Gurth, more amenable than the fiery Fritha, who led her mother a dance. He smiled. Her indomitable spirit reminded him of Niartha. He sighed, even as he smiled. Then the smith bent to lift the small pan of gold from the kiln, and other thoughts were lost as he worked his craft.

PAULINUS

I have left the peaceful kingdom of King Edwin in the safe hands of Bishop Honorius. The Pope has sent me the pallium. I am Archbishop now. Thanks be to God for granting me the saving of the soul of the greatest king of his age, and the souls of so many more.

Let us now praise famous men and our fathers that begat us.

The Lord hath wrought great glory by them through his great power from the beginning.

Such as did bear rule in their kingdoms, men renowned for their power, giving counsel by their understanding, and declaring prophecies.

Leaders of the people by their counsels, and by their learning meet for the people, wise and eloquent are their instructions,

.

Such as found out musical tunes, and recited verses in writing.

.

Rich men furnished with ability, living peaceably in their habitations.

All these were honoured in their generations, and were the glory of their times.

There be of them, that have left a name behind them, that their praises might be reported.

And some there be, which have no memorial, who are perished, as though they had never been born; and their children after them,

But these were merciful men, whose righteousness hath not been forgotten.

With their seed shall continually remain a good inheritance, and their children within the covenant.

Their seed standeth fast, and their children for their sakes.

Their seed shall remain for ever, and their glory shall not be blotted out.

Their bodies are buried in peace; but their name liveth for evermore.

So be it, Lord Jesus. Amen

BEORHTFYR

The timbers over the longship topple, crumbling into dirt. The ship is swallowed in the sand.

Deep in its master's grave, the gold-roped hilt long-since slipped from the gripless bones, the sword lies motionless, unlit.

The scabbard-case has rotted, has let mould gnaw at its body, as damp seeps through the centuries.

Yet the gold and garnets do not fade: what they embraced has died to dross, but these will shine forever.

The belt encircled, once, the living body of the warrior-king, the greatest of his age. Now only the jewels gleam in the leather's dust, to mark the girth of the great man. They sing of his strength, they measure his might.

The braids that bind the sword to its sheath are torn to shreds. So the power of the once-bright blade is now set free. Some spectral hand may slide the silent steel and fly at foes we fail to fear.

The fire is quenched, we think, but if we breathe, maybe a spark will glow.

BACKGROUND READING

Apocrypha: Ecclesiasticus

King James Authorised Version of the Holy Bible: Psalms

Richard Barber (sel.): Chronicles of the Dark Ages (The Folio Society)

Bede: Ecclesiastical History of the English People (Penguin) see Acknowledgements

Angela Care Evans: The Sutton Hoo Ship Burial (British Museum Publications)

Prof. Martin Carver: Sutton Hoo: Burial Ground of Kings? (British Museum Publications)

D.Dymond & E.Martin: Historical Atlas of Suffolk (Suffolk CC & Suffolk Inst. Arch. & Hist.)

Bill Griffiths: Aspects of Anglo-Saxon Magic (Anglo-Saxon Books)

Anne Hagen: A Handbook of Anglo-Saxon Food (Anglo-Saxon Books)

Richard Hamer (sel. & trans.): A Choice of Anglo-Saxon Verse (faber and faber)

Gabrielle Hatfield: Country Remedies (Boydell Press)

Kathleen Herbert: Looking for the Lost Gods of England (Anglo-Saxon Books)

David A.Hinton: A Smith in Lindsey (Society for Medieval Archaeology)

John Kemble: Anglo-Saxon Runes (Anglo-Saxon Books)

Tony Linsell & Brian Partridge: (Anglo-Saxon Books)

G.R.Owen-Crocker: Dress in Anglo-Saxon England (Boydell Press)

Fr. Andrew Phillips: The Hallowing of England (Anglo-Saxon Books)

Steven Plunkett: Suffolk in Anglo-Saxon Times (Tempus)

Stephen Pollington: The Mead Hall (Anglo-Saxon Books)

John Porter: Anglo-Saxon Riddles (Anglo-Saxon Books)

Oliver Rackham: The History of the Countryside (J.M.Dent)

Bernard Scudder (trans.): Egil's Saga (Penguin)

Francis Simpson: Simpson's Flora of Suffolk (Suffolk Naturalists' Society)

Prof. Tom Williamson: Sutton Hoo and its Landscape (Windgather Press/Oxbow Books)

Websites:

www.regioanglorum/weapons ...etc

Yeavering: overview
www.pastperfect.org.uk/sites/yeavering...royal centre

www.ormsgard.net

www.fordham.edu/halsall/basis/gildas-full...(for Gildas in translation)

www.suttonhoo.org

About the Author

The author lives in Suffolk, is a Sutton Hoo Society Guide at Sutton Hoo (National Trust). She lists among her other interests: family, theatre, literature, travel. She has enjoyed amateur drama, teaching English and Drama, swimming with dolphins, and scuba-diving on the Great Barrier Reef.

After studying Old English as part of her degree, she renewed her interest in the Anglo-Saxon period, language and culture, finding inspiration at Sutton Hoo.

Lightning Source UK Ltd.
Milton Keynes UK
UKOW05f0836171113

221186UK00002B/39/P